The Path Of The King by John Buchan

John Buchan was born on August 26th 1875. After a brief career in the legal profession he began a twin career as writer and politician. He was a prodigious writer not just of fiction but of such acclaimed works as a 24 volume history of World War I. It was during the war, where, as a sideline writing propaganda he wrote his most famous works 'The Thirty Nine Steps'. Its hero, Richard Hannay, continues his story in other Buchan novels, most notably Greenmantle (1916) and Mr Standfast (1919).

After the war he became a Member of Parliament and in 1935 was appointed as Governor General of Canada. This title was added to his other very impressive collection: 1st Baron Tweedsmuir PC GCMG GCVO CH.

He occupied the post of Governor General and continued to write until his death on February 11th 1940. In all he wrote 100 works including 30 novels, short stories, poems, biographies and many volumes about military history.

Index Of Contents

PROLOGUE
CHAPTER I. HIGHTOWN UNDER SUNFELL
CHAPTER II. THE ENGLISHMAN
CHAPTER III. THE WIFE OF FLANDERS
CHAPTER IV. EYES OF YOUTH
CHAPTER V. THE MAID
CHAPTER VI. THE WOOD OF LIFE
CHAPTER VII. EAUCOURT BY THE WATERS
CHAPTER VIII. THE HIDDEN CITY
CHAPTER IX. THE REGICIDE
CHAPTER X. THE MARPLOT
CHAPTER XI. THE LIT CHAMBER
CHAPTER XII. IN THE DARK LAND
CHAPTER XIII. THE LAST STAGE
CHAPTER XIV. THE END OF THE ROAD
EPILOGUE

John Buchan - A Short biography
John Buchan - A Concise Bibliography

PROLOGUE

The three of us in that winter camp in the Selkirks were talking the slow aimless talk of wearied men.

The Soldier, who had seen many campaigns, was riding his hobby of the Civil War and descanting on Lee's tactics in the last Wilderness struggle. I said something about the stark romance of it, of Jeb Stuart flitting like a wraith through the forests; of Sheridan's attack at Chattanooga, when the charging troops on the ridge were silhouetted against a harvest moon; of Leonidas Polk, last of the warrior Bishops, baptizing his fellow generals by the light of a mess candle. "Romance," I said, "attended the sombre grey and blue levies as faithfully as she ever rode with knight-errant or crusader."

The Scholar, who was cutting a raw-hide thong, raised his wise eyes.

"Does it never occur to you fellows that we are all pretty mixed in our notions? We look for romance in the well-cultivated garden-plots, and when it springs out of virgin soil we are surprised, though any fool might know it was the natural place for it."

He picked up a burning stick to relight his pipe.

"The things we call aristocracies and reigning houses are the last places to look for masterful men. They began strongly, but they have been too long in possession. They have been cosseted and comforted and the devil has gone out of their blood. Don't imagine that I undervalue descent. It is not for nothing that a great man leaves posterity. But who is more likely to inherit the fire, the elder son with his flesh-pots or the younger son with his fortune to find? Just think of it! All the younger sons of younger sons back through the generations! We none of us know our ancestors beyond a little way. We all of us may have kings' blood in our veins. The dago who blacked my boots at Vancouver may be descended by curious byways from Julius Caesar.

"Think of it!" he cried. "The spark once transmitted may smoulder for generations under ashes, but the appointed time will come, and it will flare up to warm the world. God never allows waste. And we fools rub our eyes and wonder, when we see genius come out of the gutter. It didn't begin there. We tell ourselves that Shakespeare was the son of a woolpedlar, and Napoleon of a farmer, and Luther of a peasant, and we hold up our hands at the marvel. But who knows what kings and prophets they had in their ancestry!"

After that we turned in, and as I lay looking at the frosty stars a fancy wove itself in my brain. I saw the younger sons carry the royal blood far down among the people, down even into the kennels of the outcast. Generations follow, oblivious of the high beginnings, but there is that in the stock which is fated to endure. The sons and daughters blunder and sin and perish, but the race goes on, for there is a fierce stuff of life in it. It sinks and rises again and blossoms at haphazard into virtue or vice, since the ordinary moral laws do not concern its mission. Some rags of greatness always cling to it, the dumb faith that sometime and somehow that blood drawn from kings it never knew will be royal again. Though nature is wasteful of material things, there is no waste of spirit. And then after long years there comes, unheralded and unlooked-for, the day of the Appointed Time....

This is the story which grew out of that talk by the winter fire.

CHAPTER I. HIGHTOWN UNDER SUNFELL

When Biorn was a very little boy in his father's stead at Hightown he had a play of his own making for the long winter nights. At the back end of the hall, where the men sat at ale, was a chamber which the thralls used of a morning, a place which smelt of hams and meal and good provender. There a bed had been made for him when he forsook his cot in the women's quarters. When the door was shut it was black dark, save for a thin crack of light from the wood fire and torches of the hall. The crack made on the earthen floor a line like a golden river. Biorn, cuddled up on a bench in his little bear-skin, was drawn like a moth to that stream of light. With his heart beating fast he would creep to it and stand for a moment with his small body bathed in the radiance. The game was not to come back at once, but to foray into the farther darkness before returning to the sanctuary of bed. That took all the fortitude in Biorn's heart, and not till the thing was dared and done could he go happily to sleep.

One night Leif the Outborn watched him at his game. Sometimes the man was permitted to sleep there when he had been making sport for the housecarles.

"Behold an image of life!" he had said in his queer outland speech. "We pass from darkness to darkness with but an instant of light between. You are born for high deeds, princeling. Many would venture from the dark to the light, but it takes a stout breast to voyage into the farther dark."

And Biorn's small heart swelled, for he detected praise, though he did not know what Leif meant.

In the long winter the sun never topped Sunfell, and when the gales blew and the snow drifted there were lights in the hall the day long. In Biorn's first recollection the winters were spent by his mother's side, while she and her maids spun the wool of the last clipping. She was a fair woman out of the Western Isles, all brown and golden as it seemed to him, and her voice was softer than the hard ringing speech of the Wick folk. She told him island stories about gentle fairies and good-humoured elves who lived in a green windy country by summer seas, and her air would be wistful as if she thought of her lost home. And she sang him to sleep with crooning songs which had the sweetness of the west wind in them. But her maids were a rougher stock, and they stuck to the Wicking lullaby which ran something like this:

Hush thee, my bold one, a boat will I buy thee,
A boat and stout oars and a bright sword beside,

A helm of red gold and a thrall to be nigh thee,
When fair blows the wind at the next wicking-tide.

There was a second verse, but it was rude stuff, and the Queen had forbidden the maids to sing it.

As he grew older he was allowed to sit with the men in the hall, when bows were being stretched and bowstrings knotted and spear-hafts fitted. He would sit mum in a corner, listening with both ears to the talk of the old franklins, with their endless grumbles about lost cattle and ill neighbours. Better he liked the bragging of the young warriors, the Bearsarks, who were the spear-head in all the forays. At the great feasts of Yule-tide he was soon sent packing, for there were wild scenes when the ale flowed freely, though his father, King Ironbeard, ruled his hall with a strong hand. From the speech of his elders Biorn made his picture of the world beyond the firths. It was a world of gloom and terror, yet shot with a strange brightness. The High Gods might be met with in beggar's guise at any ferry, jovial fellows and good friends to brave men, for they themselves had to fight for their lives, and the End of All Things hung over them like a cloud. Yet till the day of Ragnarok there would be feasting and fine fighting and goodly fellowship, and a stout heart must live for the hour.

Leif the Outborn was his chief friend. The man was no warrior, being lame of a leg and lean and sharp as a heron. No one knew his begetting, for he had been found as a child on the high fells. Some said he was come of the Finns, and his ill-wishers would have it that his birthplace had been behind a foss, and that he had the blood of dwarves in him. Yet though he made sport for the company, he had respect from them, for he was wise in many things, a skilled leech, a maker of runes, and a crafty builder of ships. He was a master hand at riddles, and for hours the housecarles would puzzle their wits over his efforts. This was the manner of them. "Who," Leif would ask, "are the merry maids that glide above the land to the joy of their father; in winter they bear a white shield, but black in summer?" The answer was "Snowflakes and rain." Or "I saw a corpse sitting on a corpse, a blind one riding on a lifeless steed?" to which the reply was "A dead horse on an ice-floe." Biorn never guessed any of the riddles, but the cleverness of them he thought miraculous, and the others roared with glee at their own obtuseness.

But Leif had different moods, for sometimes he would tell tales, and all were hushed in a pleasant awe. The fire on the hearth was suffered to die down, and men drew closer to each other, as Leif told of the tragic love of Helgi and Sigrun, or how Weyland outwitted King Nidad, or how Thor went as bride to Thrym in Giantland, and the old sad tale of how Sigurd Fafnirsbane, noblest of men, went down to death for the love of a queen not less noble. Leif told them well, so that his hearers were held fast with the spell of wonder and then spurred to memories of their own. Tongues would be loosened, and there would be wild recollections of battles among the skerries of the west, of huntings in the hills where strange sights greeted the benighted huntsman, and of voyaging far south into the lands of the sun where the poorest thrall wore linen and the cities were all gold and jewels. Biorn's head would be in such a whirl after a night of story-telling that he could get no sleep for picturing his own deeds when he was man enough to bear a sword and launch his ship. And sometimes in his excitement he would slip outside into the darkness, and hear far up in the frosty sky the whistle of the swans as they flew southward, and fancy them the shield-maids of Odin on their way to some lost battle.

His father, Thorwald Thorwaldson, was king over all the firths and wicks between Coldness in the south and Flatness and the mountain Rauma in the north, and inland over the Uplanders as far as the highest springs of the rivers. He was king by more than blood, for he was the tallest and strongest man in all the land, and the cunningest in battle. He was for ordinary somewhat grave and silent, a dark man with hair and beard the colour of molten iron, whence came his by-name. Yet in a fight no Bearsark could vie with him for fury, and his sword Tyrfing was famed in a thousand songs. On high days the tale of his descent would be sung in the hall, not by Leif, who was low-born and of no account, but by one or other of the chiefs of the Shield-ring. Biorn was happy on such occasions, for he himself came into the songs, since it was right to honour the gentle lady, the Queen. He heard how on the distaff side he was sprung from proud western earls, Thorwolf the Black, and Halfdan and Hallward Skullsplitter. But on the spear side he was of still loftier kin, for Odin was first in his pedigree, and after him the Volsung chiefs, and Gothfred the Proud, and, that no magnificence might be wanting, one Karlamagnus, whom Biorn had never heard of before, but who seemed from his doings to have been a puissant king.

On such occasions there would follow a braggingmatch among the warriors, for a recital of the past was meant as an augury for the future. The time was towards the close of the Wicking-tide, and the world was becoming hard for simple folk. There were endless bickerings with the Tronds in the north and the men of More in the south, and a certain Shockhead, an upsetting king in Norland, was making trouble with his neighbours. Likewise there was one Kristni, a king of the Romans, who sought to dispute with Odin himself. This Kristni was a magic-worker, who clad his followers in white linen instead of byrnies, and gave them runes in place of swords, and sprinkled them with witch water. Biorn did not like what he heard of the warlock, and longed for the day when his father Ironbeard would make an end of him.

Each year before the coming of spring there was a lean season in Hightown. Fish were scarce in the ice-holes, the stock of meal in the meal-ark grew low, and the deep snow made poor hunting in wood or on fell-side. Belts were tightened, and there were hollow cheeks among the thralls. And then one morning the wind would blow from the south, and a strange smell come into the air. The dogs left their lair by the fire and, led by the Garm the old blind patriarch, made a tour of inspection among the outhouses to the edge of the birch woods. Presently would come a rending of the ice on the firth, and patches of inky water would show between the floes. The snow would slip from the fell-side, and leave dripping rock and clammy bent, and the river would break its frosty silence and pour a mighty grey-green flood to the sea. The swans and geese began to fly northward, and the pipits woke among the birches. And at last one day the world put on a new dress, all steel-blue and misty green, and a thousand voices woke of flashing streams and nesting birds and tossing pines, and the dwellers in Hightown knew that spring had fairly come.

Then was Biorn the happy child. All through the long day, and through much of that twilight which is the darkness of a Norland summer, he was abroad on his own errands. With Grim the Hunter he adventured far up on the fells and ate cheese and bannocks in the tents of the wandering Skridfinns, or stalked the cailzie-cock with his arrows in the great pine forest, which in his own mind he called Mirkwood and feared exceedingly. Or he would go fishing with Egil the Fisherman, spearing salmon in the tails of the river pools. But best he loved to go up the firth in the boat which Leif had made him, a finished, clinker-built little model of a war galley, christened the Joy-maker, and catch the big sea fish. Monsters he caught sometimes in the deep water under the cliffs, till he thought he was destined to repeat the exploit of Thor when he went fishing with the giant Hymi, and hooked the Midgard Serpent, the brother of Fenris-wolf, whose coils encircle the earth.

Nor was his education neglected. Arnwulf the Bearsark taught him axe-play and sword-play, and he had a small buckler of his own, not of linden-wood like those of the Wick folk, but of wickerwork after the fashion of his mother's people. He learned to wrestle toughly with the lads of his own age, and to throw a light spear truly at a mark. He was fleet of foot and scoured the fells like a goat, and he could breast the tide in the pool of the great foss up to the very edge of the white water where the trolls lived.

There was a wise woman dwelt on the bay of Sigg. Katla was her name, a woman still black-browed though she was very old, and clever at mending hunters' scars. To her house Biorn went with Leif; and when they had made a meal of her barley-cakes and sour milk, and passed the news of the coast, Leif would fall to probing her craft and get but surly answers. To the boy's question she was kinder. "Let the dead things be, prince," she said. "There's small profit from foreknowledge. Better to take fates as they come sudden round a turn of the road than be watching them with an anxious heart all the way down the hill. The time will come soon enough when you must stand by the Howe of the Dead and call on the ghost-folk."

But Leif coaxed and Biorn harped on the thing, as boys do, and one night about the midsummer time her hour came upon Katla and she spoke without their seeking. There in the dim hut with the apple-green twilight dimming the fells Biorn stood trembling on the brink of the half-world, the woman huddled on the floor, her hand shading her eyes as if she were looking to a far horizon. Her body shook with gusts of passion, and the voice that came from her was not her own. Never so long as he lived did Biorn forget the terrible hour when that voice from beyond the world spoke things he could not understand. "I have been snowed on with snow," it said, "I have been beaten with the rain, I have been drenched with the dew, long have I been dead." It spoke of kings whose names he had never heard, and of the darkness gathering about the Norland, and famine and awe stalking upon the earth.

Then came a whisper from Leif asking the fortune of the young prince of Hightown.

"Death," said the weird-wife, "death, but not yet. The shears of the Norns are still blunt for him, and Skuld has him in keeping."

There was silence for a space, for the fit was passing from Katla. But the voice came again in broken syllables. "His thread runs westward, beyond the Far Isles... not he but the seed of his loins shall win great kingdoms ... beyond the sea-walls.... The All-Father dreams.... Nay, he wakes... he wakes..."

There was a horrible choking sound, and the next Biorn knew was that Leif had fetched water and was dashing it on Katla's face.

It was nearly a week before Biorn recovered his spirits after this adventure, and it was noticeable that neither Leif nor he spoke a word to each other on the matter. But the boy thought much, and from that night he had a new purpose. It seemed that he was fated to travel far, and his fancy forsook the homely life of his own wicks and fells and reached to that outworld of which he had heard in the winter's talk by the hall fire.

There were plenty of folk in Hightown to satisfy his curiosity. There were the Bearsarks, who would spin tales of the rich Frankish lands and the green isles of the Gael. From the Skridfinns he heard of the bitter country in the north where the Jotuns dwelt, and the sun was not and the frost split the rocks to dust, while far underground before great fires the dwarves were hammering gold. But these were only old wives' tales, and he liked better the talk of the sea-going franklins, who would sail in the summer time on trading ventures and pushed farther than any galleys of war. The old sailor, Othere Cranesfoot, was but now back from a voyage which had taken him to Snowland, or, as we say, Iceland. He could tell of the Curdled Sea, like milk set apart for cheese-making, which flowed as fast as a river, and brought down ghoulish beasts and great dragons in its tide. He told, too, of the Sea-walls which were the end of the world, waves higher than any mountain, which ringed the whole ocean. He had seen them, blue and terrible one dawn, before he had swung his helm round and fled southwards. And in Snowland and the ports of the Isles this Othere had heard talk from others of a fine land beyond the sunset, where corn grew unsown like grass, and the capes looked like crusted cow-pats they were so thick with deer, and the dew of the night was honey-dew, so that of a morning a man might breakfast delicately off the face of the meadows.

Full of such marvels, Biorn sought Leif and poured out his heart to him. For the first time he spoke of the weird-wife's spaeing. If his fortune lay in the west, there was the goal to seek. He would find the happy country and reign over it. But Leif shook his head, for he had heard the story before. "To get there you will have to ride over Bilrost, the Rainbow Bridge, like the Gods. I know of the place. It is called Gundbiorn's Reef and it is beyond the world."

All this befell in Biorn's eleventh summer. The winter which followed brought ill luck to Hightown and notably to Ironbeard the King. For in the autumn the Queen, that gentle lady, fell sick, and, though leeches were sought for far and near, and spells and runes were prepared by all who had skill of them, her life ebbed fast and ere Yule she was laid in the Howe of the Dead. The loss of her made Thorwald grimmer and more silent than before, and there was no feasting at the Yule high-tide and but little at the spring merry-making. As for Biorn he sorrowed bitterly for a week, and then, boylike, forgot his grief in the wonder of living.

But that winter brought death in another form. Storms never ceased, and in the New Year the land lay in the stricture of a black frost which froze the beasts in the byres and made Biorn shiver all the night through, though in ordinary winter weather he was hardy enough to dive in the ice-holes. The stock of meal fell low, and when spring tarried famine drew very near. Such a spring no man living remembered. The snow lay deep on the shore till far into May. And when the winds broke they were cold sunless gales which nipped the young life in the earth. The ploughing was backward, and the seed-time was a month too late. The new-born lambs died on the fells and there fell a wasting sickness among the cattle. Few salmon ran up the streams, and the sea-fish seemed to have gone on a journey. Even in summer, the pleasant time, food was scarce, for the grass in the pastures was poor and the cows gave little milk, and the children died. It foreboded a black harvest-time and a blacker winter.

With these misfortunes a fever rose in the blood of the men of Hightown. Such things had happened before for the Norland was never more than one stage distant from famine; and in the old days there had been but a single remedy. Food and wealth must be won from a foray overseas. It was years since Ironbeard had ridden Egir's road to the rich lowlands, and the Bearsarks were growing soft from idleness. Ironbeard himself was willing, for his hall was hateful to him since the Queen's death. Moreover, there was no other way. Food must be found for the winter or the folk would perish.

So a hosting was decreed at harvest-tide, for few men would be needed to win the blasted crops; and there began a jointing of shields and a burnishing of weapons, and the getting ready of the big ships. Also there was a great sortilege-making. Whither to steer, that was the question. There were the rich coasts of England, but they were well guarded, and many of the Norland race were along the wardens. The isles of the Gael were in like case, and, though they were the easier prey, there was less to be had from them. There were soon two parties in the hall, one urging Ironbeard to follow the old track of his kin westward, another looking south to the Frankish shore. The King himself, after the sacrifice of a black heifer, cast the sacred twigs, and they seemed to point to Frankland. Old Arnwulf was deputed on a certain day to hallow three ravens and take their guidance, but, though he said three times the Ravens' spell, he got no clear counsel from the wise birds. Last of all, the weird-wife Katla came from Sigg, and for the space of three days sat in the hall with her head shrouded, taking no meat or drink. When at last she spoke she prophesied ill. She saw a red cloud and it descended on the heads of the warriors, yea of the King himself. As for Hightown she saw it frozen deep in snow like Jotunheim, and rime lay on it like a place long dead. But she bade Ironbeard go to Frankland, for it was so written. "A great kingdom waits," she said, "not for you, but for the seed of your loins." And Biorn shuddered, for they were the words spoken in her hut on that unforgotten midsummer night.

The boy was in an agony lest he should be left behind. But his father decreed that he should go. "These are times when manhood must come fast," he said. "He can bide within the Shield-ring when blows are going. He will be safe enough if it holds. If it breaks, he will sup like the rest of us with Odin."

Then came days of bustle and preparation. Biorn was agog with excitement and yet solemnised, for there was strange work afoot in Hightown. The King made a great festival in the Gods' House, the dark hall near the Howe of the Dead, where no one ventured except in high noon. Cattle were slain in honour of Thor, the God who watched over forays, and likewise a great boar for Frey. The blood was caught up in the sacred bowls, from which the people were sprinkled, and smeared on the altar of blackened fir. Then came the oath-taking, when Ironbeard and his Bearsarks swore brotherhood in battle upon the ship's bulwarks, and the shield's rim, and the horse's shoulder, and the brand's edge. There followed the mixing of blood in the same footprint, a rite to which Biorn was admitted, and a lesser oath for all the people on the great gold ring which lay on the altar. But most solemn of all was the vow the King made to his folk, warriors and franklins alike, when he swore by the dew, the eagle's path, and the valour of Thor.

Then it was Biorn's turn. He was presented to the High Gods as the prince and heir.

Old Arnwulf hammered on his left arm a torque of rough gold, which he must wear always, in life and in death.

"I bring ye the boy, Biorn Thorwaldson When the Gods call for Thorwald it will be his part to lead the launchings and the seafarings and be first when blows are going. Do ye accept him, people of Hightown?"

There was a swelling cry of assent and a beating of hafts on shields. Biorn's heart was lifted with pride, but out of a corner of his eye he saw his father's face. It was very grave, and his gaze was on vacancy.

Though it was a time of bustle, there was no joy in it, as there had been at other hostings. The folk were too hungry, the need was too desperate, and there was something else, a shadow of fate, which lay over Hightown. In the dark of night men had seen the bale-fires burning on the Howe of the Dead. A grey seal had been heard speaking with tongues off

Siggness, and speaking ill words, said the fishermen who saw the beast. A white reindeer had appeared on Sunfell, and the hunter who followed it had not been seen again. By day, too, there was a brooding of hawks on the tide's edge, which was strange at that season. Worst portent of all, the floods of August were followed by high north-east winds that swept the clouds before them, so that all day the sky was a scurrying sea of vapour, and at night the moon showed wild grey shapes moving ever to the west. The dullest could not mistake their meaning; these were the dark horses, and their riders, the Helmed Maidens, mustering for the battle to which Hightown was faring.

As Biorn stared one night at the thronged heavens, he found Leif by his elbow. In front of the dark company of the sky a white cloud was scudding, tinged with the pale moon. Leif quoted from the speech of the Giant-wife Rimegerd to Helgi in the song:

"Three nines of maiden, ride,
But one rides before them,
A white maid helmed:
From their manes the steeds shake
Dew into the deep dales,
Hail upon the high woods."

"It bodes well," said Biorn. "They ride to choose those whom we slay. There will be high doings ere Yule."

"Not so well," said Leif. "They come from the Norland, and it is our folk they go to choose. I fear me Hightown will soon be full of widow women."

At last came the day of sailing. The six galleys of war were brought down from their sheds, and on the rollers for the launching he-goats were bound so that the keels slid blood-stained into the sea. This was the 'roller-reddening,' a custom bequeathed from their forefathers, though the old men of the place muttered darkly that the ritual had been departed from, and that in the great days it was the blood not of goats, but of captive foemen that had reddened the galleys and the tide.

The thralls sat at the thwarts, for there was no breeze that day in the narrow firth. Then came the chief warriors in short fur jackets, splendid in glittering helms and byrnies, and each with his thrall bearing his battle-axe. Followed the fighting commonalty with axe and spear. Last came Ironbeard, stern as ever, and Biorn with his heart torn between eagerness and regret. Only the children, the women, and the old men were left in Hightown, and they stood on the shingle watching till the last galley had passed out of sight beyond Siggness, and was swallowed up in the brume that cloaked the west. There were no tears in that grim leave-taking. Hightown had faced the like before with a heavy heart, but with dry eyes and a proud head. Leif, though a cripple, went with the Wickings, for he had great skill of the sea.

There was not a breath of wind for three days and three nights, as they coasted southward, with the peaks of the Norland on their port, and to starboard the skerries that kept guard on the firths. Through the haze they could now and then see to landward trees and cliffs, but never a human face. Once there was an alarm of another fleet, and the shields were slung outboard, but it proved to be only a wedding-party passing from wick to wick, and they gave it greeting and sailed on. These were eerie cheerless days. The thralls sweated in shifts at the oars, and the betterborn talked low among themselves, as if the air were full of ears. "Ran is heating her ovens," said Leif, as he watched the warm fog mingle with the oarthresh.

On the fourth morning there came a break in the clouds, and the sight of a high hill gave Leif the clue for his reckoning. The prows swung seaward, and the galleys steered for the broad ocean. That afternoon there sprang up the north-east wind for which they had been waiting. Sails were hoisted on the short masts, oars were shipped and lashed under the bulwarks, and the thralls clustered in the prows to rest their weary limbs and dice with knucklebones. The spirits of all lightened, and there was loud talk in the sterns among the Bearsarks. In the night the wind freshened, and the long shallow boats rolled filthily so that the teeth shook in a man's head, and over the swish of the waves and the creaking of the sheets there was a perpetual din of arms clashing. Biorn was miserably ill for some hours, and made sport for the seasoned voyagers.

"It will not hold," Leif prophesied. "I smell rime ahead and quiet seas."

He had spoken truly, for the sixth day the wind fell and they moved once more over still, misty waters. The thralls returned to their oars and the voices of the well-born fell low again. These were ghoulish days for Biorn, who had been accustomed to the clear lights and the clear darkness of his own land. Only once in four days they saw the sun, and then it was as red as blood, so that his heart trembled.

On the eleventh day Ironbeard summoned Leif and asked his skill of the voyage. "I know not," was the answer. "I cannot steer a course except under clean skies. We ran well with the wind aback, but now I am blind and the Gods are pilots. Some day soon we must make landfall, but I know not whether on English or Frankish shores."

After that Leif would sit in long spells of brooding, for he had a sense in him of direction to which he sought to give free play, a sense built up from old voyages over these very seas. The result of his meditations was that he swung more to the south, and events proved him wise. For on the fifteenth day came a lift in the fog and with it the noise of tides washing near at hand on a rough coast. Suddenly almost overhead they were aware of a great white headland, on the summit of which the sun shone on grass.

Leif gave a shout. "My skill has riot failed me," he cried. "We enter the Frankish firth. See, there is the butt of England!"

After that the helms were swung round, and a course laid south by west. And then the mist came again, but this time it was less of a shroud, for birds hovered about their wake, so that they were always conscious of land. Because of the strength of the tides the rowers made slow progress, and it was not till the late afternoon of the seventeenth day that Leif approached Ironbeard with a proud head and spoke a word. The King nodded, and Leif took his stand in the prow with the lead in his hand. The sea mirroring the mist was leaden dull, but the old pilot smelt shoal water.

Warily he sounded, till suddenly out of the gloom a spit of land rose on the port, and it was clear that they were entering the mouth of a river. The six galleys jolted across the sandbar, Leif in the foremost peering ahead and shouting every now and then an order. It was fine weather for a surprise landing. Biorn saw only low sand-dunes green with coarse grasses and, somewhere behind, the darkness of a forest. But he could not tear his eyes from it, for it was the long-dreamed-of Roman land.

Then a strange thing befell. A madness seemed to come on Leif. He left his pilot's stand and rushed to the stern where the King stood. Flinging himself on his knees, he clasped Ironbeard's legs and poured out supplications.

"Return!" he cried. "While there is yet time, return. Seek England, Gael-land, anywhere, but not this place. I see blood in the stream and blood on the strand. Our blood, your blood, my King! There is doom for the folk of Thorwald by this river!"

The King's face did not change. "What will be, will be," he said gravely. "We abide by our purpose and will take what Thor sends with a stout heart. How say you, my brave ones?"

And all shouted to go forward, for the sight of a new country had fired their blood. Leif sat huddled by the bulwarks, with a white face and a gasp in his throat, like one coming out of a swoon.

They went ashore at a bend of the stream where was a sandy cape, beached the galleys, felled trees from the neighbouring forest and built them a stockade. The dying sun flushed water and wood with angry crimson, and Biorn observed that the men wrought as it were in a world of blood. "That is the meaning of Leif's whimsies," he thought, and so comforted himself.

That night the Northmen slept in peace, but the scouts brought back word of a desert country, no men or cattle, and ashes where once had been dwellings.

"Our kinsfolk have been here before us," said King Ironbeard grimly. He did not love the Danes, though he had fought by their side.

Half the force was left as a guard by the ships, and next day the rest went forward up the valley at a slant from the river's course. For that way, ran the tale, lay a great Roman house, a palace of King Kristni, where much gold was to be had for the lifting. By midday they were among pleasant meadows, but the raiders had been there, for the houses were fired and the orchards hacked down. Then came a shout and, turning back, they saw a flame spring to the pale autumn skies. "The ships!" rose the cry, and the lightest of foot were sent back for news.

They returned with a sorry tale. Of the ships and the stockade nothing remained but hot cinders. Half the guard were dead, and old Arnwulf, the captain, lay blood-eagled on the edge of the tide. The others had gone they knew not where, but doubtless into the forests.

"Our kinsfolks' handiwork," said Ironbeard. "We are indeed forestalled, my heroes."

A council was held and it was resolved to make a camp by the stream and defend it against all comers, till such time as under Leif's guidance new ships could be built.

"Axes will never ring on them," said Leif under his breath. He walked now like a man who was fey and his face was that of another world.

He spoke truth, for as they moved towards the riverbank, just before the darkening, in a glade between two forests Fate met them. There was barely time to form the Shield-ring ere their enemies were upon them, a mass of wild men in wolves' skins and at their head mounted warriors in byrnies, with long swords that flashed and fell.

Biorn saw little of the battle, wedged in the heart of the Shield-ring. He heard the shouts of the enemy, and the clangour of blows, and the sharp intake of breath, but chiefly he heard the beating of his own heart. The ring swayed and moved as it gave before the onset or pressed to an attack of its own, and Biorn found himself stumbling over the dead. "I am Biorn, and my father is King," he repeated to himself, the spell he had so often used when on the fells or the firths he had met fear.

Night came and a young moon, and still the fight continued. But the Shield-ring was growing ragged, for the men of Hightown were fighting one to eight, and these are odds that cannot last. Sometimes it would waver, and an enemy would slip inside, and before he sank dead would have sorely wounded one of Ironbeard's company.

And now Biorn could see his father, larger than human, it seemed, in the dim light, swinging his sword Tyrfing, and crooning to himself as he laid low his antagonists. At the sight a madness rose in the boy's heart. Behind in the sky clouds were banking, dark clouds like horses, with one ahead white and moontipped, the very riders he had watched with Leif from the firth shore. The Walkyries were come for the chosen, and he would fain be one of them. All fear had gone from him. His passion was to be by his father's side and strike his small blow, beside those mighty ones which Thor could not have bettered.

But even as he was thus uplifted the end came. Thorwald Thorwaldson tottered and went down, for a hurled axe had cleft him between helm and byrnie. With him fell the last hope of Hightown and the famished clan under Sunfell. The Shield-ring was no more. Biorn found himself swept back as the press of numbers overbore the little knot of sorely wounded men. Someone caught him by the arm and snatched him from the mellay into the cover of a thicket. He saw dimly that it was Leif.

He was giddy and retching from weariness, and something inside him was cold as ice, though his head burned. It was not rage or grief, but awe, for his father had fallen and the end of the world had come. The noise of the battle died, as the two pushed through the undergrowth and came into the open spaces of the wood. It was growing very dark, but still Leif dragged him onwards. Then suddenly he fell forward on his face, and Biorn, as he stumbled over him found his hands wet with blood.

"I am for death," Leif whispered. "Put your ear close, prince. I am Leif the Outborn and I know the hidden things.... You are the heir of Thorwald Thorwaldson and you will not die.... I see a long road, but at the end a great kingdom. Farewell, little Biorn. We have been good comrades, you and I. Katla from Sigg spoke the true word..."

And when Biorn fetched water in his horn from a woodland pool he found Leif with a cold brow.

Blind with sorrow and fatigue, the boy stumbled on, without purpose. He was lonely in the wide world, many miles from his home, and all his kin were slain. Rain blew from the south-west and beat in his face, the brambles tore his legs, but he was dead to all things. Would that the Shield Maids had chosen him to go with that brave company to the bright hall of Odin! But he was only a boy and they did not choose striplings.

Suddenly in a clearing a pin-point of light pricked the darkness.

The desire for human companionship came over him, even though it were that of enemy or outcast. He staggered to the door and beat on it feebly. A voice spoke from within, but he did not hear what it said.

Again he beat and again the voice came. And now his knocking grew feebler, for he was at the end of his strength.

Then the bar was suddenly withdrawn and he was looking inside a poor hut, smoky from the wood-fire in the midst of it. An old woman sat by it with a bowl in her hand, and an oldish man with a cudgel stood before him. He did not understand their speech, but he gathered he was being asked his errand.

"I am Biorn," he said, "and my father was Ironbeard, the King."

They shook their heads, but since they saw only a weary, tattered boy they lost their fears. They invited him indoors, and their voices were kindly. Nodding with exhaustion, he was given a stool to sit on and a bowl of coarse porridge was put into his hands. They plied him with questions, but he could make nothing of their tongue.

Then the thrall rose, yawned, and dropped the bar over the door. The sound was to the boy like the clanging of iron gates on his old happy world. For a moment he was on the brink of tears. But he set his teeth and stiffened his drooping neck.

"I am Biorn," he said aloud, "and my father was a king."

They nodded to each other and smiled. They thought his words were a grace before meat.

CHAPTER II. THE ENGLISHMAN

Part I

The little hut among the oak trees was dim in the October twilight on the evening of St. Callixtus' Day. It had been used by swineherds, for the earthen floor was puddled by the feet of generations of hogs, and in the corner lay piles of rotting acorns. Outside the mist had filled the forest, and the ways were muffled with fallen leaves, so that the four men who approached the place came as stealthily as shades.

They reconnoitred a moment at the entrance, for it was a country of war.

"Quarters for the night," said one, and put his shoulder to the door of oak-toppings hinged on strips of cowhide.

But he had not taken a step inside before he hastily withdrew.

"There is something there," he cried, "something that breathes. A light, Gil."

One of the four lit a lantern from his flint and poked it within. It revealed the foul floor and the rotting acorns, and in the far corner, on a bed of withered boughs, something dark which might be a man. They stood still and listened. There was the sound of painful breathing, and then the gasp with which a sick man wakens. A figure disengaged itself from the shadows. Seeing it was but one man, the four pushed inside, and the last pulled the door to behind him.

"What have we here?" the leader cried. A man had dragged himself to his feet, a short, square fellow who held himself erect with a grip on a side-post. His eyes were vacant, dazzled by the light and also by pain. He seemed to have had hard usage that day, for his shaggy locks were matted with blood from a sword-cut above his forehead, one arm hung limp, and his tunic was torn and gashed. He had no weapons but a knife which he held blade upwards in the hollow of his big hand.

The four who confronted him were as ill-looking a quartet as Duke William's motley host could show. One, the leader, was an unfrocked priest of Rouen; one was a hedge-robber from the western marches who had followed Alan of Brittany; a third had the olive cheeks and the long nose of the south; and the fourth was a heavy German from beyond the Rhine. They were the kites that batten on the offal of war, and the great battle on the seashore having been won by better men, were creeping into the conquered land for the firstfruits of its plunder.

"An English porker," cried the leader. "We will have the tusks off him." Indeed, in the wild light the wounded man, with his flat face and forked beard, had the look of a boar cornered by hounds.

"'Ware his teeth," said the one they called Gil. "He has a knife in his trotter."

The evil faces of the four were growing merry. They were worthless soldiers, but adepts in murder. Loot was their first thought, but after that furtive slaying. There seemed nothing to rob here, but there was weak flesh to make sport of.

Gil warily crept on one side, where he held his spear ready. The ex-priest, who had picked up somewhere a round English buckler, gave the orders. "I will run in on him, and take his stroke, so you be ready to close. There is nothing to be feared from the swine. See, he is blooded and faints."

The lantern had been set on the ground by the door and revealed only the lower limbs of the four. Their heads were murky in shadow. Their speech was foreign to the wounded man, but he saw their purpose. He was clearly foredone with pain, but his vacant eyes kindled to slow anger, and he shook back his hair so that the bleeding broke out again on his forehead. He was as silent as an old tusker at bay.

The ex-priest gave the word and the four closed in on him. He defeated their plan by hurling himself on the leader's shield, so that his weight bore him backwards and he could not use his weapon. The spears on the flanks failed for the same reason, and the two men posted there had well-nigh been the death of each other. The fourth, the one from the south, whose business it had been to support the priest, tripped and fell sprawling beside the lantern.

The Englishman had one arm round the priest's neck and was squeezing the breath out of him. But the blood of the four was kindling, and they had vengeance instead of sport to seek. Mouthing curses, the three of them went to the rescue of the leader, and a weaponless and sore-wounded man cannot strive with such odds. They overpowered him, bending his arms viciously back and kicking his broken head. Their oaths filled the hut with an ugly clamour, but no sound came from their victim.

Suddenly a gust of air set the lantern flickering, and a new-comer stood in the doorway. He picked up the light and looked down on the struggle. He was a tall, very lean man, smooth faced, and black haired, helmetless and shieldless, but wearing the plated hauberk of the soldier. There was no scabbard on his left side, but his right hand held a long bright sword.

For a second he lifted the light high, while he took in the scene. His eyes were dark and dancing, like the ripples on a peat stream. "So-ho!" he said softly. "Murder! And by our own vermin!"

He appeared to brood for a second, and then he acted. For he set the light very carefully in the crook of a joist so that it illumined the whole hut. Then he reached out a hand, plucked the ex-priest from his quarry, and, swinging him in both arms, tossed him through the door into the darkness. It would seem that he fell hard, for there was a groan and then silence.

"One less," he said softly.

The three had turned to face him, warned by Gil's exclamation, and found themselves looking at the ominous bar of light which was his sword. Cornered like rats, they took small comfort from the odds. They were ready to surrender, still readier to run, and they stood on their defence with no fight in their faces, whining in their several patois. All but the man from the south. He was creeping round in the darkness by the walls, and had in his hands a knife. No mailed hauberk protected the interloper's back and there was a space there for steel to quiver between his shoulder blades.

The newcomer did not see, but the eyes of the wounded man seemed to have been cleared by the scuffle. He was now free, and from the floor he snatched the round shield which the ex-priest had carried, and hurled it straight at the creeping miscreant. It was a heavy oaken thing with rim and boss of iron, and it caught him fairly above the ear, so that he dropped like a poled ox. The stranger turned his head to see what was happening. "A lucky shot, friend," he cried. "I thank you." And he addressed himself to the two pitiful bandits who remained.

But their eyes were looking beyond him to the door, and their jaws had dropped in terror. For from outside came the sound of horses' hooves and bridles, and two riders had dismounted and were peering into the hut. The first was a very mountain of a man, whose conical helmet surmounted a vast pale face, on which blond moustaches hung like the teeth of a walrus. The said helmet was grievously battered, and the nose-piece was awry as if from some fierce blow, but there was no scar on the skin. His long hauberk was wrought in scales of steel and silver, and the fillets which bound his great legs were of fine red leather. Behind him came a grizzled squire, bearing a kite-shaped shield painted with the cognisance of a dove.

"What have we here?" said the knight in a reedy voice like a boy's. His pale eyes contemplated the figures, the wounded man, now faint again with pain and half-fallen on the litter of branches; his deliverer, tall and grim, but with laughing face; the two murderers cringing in their fear; in a corner the huddled body of the man from the south half hidden by the shield. "Speak, fellow," and he addressed the soldier. "What work has been toward?

Have you not had your bellyfull of battles that you must scrabble like rats in this hovel? What are you called, and whence come you?"

The soldier lifted his brow, looked his questioner full in the face, and, as if liking what he found there, bowed his head in respect. The huge man had the air of one to be obeyed.

"I am of the Duke's army," he said, "and was sent on to reconnoitre the forest roads I stumbled on this hut and found four men about to slay a wounded English. One lies outside where I flung him, another is there with a cracked skull, and you have before you the remnant."

The knight seemed to consider. "And why should a soldier of the Duke's be so careful of English lives?" he asked.

"I would help my lord Duke to conquer this land," was the answer. "We have broken their army and the way is straight before us. We shall have to fight other armies, but we cannot be fighting all our days, and we do not conquer England till England accepts us. I have heard enough of that stubborn people to know that the way to win them is not by murder. A fair fight, and then honest dealing and mercy, say I."

The knight laughed. "A Solomon in judgment," he cried. "But who are you that bear a sword and wear gold on your finger?"

The old squire broke in. "My lord Count, I know the man. He is a hunter of the Lord Odo's, and has a name for valour. He wrought mightily this morning on the hill. They call him Jehan the Hunter, and sometimes Jehan the Outborn, for no man knows his comings. There is a rumour that he is of high blood, and truly in battle he bears himself like a prince. The monks loved him not, but the Lord Odo favoured him."

The knight looked steadily for the space of a moment at the tall soldier, and his light eyes seemed to read deep. "Are you that man," he asked at last, and got the reply: "I am Jehan the Hunter."

"Bid my fellows attend to yon scum," he told his squire. "The camp marshal will have fruit for his gallows. The sweepings of all Europe have drifted with us to England, and it is our business to make bonfire of them before they breed a plague.... See to the wounded man, likewise. He may be one of the stout house-carles who fought with Harold at Stamford, and to meet us raced like a gale through the length of England. By the Mount of the Archangel, I would fain win such mettle to our cause."

Presently the hut was empty save for the two soldiers, who faced each other while the lantern flickered to its end on the rafters.

"The good Odo is dead," said the knight. "An arrow in the left eye has bereft our Duke of a noble ally and increased the blessedness of the City of Paradise. You are masterless now.

Will you ride with me on my service, you Jehan the Hunter? It would appear that we are alike in our ways of thinking. They call me the Dove from the shield I bear, and a dove I seek to be in the winning of England. The hawk's task is over when the battle is won, and he who has but the sword for weapon is no hawk, but carrion-crow. We have to set our Duke on the throne, but that is but the first step. There are more battles before us, and when they are ended begins the slow task of the conquest of English hearts. How say you, Jehan? Will you ride north with me on this errand, and out of the lands which are granted me to govern have a corner on which to practise your creed?"

So it befell that Jehan the Hunter, sometimes called Jehan the Outborn, joined the company of Ivo of Dives, and followed him when Duke William swept northward laughing his gross jolly laughter and swearing terribly by the splendour of God.

Part II

Two years later in the same month of the year Jehan rode east out of Ivo's new castle of Belvoir to visit the manor of which, by the grace of God and the King and the favour of the Count of Dives, he was now the lord. By the Dove's side he had been north to Durham and west to the Welsh marches, rather on falcon's than on dove's errands, for Ivo held that the crooning of peace notes came best after hard blows. But at his worst he was hawk and not crow, and malice did not follow his steps. The men he beat had a rude respect for one who was just and patient in victory, and whose laughter did not spare himself. Like master like man; and Jehan was presently so sealed of Ivo's brotherhood that in the tales of the time the two names were rarely separate. The jealous, swift to deprecate good fortune, spared the Outborn, for it was observed that he stood aside while others scrambled for gain. Also, though no man knew his birth, he bore himself with the pride of a king.

When Ivo's raw stone towers faded in the blue distance, the road led from shaggy uplands into a forested plain, with knolls at intervals which gave the traveller a prospect of sullen levels up to the fringe of the fens and the line of the sea. Six men-at-arms jolted at his back on little country-red horses, for Jehan did his tasks with few helpers; and they rode well in the rear, for he loved to be alone. The weather was all October gleams and glooms, now the sunshine of April, now the purple depths of a thunderstorm. There was no rain in the air, but an infinity of mist, which moved in fantastic shapes, rolling close about the cavalcade, so that the very road edge was obscured, now dissolving into clear light, now opening up corridors at the end of which some landmark appeared at an immeasurable distance. In that fantastic afternoon the solid earth seemed to be dissolving, and Jehan's thoughts as he journeyed ranged like the mists.

He told himself that he had discovered his country. He, the Outborn, had come home; the landless had found his settlement. He loved every acre of this strange England, its changing skies, the soft pastures in the valleys, the copses that clung like moss to the hills, the wide moorland that lay quiet as a grave from mountain to mountain. But this day something new had been joined to his affection. The air that met him from the east had that in it which stirred some antique memory. There was brine in it from the unruly eastern sea, and the sourness of marsh water, and the sweetness of marsh herbage. As the forest thinned into scrub again it came stronger and fresher, and he found himself sniffing it like a hungry man at the approach of food. "If my manor of Highstead is like this," he told himself, "I think I will lay my bones there."

At a turn of the road where two grassy tracks forked, he passed a graven stone now chipped and moss-grown, set on noble eminence among reddening thorns. It was an altar to the old gods of the land, there had been another such in the forest of his childhood. The priest had told him it was the shrine of the Lord Apollo and forbade him on the pain of a mighty cursing to do reverence to it. Nevertheless he had been wont to doff his cap when he passed it, for he respected a god that lived in the woods instead of a clammy church. Now the sight of the ancient thing seemed an omen. It linked up the past and the present. He waved a greeting to it. "Hail, old friend," he said. "Bid your master be with me, whoever he be, for I go to find a home."

One of his fellows rode up to his side. "We are within a mile of Highstead," he told him. "Better go warily, for the King's law runs limpingly in the fanlands. I counsel that a picket be sent forward to report if the way be clear. Every churl that we passed on the road will have sent news of our coming."

"So much the better," said Jehan. "Man, I come not as a thief in the night. This is a daylight business. If I am to live my days here I must make a fair conquest."

The man fell back sullenly, and there were anxious faces in the retinue jogging twenty yards behind. But no care sat on Jehan's brow. He plucked sprays of autumn berries and tossed and caught them, he sang gently to himself and spoke his thoughts to his horse. Harm could not come to him when air and scene woke in his heart such strange familiarity.

A last turn of the road showed Highstead before him, two furlongs distant. The thatched roof of the hall rose out of a cluster of shingled huts on a mound defended by moat and palisade. No smoke came from the dwelling, and no man was visible, but not for nothing was Jehan named the Hunter. He was aware that every tuft of reed and scrog of wood concealed a spear or a bowman. So he set his head stiff and laughed, and hummed a bar of a song which the ferry-men used to sing on Seine side. "A man does not fight to win his home," he told his horse, "but only to defend it when he has won it. If God so wills I shall be welcomed with open gates: otherwise there will be burying ere nightfall."

In this fashion he rode steadfastly toward the silent burg. Now he was within a stone's throw of it, and no spear had been launched; now he was before the massive oaken gate.

Suddenly it swung open and a man came out. He was a short, square fellow who limped, and, half hidden by his long hair, a great scar showed white on his forehead.

"In whose name?" he asked in the English tongue.

"In the name of our lord the King and the Earl Ivo."

"That is no passport," said the man.

"In my own name, then, in the name of Jehan the Hunter."

The man took two steps forward and laid a hand on the off stirrup. Jehan leaped to the ground and kissed him on both cheeks.

"We have met before, friend," he said, and he took between his palms the joined hands of his new liege.

"Two years back on the night of Hastings," said the man. "But for that meeting, my lord, you had tasted twenty arrows betwixt Highstead and the forest."

Part III

"I go to visit my neighbours," said Jehan next morning.

Arn the Steward stared at his master with a puzzled face. "You will get a dusty welcome," he said. "There is but the Lady Hilda at Galland, and her brother Aelward is still at odds with your Duke."

Nevertheless Jehan rode out in a clear dawn of St. Luke's summer, leaving a wondering man behind him, and he rode alone, having sent back his men-at-arms to Ivo. "He has the bold heart," said Arn to himself. "If there be many French like him there will assuredly be a new England."

At Galland, which is low down in the fen country, he found a sullen girl. She met him at the bridge of the Galland fen and her grey eyes flashed fire. She was a tall maid, very fair to look upon, and the blue tunic which she wore over her russet gown was cunningly embroidered. Embroidered too with gold was the hood which confined her plaited yellow hair.

"You find a defenceless house and a woman to conquer," she railed.

"Long may it need no other warder," said Jehan, dismounting and looking at her across the water.

"The fortune of war has given me a home, mistress. I would dwell in amity with my neighbours."

"Amity!" she cried in scorn. "You will get none from me. My brother Aelward will do the parleying."

"So be it," he said. "Be assured I will never cross this water into Galland till you bid me."

He turned and rode home, and for a month was busied with the work of his farms. When he came again it was on a dark day in November, and every runnel of the fens was swollen. He got the same answer from the girl, and with it a warning "Aelward and his men wait for you in the oakshaw," she told him. "I sent word to them when the thralls brought news of you." And her pretty face was hard and angry.

Jehan laughed. "Now, by your leave, mistress, I will wait here the hour or two till nightfall. I am Englishman enough to know that your folk do not strike in the dark."

He returned to Highstead unscathed, and a week later came a message from Aelward. "Meet me," it ran, "to-morrow by the Danes' barrow at noon, and we will know whether Englishman or Frenchman is to bear rule in this land."

Jehan donned his hauberk and girt himself with his long sword. "There will be hot work to-day in that forest," he told Arn, who was busied with the trussing of his mail.

"God prosper you, master," said the steward. "Frenchman or no, you are such a man as I love. Beware of Aelward and his downward stroke, for he has the strength of ten."

At noon by the Danes' barrow Jehan met a young tow-headed giant, who spoke with the back of his throat and made surly-response to the other's greeting. It was a blue winter's day, with rime still white on the grass, and the forest was very still. The Saxon had the shorter sword and a round buckler; Jehan fought only with his blade.

At the first bout they strove with steel, and were ill-matched at that, for the heavy strength of the fenman was futile against the lithe speed of the hunter. Jehan ringed him in circles of light, and the famous downward stroke was expended on vacant air. He played with him till he breathed heavily like a cow, and then by a sleight of hand sent his sword spinning among the oak mast. The young giant stood sulkily before him, unarmed, deeply shamed, waiting on his death, but with no fear in his eyes.

Jehan tossed his own blade to the ground, and stripped off his hauberk. "We have fought with weapons," he said, "now we will fight in the ancient way."

There followed a very different contest. Aelward lost his shamefastness and his slow blood fired as flesh met flesh and sinew strained against sinew. His great arms crushed the Frenchman till the ribs cracked, but always the other slipped through and evaded the fatal hug. And as the struggle continued Aelward's heart warmed to his enemy. When their swords crossed he had hated him like death; now he seemed to be striving with a kinsman.

Suddenly, when victory looked very near, he found the earth moving from beneath him, and a mountain descended on his skull. When he blinked himself into consciousness again, Jehan was laving his head from a pool in an oak-root.

"I will teach you that throw some day, friend," he was saying. "Had I not known the trick of it, you had mauled me sadly. I had liefer grapple with a bear."

Aelward moistened his lips. "You have beat me fairly, armed and weaponless," he said, and his voice had no anger in it.

"Talk not of beating between neighbours," was the answer. "We have played together and I have had the luck of it. It will be your turn to break my head to-morrow."

"Head matters little," grumbled Aelward. "Mine has stood harder dints. But you have broken my leg, and that means a month of housekeeping."

Jehan made splints of ash for the leg, and set him upon his horse, and in this wise they came to the bridge of Galland fen. On the far side of the water stood the Lady Hilda. He halted and waited on her bidding. She gazed speechless at the horse whereon sat her brother with a clouted scalp.

"What ails you, Frenchman?" said Aelward. "It is but a half-grown girl of my father's begetting."

"I have vowed not to pass that bridge till yonder lady bids me."

"Then for the pity of Christ bid him, sister. He and I are warm with play and yearn for a flagon."

In this manner did Jehan first enter the house of Galland, whence in the next cowslip-time he carried a bride to Highstead.

The months passed smoothly in the house on the knoll above the fat fen pastures. Jehan forsook his woodcraft for the work of byre and furrow and sheepfold, and the yield of his lands grew under his wardenship. He brought heavy French cattle to improve the little native breed, and made a garden of fruit trees where once had been only bent and sedge. The thralls wrought cheerfully for him, for he was a kindly master, and the freemen of the manor had no complaint against one who did impartial justice and respected their slow and ancient ways. As for skill in hunting, there was no fellow to the lord of Highstead between Trent and Thames.

Inside the homestead the Lady Hilda moved happily, a wife smiling and well content. She had won more than a husband; it seemed she had made a convert; for daily Jehan grew into the country-side as if he had been born in it. Something in the soft woodland air and the sharper tang of the fens and the sea awoke response from his innermost soul. An aching affection was born in him for every acre of his little heritage. His son, dark like his father, who made his first diffident pilgrimages in the sunny close where the pigeons cooed, was not more thirled to English soil.

They were quiet years in that remote place, for Aelward over at Galland had made his peace with the King. But when the little Jehan was four years old the tides of war lapped again to the forest edges. One Hugo of Auchy, who had had a usurer to his father and had risen in an iron age by a merciless greed, came a-foraying from the north to see how he might add to his fortunes. Men called him the Crane, for he was tall and lean and parchment-skinned, and to his banner resorted all malcontents and broken men. He sought to conduct a second Conquest, making war on the English who still held their lands, but sparing the French manors. The King's justice was slow-footed, and the King was far away, so the threatened men, banded together to hold their own by their own might.

Aelward brought the news from Galland that the Crane had entered their borders. The good Ivo was overseas, busy on the Brittany marches, and there was no ruler in Fenland.

"You he will spare," Aelward told his sister's husband. "He does not war with you new-comers. But us of the old stock he claims as his prey. How say you, Frenchman? Will you reason with him? Hereaways we are peaceful folk, and would fain get on with our harvest."

"I will reason with him," said Jehan, "and by the only logic that such carrion understands. I am by your side, brother. There is but the one cause for all us countrymen."

But that afternoon as he walked abroad in his cornlands he saw a portent. A heron rose out of the shallows, and a harrier-hawk swooped to the pounce, but the long bird flopped securely into the western sky, and the hawk dropped at his feet, dead but with no mark of a wound.

"Here be marvels," said Jehan, and with that there came on him the foreknowledge of fate, which in the brave heart wakes awe, but no fear. He stood silent for a time and gazed over his homelands. The bere was shaking white and gold in the light evening wind; in the new orchard he had planted the apples were reddening; from the edge of the forest land rose wreaths of smoke where the thralls were busy with wood-clearing. There was little sound in the air, but from the steading came the happy laughter of a child. Jehan stood very still, and his wistful eyes drank the peace of it.

"Non nobis, Domine," he said, for a priest had once had the training of him. "But I leave that which shall not die."

He summoned his wife and told her of the coming of the Crane. From a finger of his left hand he took the thick ring of gold which Ivo had marked years before in the Wealden hut.

"I have a notion that I am going a long journey," he told her. "If I do not return, the Lord Ivo will confirm the little lad in these lands of ours. But to you and for his sake I make my own bequest. Wear this ring for him till he is a man, and then bid him wear it as his father's guerdon. I had it from my father, who had it from his, and my grandfather told me the tale of it. In his grandsire's day it was a mighty armlet, but in the famine years it was melted and part sold, and only this remains. Some one of us far back was a king, and this is the badge of a king's house. There comes a day, little one, when the fruit of our bodies shall possess a throne. See that the lad be royal in thought and deed, as he is royal in blood."

Next morning he kissed his wife and fondled his little son, and with his men rode northward, his eyes wistful but his mouth smiling.

What followed was for generations a tale among humble folk in England, who knew nothing of the deeds of the King's armies. By cottage fires they wove stories about it and made simple songs, the echo of which may still be traced by curious scholars. There is something of it in the great saga of Robin Hood, and long after the fens were drained women hushed their babies with snatches about the Crane and the Falcon, and fairy tales of a certain John of the Shaws, who became one with Jack the Giant-killer and all the nursery heroes.

Jehan and his band met Aelward at the appointed rendezvous, and soon were joined by a dozen knots of lusty yeomen, who fought not only for themselves but for the law of England and the peace of the new king. Of the little force Jehan was appointed leader, and once again became the Hunter, stalking a baser quarry than wolf or boar. For the Crane and his rabble, flushed with easy conquest, kept ill watch, and the tongues of forest running down to the fenland made a good hunting ground for a wary forester.

Jehan's pickets found Hugo of Auchy by the Sheen brook and brought back tidings. Thereupon a subtle plan was made. By day and night the invaders' camp was kept uneasy; there would be sudden attacks, which died down after a few blows; stragglers disappeared, scouts never returned; and when a peasant was brought in and forced to speak, he told with scared face a tale of the great mustering of desperate men in this or that quarter. The Crane was a hardy fighter, but the mystery baffled him, and he became cautious, and, after the fashion of his kind credulous. Bit by bit Jehan shepherded him into the trap he had prepared. He had but one man to the enemy's six, and must drain that enemy's strength before he struck. Meantime the little steadings went up in flames, but with every blaze seen in the autumn dusk the English temper grew more stubborn. They waited confidently on the reckoning.

It came on a bleak morning when the east wind blew rain and fog from the sea. The Crane was in a spit of open woodland, with before him and on either side deep fenland with paths known only to its dwellers. Then Jehan struck. He drove his enemy to the point of the dry ground, and thrust him into the marshes. Not since the time of the Danes had the land known such a slaying. The refuse of France and the traitor English who had joined them went down like sheep before wolves. When the Lord Ivo arrived in the late afternoon, having ridden hot-speed from the south coast when he got the tidings, he found little left of the marauders save the dead on the land and the scum of red on the fen pools.

Jehan lay by a clump of hazels, the blood welling from an axe-wound in the neck. His face was ashen with the oncoming of death, but he smiled as he looked up at his lord.

"The Crane pecked me," he said. "He had a stout bill, if a black heart."

Ivo wept aloud, being pitiful as he was brave. He would have scoured the country for a priest.

"Farewell, old comrade," he sobbed. "Give greeting to Odo in Paradise, and keep a place for me by your side. I will nourish your son, as if he had been that one of my own whom Heaven has denied me. Tarry a little, dear heart, and the Priest of Glede will be here to shrive you."

Through the thicket there crawled a mighty figure, his yellow hair dabbled in blood, and his breath labouring like wind in a threshing-floor. He lay down by Jehan's side, and with a last effort kissed him on the lips.

"Priest!" cried the dying Aelward. "What need is there of priest to help us two English on our way to God?"

CHAPTER III. THE WIFE OF FLANDERS

From the bed set high on a dais came eerie spasms of laughter, a harsh cackle like fowls at feeding time.

"Is that the last of them, Anton?" said a voice.

A little serving-man with an apple-hued face bowed in reply. He bowed with difficulty, for in his arms he held a huge grey cat, which still mewed with the excitement of the chase. Rats had been turned loose on the floor, and it had accounted for them to the accompaniment of a shrill urging from the bed. Now the sport was over, and the domestics who had crowded round the door to see it had slipped away, leaving only Anton and the cat.

"Give Tib a full meal of offal," came the order, "and away with yourself. Your rats are a weak breed. Get me the stout grey monsters like Tuesday se'ennight."

The room was empty now save for two figures both wearing the habit of the religious. Near the bed sat a man in the full black robe and hood of the monks of Cluny. He warmed plump hands at the brazier and seemed at ease and at home. By the door stood a different figure in the shabby clothes of a parish priest, a curate from the kirk of St. Martin's who had been a scandalised spectator of the rat hunt. He shuffled his feet as if uncertain of his next step, a thin, pale man with a pinched mouth and timid earnest eyes.

The glance from the bed fell on him "What will the fellow be at?" said the voice testily. "He stands there like a sow about to litter, and stares and grunts. Good e'en to you, friend. When you are wanted you will be sent for Jesu's name, what have I done to have that howlet glowering at me?"

The priest at the words crossed himself and turned to go, with a tinge of red in his sallow cheeks. He was faithful to his duties and had come to console a death bed, though he was well aware that his consolations would be spurned.

As he left there came again the eerie laughter from the bed. "Ugh, I am weary of that incomparable holiness. He hovers about to give me the St. John's Cup, and would fain speed my passing. But I do not die yet, good father. There's life still in the old wolf."

The monk in a bland voice spoke some Latin to the effect that mortal times and seasons were ordained of God. The other stretched out a skinny hand from the fur coverings and rang a silver bell. When Anton appeared she gave the order "Bring supper for the reverend father," at which the Cluniac's face mellowed into complacence.

It was a Friday evening in a hard February. Out-of-doors the snow lay deep in the streets of Bruges, and every canal was frozen solid so that carts rumbled along them as on a street. A wind had risen which drifted the powdery snow and blew icy draughts through every chink. The small-paned windows of the great upper-room were filled with oiled vellum, but they did not keep out the weather, and currents of cold air passed through them to the doorway, making the smoke of the four charcoal braziers eddy and swirl. The place was warm, yet shot with bitter gusts, and the smell of burning herbs gave it the heaviness of a chapel at high mass. Hanging silver lamps, which blazed blue and smoky, lit it in patches, sufficient to show the cleanness of the rush-strewn floor, the glory of the hangings of cloth-of-gold and damask, and the burnished sheen of the metal-work. There was no costlier chamber in that rich city.

It was a strange staging for death, for the woman on the high bed was dying. Slowly, fighting every inch of the way with a grim tenacity, but indubitably dying. Her vital ardour had sunk below the mark from which it could rise again, and was now ebbing as water runs from a little crack in a pitcher. The best leeches in all Flanders and Artois had come to doctor her. They had prescribed the horrid potions of the age: tinctures of earth-worms; confections of spiders and wood-lice and viper's flesh; broth of human skulls, oil, wine, ants' eggs, and crabs' claws; the bufo preparatus, which was a live toad roasted in a pot and ground to a powder; and innumerable plaisters and electuaries. She had begun by submitting meekly, for she longed to live, and had ended, for she was a shrewd woman, by throwing the stuff at the apothecaries' heads. Now she ordained her own diet, which was of lamb's flesh lightly boiled, and woman's milk, got from a wench in the purlieus of St. Sauveur. The one medicine which she retained was powdered elk's horn, which had been taken from the beast between two festivals of the Virgin. This she had from the foresters in the Houthulst woods, and swallowed it in white wine an hour after every dawn.

The bed was a noble thing of ebony, brought by the Rhine road from Venice, and carved with fantastic hunting scenes by Hainault craftsmen. Its hangings were stiff brocaded silver, and above the pillows a great unicorn's horn, to protect against poisoning, stood out like the beak of a ship. The horn cast an odd shadow athwart the bed, so that a big claw seemed to lie on the coverlet curving towards the throat of her who lay there. The parish priest had noticed this at his first coming that evening, and had muttered fearful prayers.

The face on the pillows was hard to discern in the gloom, but when Anton laid the table for the Cluniac's meal and set a lamp on it, he lit up the cavernous interior of the bed, so that it became the main thing in the chamber. It was the face of a woman who still retained the lines and the colouring of youth. The voice had harshened with age, and the hair was white as wool, but the cheeks were still rosy and the grey eyes still had fire. Notable beauty had once been there. The finely arched brows, the oval of the face which the years had scarcely sharpened, the proud, delicate nose, all spoke of it. It was as if their possessor recognised those things and would not part with them, for her attire had none of the dishevelment of a sickroom. Her coif of fine silk was neatly adjusted, and the great robe of marten's fur which cloaked her shoulders was fastened with a jewel of rubies which glowed in the lamplight like a star.

Something chattered beside her. It was a little brown monkey which had made a nest in the warm bedclothes.

She watched with sharp eyes the setting of the table. It was a Friday's meal and the guest was a monk, so it followed a fashion, but in that house of wealth, which had links with the ends of the earth, the monotony was cunningly varied. There were oysters from the Boulogne coast, and lampreys from the Loire, and pickled salmon from England. There was a dish of liver dressed with rice and herbs in the manner of the Turk, for liver, though contained in flesh, was not reckoned as flesh by liberal churchmen. There was a roast goose from the shore marshes, that barnacle bird which pious epicures classed as shell-fish and thought fit for fast days. A silver basket held a store of thin toasted rye-cakes, and by the monk's hand stood a flagon of that drink most dear to holy palates, the rich syrupy hippocras.

The woman looked on the table with approval, for her house had always prided itself upon its good fare. The Cluniac's urbane composure was stirred to enthusiasm. He said a Confiteor tibi Domine, rolling the words on his tongue as if in anticipation of the solider mouthfuls awaiting him. The keen weather had whetted his appetite and he thanked God that his northern peregrinations had brought him to a house where the Church was thus honoured. He had liked the cavalier treatment of the lean parish priest, a sour dog who brought his calling into disfavour with the rich and godly. He tucked back his sleeves, adjusted the linen napkin comfortably about his neck, and fell to with a will. He raised his first glass of hippocras and gave thanks to his hostess. A true mother in Israel!

She was looking at him with favour. He was the breed of monk that she liked, suave, well-mannered, observant of men and cities. Already he had told her entertaining matter about the French King's court, and the new Burgrave of Ghent, and the escapades of Count Baldwin. He had lived much among gentlefolk and kept his ears open.... She felt stronger and cheerfuller than she had been for days. That rat-hunt had warmed her blood. She was a long way from death in spite of the cackle of idiot chirurgeons, and there was much savour still in the world. There was her son, too, the young Philip.... Her eye saw clearer, and she noted the sombre magnificence of the great room, the glory of the brocade, the gleam of silver. Was she not the richest woman in all Bruges, aye, and in all Hainault and Guelderland? And the credit was her own. After the fashion of age in such moods her mind flew backward, and she saw very plain a narrow street in a wind-swept town looking out on a bleak sea. She had been cold, then, and hungry, and deathly poor. Well, she had travelled some way from that hovel. She watched the thick carved stems of the candlesticks and felt a spacious ease and power.

The Cluniac was speaking. He had supped so well that he was in love with the world.

"Your house and board, my lady, are queen-like. I have seen worse in palaces."

Her laugh was only half pleased. "Too fine, you would add, for a burgher wife. Maybe, but rank is but as man makes it. The Kings of England are sprung of a tanner. Hark you, father! I made a vow to God when I was a maid, and I have fulfilled my side of the bargain. I am come of a nobler race than any Markgrave, aye, than the Emperor himself, and I swore to set the seed of my body, which the Lord might grant me, again among the great ones. Have I not done it? Is not Philip, my son, affianced to that pale girl of Avesnes, and with more acres of pleasant land to his name than any knightlet in Artois?"

The Cluniac bowed a courtly head. "It is a great alliance, but not above the dignity of your house."

"House you call it, and I have had the making of it. What was Willebald but a plain merchant-man, one of many scores at the Friday Market? Willebald was clay that I moulded and gilded till God put him to bed under a noble lid in the New Kirk. A worthy man, but loutish and slow like one of his own hookers. Yet when I saw him on the plainstones by the English harbour I knew that he was a weapon made for my hand."

Her voice had become even and gentle as of one who remembers far-away things. The Cluniac, having dipped his hands in a silver basin, was drying them in the brazier's heat. Presently he set to picking his teeth daintily with a quill, and fell into the listener's pose.

From long experience he knew the atmosphere which heralds confidences, and was willing to humour the provider of such royal fare.

"You have never journeyed to King's Lynn?" said the voice from the bed. "There is little to see there but mudbars and fens and a noisy sea. There I dwelt when I was fifteen years of age, a maid hungry in soul and body. I knew I was of the seed of Forester John and through him the child of a motley of ancient kings, but war and famine had stripped our house to the bone. And now I, the last of the stock, dwelt with a miserly mother's uncle who did shipwright's work for the foreign captains. The mirror told me that I was fair to look on, though ill-nourished, and my soul assured me that I had no fear. Therefore I had hope, but I ate my heart out waiting on fortune."

She was looking at the monk with unseeing eyes, her head half turned towards him.

"Then came Willebald one March morning. I saw him walk up the jetty in a new red cloak, a personable man with a broad beard and a jolly laugh. I knew him by repute as the luckiest of the Flemish venturers. In him I saw my fortune. That night he supped at my uncle's house and a week later he sought me in marriage. My uncle would have bargained, but I had become a grown woman and silenced him. With Willebald I did not chaffer, for I read his heart and knew that in a little he would be wax to me. So we were wed, and I took to him no dowry but a ring which came to me from my forebears, and a brain that gold does not buy."

The monkey by her side broke into a chattering.

"Peace, Peterkin," she said. "You mind me of the babbling of the merchant-folk, when I spurred Willebald into new roads. He had done as his father before him, and bought wool and salted fish from the English, paying with the stuffs of our Flemish looms. A good trade of small and sure profits, but I sought bigger quarries. For, mark you, there was much in England that had a value in this country of ours which no Englishman guessed."

"Of what nature?" the monk asked with curiosity in his voice.

"Roman things. Once in that land of bogs and forests there were bustling Roman towns and rich Roman houses, which disappeared as every tide brought in new robbers from the sea. Yes, but not all. Much of the preciousness was hidden and the place of its hiding forgotten. Bit by bit the churls found the treasure-trove, but they did not tell their lords. They melted down jewels and sold them piecemeal to Jews for Jews' prices, and what they did not recognise as precious they wantonly destroyed. I have seen the marble heads of heathen gods broken with the hammer to make mortar of, and great cups of onyx and alabaster used as water troughs for a thrall's mongrels.... Knowing the land, I sent pedlars north and west to collect such stuff, and what I bought for pence I sold for much gold in the Germanies and throughout the French cities. Thus Willebald amassed wealth, till it was no longer worth his while to travel the seas. We lived snug in Flanders, and our servants throughout the broad earth were busy getting us gear."

The Cluniac was all interest. The making of money lay very near the heart of his Order. "I have heard wondrous tales of your enterprise," he told her. "I would fain know the truth."

"Packman's tricks," she laughed. "Nevertheless it is a good story. For I turned my eyes to the East, whence come those things that make the pride of life. The merchants of Venice were princes, and it was in my head to make those of Bruges no worse. What did it profit that the wind turned daily the sails of our three hundred mills if we limited ourselves to common burgher wares and the narrow northern markets? We sent emissaries up the Rhine and beyond the Alps to the Venice princes, and brought hither the spices and confections of Egypt and the fruits and wines of Greece, and the woven stuffs of Asia till the marts of Flanders had the savour of Araby. Presently in our booths could be seen silks of Italy, and choice metals from Innsbruck, and furs from Muscovy, and strange birds and beasts from Prester John's country, and at our fairs such a concourse of outlandish traders as put Venice to shame. 'Twas a long fight and a bitter for Willebald and me, since, mark you, we had to make a new road over icy mountains, with a horde of freebooters hanging on the skirts of our merchant trains and every little burg on the way jealous to hamper us. Yet if the heart be resolute, barriers will fall. Many times we were on the edge of beggary, and grievous were our losses, but in the end we triumphed. There came a day when we had so many bands of the Free Companions in our pay that the progress of our merchandise was like that of a great army, and from rivals we made the roadside burgs our allies, sharing modestly in our ventures. Also there were other ways. A pilgrim travels unsuspect, for who dare rob a holy man? and he is free from burgal dues; but if the goods be small and very precious, pilgrims may carry them."

The monk, as in duty bound, shook a disapproving head.

"Sin, doubtless," said the woman, "but I have made ample atonement. Did I not buy with a bushel of gold a leg of the blessed St. George for the New Kirk, and give to St. Martin's a diamond as big as a thumb nail and so bright that on a dark day it is a candle to the shrine? Did not I give to our Lady at Aix a crown of ostrich feathers the marrow of which is not in Christendom?"

"A mother in Israel, in truth," murmured the cleric.

"Yea, in Israel," said the old wife with a chuckle. "Israel was the kernel of our perplexities. The good Flemings saw no farther than their noses, and laughed at Willebald when he began his ventures. When success came, it was easy to win them over, and by admitting them to a share in our profits get them to fling their caps in the air and huzza for their benefactors. But the Jews were a tougher stock. Mark you, father, when God blinded their eyes to the coming of the Lord Christ, He opened them very wide to all lower matters. Their imagination is quick to kindle, and they are as bold in merchantcraft as Charlemagne in war. They saw what I was after before I had been a month at it, and were quick to profit by my foresight. There are but two ways to deal with Israelites, root them from the face of the earth or make them partners with you. Willebald would have fought them; I, more wise, bought them at a price. For two score years they have wrought faithfully for me. You say well, a mother in Israel!"

"I could wish that a Christian lady had no dealings with the accursed race," said the Cluniac.

"You could wish folly," was the tart answer. "I am not as your burgher folk, and on my own affairs I take no man's guiding, be he monk or merchant. Willebald is long dead; may he sleep in peace, He was no mate for me, but for what he gave me I repaid him in the coin he loved best. He was a proud man when he walked through the Friday Market with every cap doffed. He was ever the burgher, like the child I bore him."

"I had thought the marriage more fruitful. They spoke of two children, a daughter and a son."

The woman turned round in her bed so that she faced him. The monkey whimpered and she cuffed its ears. Her face was sharp and exultant, and for a sick person her eyes were oddly bright.

"The girl was Willebald's. A poor slip of vulgar stock with the spirit of a house cat. I would have married her well, for she was handsome after a fashion, but she thwarted me and chose to wed a lout of a huckster in the Bredestreet. She shall have her portion from Willebald's gold, but none from me. But Philip is true child of mine, and sprung on both sides of high race. Nay, I name no names, and before men he is of my husband's getting. But to you at the end of my days I speak the truth. That son of wrath has rare blood in him. Philip..."

The old face had grown kind. She was looking through the monk to some happy country of vision. Her thoughts were retracing the roads of time, and after the way of age she spoke them aloud. Imperiously she had forgotten her company.

"So long ago," came the tender voice. "It is years since they told me he was dead among the heathen, fighting by the Lord Baldwin's side. But I can see him as if it were yesterday, when he rode into these streets in spring with April blooms at his saddle-bow. They called him Phadbus in jest, for his face was like the sun.... Willebald, good dull man, was never jealous, and was glad that his wife should be seen in brave company. Ah, the afternoons at the baths when we sported like sea-nymphs and sang merry ballads! And the proud days of Carnival where men and women consorted freely and without guile like the blessed in Paradise! Such a tide for lovers!... Did I not lead the dance with him at the Burgrave's festival, the twain of us braver than morning? Sat I not with him in the garden of St. Vaast, his head in my lap, while he sang me virelays of the south? What was Willebald to me or his lean grey wife to him? He made me his queen, me the burgher wife, at the jousting at Courtrai, when the horses squealed like pigs in the mellay and I wept in fear for him. Ah, the lost sweet days!

Philip, my darling, you make a brave gentleman, but you will not equal him who loved your mother."

The Cluniac was a man of the world whom no confidences could scandalise. But he had business of his own to speak of that night, and he thought it wise to break into this mood of reminiscence.

"The young lord, Philip, your son, madam? You have great plans for him? What does he at the moment?"

The softness went out of the voice and the woman's gaze came back to the chamber. "That I know not. Travelling the ways of the world and plucking roadside fruits, for he is no home-bred and womanish stripling. Wearing his lusty youth on the maids, I fear. Nay, I forget. He is about to wed the girl of Avesnes and is already choosing his bridal train. It seems he loves her. He writes me she has a skin of snow and eyes of vair. I have not seen her. A green girl, doubtless with a white face and cat's eyes. But she is of Avesnes, and that blood comes pure from Clovis, and there is none prouder in Hainault. He will husband her well, but she will be a clever woman if she tethers to her side a man of my bearing. He will be for the high road and the battle-front."

"A puissant and peaceable knight, I have heard tell," said the Cluniac.

"Puissant beyond doubt, and peaceable when his will is served. He will play boldly for great things and will win them. Ah, monk! What knows a childless religious of a mother's certainty? 'Twas not for nothing that I found Willebald and changed the cobbles of King's Lynn for this fat country. It is gold that brings power, and the stiffest royal neck must bend to him who has the deep coffers. It is gold and his high hand that will set my Philip by the side of kings. Lord Jesus, what a fortune I have made for him! There is coined money at the goldsmiths' and in my cellars, and the ships at the ports, and a hundred busy looms, and lands in Hainault and Artois, and fair houses in Bruges and Ghent. Boats on the Rhine and many pack trains between Antwerp and Venice are his, and a wealth of preciousness lies in his name with the Italian merchants. Likewise there is this dwelling of mine, with plenishing which few kings could buy. My sands sink in the glass, but as I lie a-bed I hear the bustle of wains and horses in the streets, and the talk of shipfolk, and the clatter of my serving men beneath, and I know that daily, hourly, more riches flow hither to furnish my son's kingdom."

The monk's eyes sparkled at this vision of wealth, and he remembered his errand.

"A most noble heritage. But if the Sire God in His inscrutable providence should call your son to His holy side, what provision have you made for so mighty a fortune? Does your daughter then share?"

The face on the pillows became suddenly wicked and very old. The eyes were lit with hate.

"Not a bezant of which I have the bequeathing. She has something from Willebald, and her dull husband makes a livelihood. 'Twill suffice for the female brats, of whom she has brought three into the world to cumber it.... By the Gospels, she will lie on the bed she has made. I did not scheme and toil to make gold for such leaden souls."

"But if your most worthy son should die ere he has begot children, have you made no disposition?" The monk's voice was pointed with anxiety, for was not certainty on this point the object of his journey? The woman perceived it and laughed maliciously.

"I have made dispositions. Such a chapel will be builded in the New Kirk as Rome cannot equal. Likewise there will be benefactions for the poor and a great endowment for the monks at St. Sauveur. If my seed is not to continue on earth I will make favour in Paradise."

"And we of Cluny, madam?" The voice trembled in spite of its training.

"Nay I have not forgotten Cluny. Its Abbot shall have the gold flagons from Jerusalem and some wherewithal in money. But what is this talk? Philip will not die, and like his mother he loves Holy Church and will befriend her in all her works.... Listen, father, it is long past the hour when men cease from labour, and yet my provident folk are busy. Hark to the bustle below. That will be the convoy from the Vermandois. Jesu, what a night!"

Flurries of snow beat on windows, and draughts stirred the hot ashes in the braziers and sent the smoke from them in odd spirals about the chamber. It had become perishing cold, and the monkey among the bedclothes whimpered and snuggled closer into his nest. There seemed to be a great stir about the house-door. Loud voices were heard in gusts, and a sound like a woman's cry. The head on the pillow was raised to listen.

"A murrain on those folk. There has been bungling among the pack-riders. That new man Derek is an oaf of oafs."

She rang her silver bell sharply and waited on the ready footsteps. But none came. There was silence now below, an ominous silence.

"God's curse upon this household," the woman cried. The monkey whimpered again, and she took it by the scruff and tossed it to the floor. "Peace, ape, or I will have you strangled. Bestir yourself, father, and call Anton. There is a blight of deafness in this place."

The room had suddenly lost its comfort and become cold and desolate. The lamps were burning low and the coloured hangings were in deep shadow. The storm was knocking fiercely at the lattice.

The monk rose with a shiver to do her bidding, but he was forestalled. Steps sounded on the stairs and the steward entered. The woman in the bed had opened her mouth to upbraid, when something in his dim figure struck her silent.

The old man stumbled forward and fell on his knees beside her.

"Madam, dear madam," he stammered, "ill news has come to this house.... There is a post in from Avesnes.... The young master..."

"Philip," and the woman's voice rose to a scream. "What of my son?"

"The lord has taken away what He gave. He is dead, slain in a scuffle with highway robbers.... Oh, the noble young lord! The fair young knight! Woe upon this stricken house!"

The woman lay very still, white the old man on his knees drifted into broken prayers. Then he observed her silence, scrambled to his feet in a panic, and lit two candles from the nearest brazier. She lay back on the pillows in a deathly faintness, her face drained of blood. Only her tortured eyes showed that life was still in her.

Her voice came at last, no louder than a whisper. It was soft now, but more terrible than the old harshness.

"I follow Philip," it said. "Sic transit gloria.... Call me Arnulf the goldsmith and Robert the scrivener.... Quick, man, quick. I have much to do ere I die."

As the steward hurried out, the Cluniac, remembering his office, sought to offer comfort, but in his bland worldling's voice the consolations sounded hollow. She lay motionless, while he quoted the Scriptures. Encouraged by her docility, he spoke of the certain reward promised by Heaven to the rich who remembered the Church at their death. He touched upon the high duties of his Order and the handicap of its poverty. He bade her remember her debt to the Abbot of Cluny.

She seemed about to speak and he bent eagerly to catch her words.

"Peace, you babbler," she said. "I am done with your God. When I meet Him I will outface Him. He has broken His compact and betrayed me. My riches go to the Burgrave for the comfort of this city where they were won. Let your broken rush of a Church wither and rot!"

Scared out of all composure by this blasphemy, the Cluniac fell to crossing himself and mumbling invocations. The diplomat had vanished and only the frightened monk remained. He would fain have left the room had he dared, but the spell of her masterful spirit held him. After that she spoke nothing....

Again there was a noise on the stairs and she moved a little, as if mustering her failing strength for the ultimate business. But it was not Arnulf the gold smith. It was Anton, and he shook like a man on his way to the gallows.

"Madam, dear madam," he stammered, again on his knees. "There is another message. One has come from the Bredestreet with word of your lady daughter. An hour ago she has borne a child...A lusty son, madam."

The reply from the bed was laughter.

It began low and hoarse like a fit of coughing, and rose to the high cackling mirth of extreme age. At the sound both Anton and the monk took to praying. Presently it stopped, and her voice came full and strong as it had been of old.

"Mea culpa," it said, "mea maxima culpa. I judged the Sire God over hastily. He is merry and has wrought a jest on me. He has kept His celestial promise in His own fashion. He takes my brave Philip and gives me instead a suckling.... So be it. The infant has my blood, and the race of Forester John will not die. Arnulf will have an easy task. He need but set the name of this new-born in Philip's place. What manner of child is he, Anton? Lusty, you say, and well-formed? I would my arms could have held him.... But I must be about my business of dying. I will take the news to Philip."

Hope had risen again in the Cluniac's breast. It seemed that here was a penitent. He approached the bed with a raised crucifix, and stumbled over the whimpering monkey. The woman's eyes saw him and a last flicker woke in them.

"Begone, man," she cried. "I have done with the world. Anton, rid me of both these apes. And fetch the priest of St. Martin's, for I would confess and be shriven. Yon curate is no doubt a fool, but he serves my jesting God."

CHAPTER IV. EYES OF YOUTH

On the morning of Shrove Tuesday, in the year of our Lord 1249, Sir Aimery of Beaumanoir, the envoy of the most Christian king, Louis of France, arrived in the port of Acre, having made the voyage from Cyprus with a fair wind in a day and a night in a ship of Genoa flying the red and gold banner of the Temple. Weary of the palms and sun-baked streets of Limasol and the eternal wrangling of the Crusading hosts, he looked with favour at the noble Palestine harbour, and the gilt steeples and carven houses of the fair city. From the quay he rode to the palace of the Templars and was admitted straightway to an audience with the Grand Master. For he had come in a business of some moment.

The taste of Cyprus was still in his mouth; the sweet sticky air of the coastlands; the smell of endless camps of packed humanity, set among mountains of barrels and malodorous sprouting forage-stuffs; the narrow streets lit at night by flares of tarry staves; and over all that rotting yet acrid flavour which is the token of the East. The young damoiseau of Beaumanoir had grown very sick of it all since the royal dromonds first swung into Limasol Bay. He had seen his friends die like flies of strange maladies, while the host waited on Hugh of Burgundy. Egypt was but four days off across the waters, and on its sands Louis had ordained that the War of the Cross should begin.

... But the King seemed strangely supine. Each day the enemy was the better forewarned, and each day the quarrels of Templar and Hospitaller grew more envenomed, and yet he sat patiently twiddling his thumbs, as if all time lay before him and not a man's brief life. And now when at long last the laggards of Burgundy and the Morea were reported on their way, Sir Aimery had to turn his thoughts from the honest field of war. Not for him to cry Montjole St. Denis by the Nile. For behold he was now speeding on a crazy errand to the ends of the earth.

There had been strange councils in the bare little chamber of the Most Christian King. Those locusts of the dawn whom men called Tartars, the evil seed of the Three Kings who had once travelled to Bethlehem, had, it seemed, been vouchsafed a glimpse of grace. True, they had plundered and eaten the faithful and shed innocent blood in oceans, but they hated the children of Mahound worse than the children of Christ. On the eve of Christmas-tide four envoys had come from their Khakan, monstrous men with big heads that sprang straight from the shoulder, and arms that hung below the knee, and short thin legs like gnomes. For forty weeks they had been on the road, and they brought gifts such as no eye had seen before, silks like gossamer woven with wild alphabets, sheeny jars of jade, and pearls like moons. Their Khakan, they said, had espoused the grandchild of Prester John, and had been baptized into the Faith. He marched against Bagdad, and had sworn to root the heresy of Mahound from the earth. Let the King of France make a league with him, and between them, pressing from east and west, they would accomplish the holy task. Let him send teachers to expound the mysteries of God, and let him send knights who would treat on mundane things. The letter, written in halting Latin and sealed with a device like a spider's web, urged instant warfare with Egypt. "For the present we dwell far apart," wrote the Khakan; "therefore let us both get to business."

So Aimery had been summoned to the King's chamber, where he found his good master, the Count of St. Pol, in attendance with others. After prayer, Louis opened to them his mind. Pale from much fasting and nightly communing with God, his face was lit again with that light which had shone in it when on the Friday after Pentecost the year before he had received at St. Denis the pilgrim's scarf and the oriflamme of France.

"God's hand is in this, my masters," he said. "Is it not written that many shall come from the east and from the west to sit down with Abraham in his kingdom? I have a duty towards those poor folk, and I dare not fail."

There was no man present bold enough to argue with the white fire in the King's eyes. One alone cavilled. He was a Scot, Sir Patrick, the Count of Dunbar, who already shook with the fever which was to be his death.

"This Khakan is far away, sire," he said. "If it took his envoys forty weeks to reach us, it will be a good year before his armies are on the skirts of Egypt. As well make alliance with a star."

But Louis was in missionary mood. "God's ways are not as our ways. To Him a thousand years are a day, and He can make the weakest confound a multitude. This far-away King asks for instruction, and I will send him holy men to fortify his young faith. And this knight, of whom you, my lord of St. Pol, speak well, shall bear the greetings of a soldier."

Louis' face, which for usual was grave like a wise child's, broke into a smile which melted Aimery's heart. He scarcely heard the Count of St. Pol as that stout friend enlarged on his merits. "The knight of Beaumanoir," so ran the testimony, "has more learning than any clerk. In Spain he learned the tongues of the heathen, and in Paris he read deep in their philosophy. Withal he is a devout son of Holy Church."

The boy blushed at the praise and the King's kindly regard. But St. Pol spoke truth, for Aimery, young as he was, had travelled far both on the material globe and in the kingdom of the spirit. As a stripling he had made one of the Picardy Nation in the schools of Paris. He had studied the metaphysics of Aristotle under Aquinas, and voyaged strange seas of thought piloted by Roger, the white-bearded Englishman. Thence, by the favour of the Queen-mother, he had gone as squire to Alphonso's court of Castile, where the Spanish doctors had opened windows for him into the clear dry wisdom of the Saracens. He had travelled with an embassy to the Emperor, and in Sicily had talked with the learned Arabs who clustered around the fantastic Frederick. In Italy he had met adventurers of Genoa and Venice who had shown him charts of unknown oceans and maps of Prester John's country and the desert roads that led to Cambaluc, that city farther than the moon, and told him tales of awful and delectable things hidden beyond the dawn. He had returned to his tower by the springs of Canche, a young man with a name for uncanny knowledge, a searcher after concealed matters, negligent of religion and ill at ease in his world.

Then Louis cast his spell over him. He saw the King first at a great hunting in Avesnes and worshipped from afar the slight body, royal in every line of it, and the blue eyes which charmed and compelled, for he divined there a spirit which had the secret of both earth and heaven. While still under the glamour he was given knighthood at the royal hands, and presently was weaned from unwholesome fancies by falling in love. The girl, Alix of Valery, was slim like a poplar and her eyes were grey and deep as her northern waters. She had been a maid of Blanche the Queen, and had a nun's devoutness joined to a merry soul. Under her guiding Aimery made his peace with the Church, and became notable for his gifts to God, for he derived great wealth from his Flemish forbears. Yet the yeast of youth still wrought in him, and by Alix's side at night he dreamed of other lands than his grey-green Picardy. So, when the King took the croix d'outre mer and summoned his knights to the freeing of Jerusalem, Sir Aimery of Beaumanoir was the first to follow. For to him, as to others like him, the goal was no perishable city made by mortal hands, but that beata urbs without foundations which youth builds of its dreams.

He heard mass by the King's side and, trembling with pride, kissed the royal hands and set out on his journey. His last memory of Louis was of a boyish figure in a surcoat of blue samite, gazing tenderly on him as of bidding farewell to a brother.

The Grand Master of the Templars, sitting in a furred robe in a warm upper chamber, for he had an ague on him, spoke gloomily of the mission. He would have preferred to make alliance with the Soldan of Egypt, and by his aid recover the Holy Cities. "What Khakan is this?" he cried, "to whom it is a journey of a lifetime to come nigh? What kind of Christian will you make of men that have blood for drink and the flesh of babes for food, and blow hither and thither on horses like sandstorms? Yours is a mad venture, young sir, and I see no good that can come of it." Nevertheless he wrote letters of commendation to the Prince of Antioch and the Constable of Armenia; and he brought together all those about the place who had travelled far inland to make a chart of the journey.

Aimery heeded little the Templar's forebodings, for his heart had grown high again and romance was kindling his fancy. There was a knuckle of caution in him, for he had the blood of Flemish traders in his veins, though enriched by many nobler streams. "The profit is certain," a cynic had whispered to him ere they left Aigues Mortes. "Should we conquer we shall grow rich, and if we fail we shall go to heaven." The phrase had fitted some of his moods, notably the black ones at Limasol, but now he was all aflame with the quixotry of the Crusader. He neither needed nor sought wealth, nor was he concerned about death. His feet trod the sacred soil of his faith, and up in the hills which rimmed the seaward plain lay all the holiness of Galilee and Nazareth, the three tabernacles built by St. Peter on the Mount of Transfiguration, the stone whence Christ ascended into heaven, the hut at Bethlehem which had been the Most High's cradle, the sanctuary of Jerusalem whose every stone was precious. Presently his King would win it all back for God. But for him was the sterner task, no clean blows in the mellay among brethren, but a lone pilgrimage beyond the east wind to the cradle of all marvels. The King had told him that he carried the hopes of Christendom in his wallet; he knew that he bore within himself the delirious expectation of a boy. Youth swelled his breast and steeled his sinews and made a golden mist for his eyes. The new, the outlandish, the undreamed-of! Surely no one of the Seven Champions had had such fortune! Scribes long after would write of the deeds of Aimery of Beaumanoir, and minstrels would sing of him as they sang of Roland and Tristan.

The Count of Jaffa, whose tower stood on the borders and who was therefore rarely quit of strife, convoyed him a stage or two on his way. It was a slender company: two Franciscans bearing the present of Louis to the Khakan, a chapel-tent of scarlet cloth embroidered inside with pictures of the Annunciation and the Passion; two sumpter mules with baggage; Aimery's squire, a lad from the Boulonnais; and Aimery himself mounted on a Barbary horse warranted to go far on little fodder. The lord of Jaffa turned back when the snows of Lebanon were falling behind on their right. He had nodded towards the mountains.

"There lives the Old Man and his Ishmaelites. Fear nothing, for his fangs are drawn." And when Aimery asked the cause of the impotence of the renowned Assassins, he was told, "That Khakan whom ye seek."

After that they made good speed to the city of Antioch, where not so long before angels from heaven had appeared as knights in white armour to do battle for the forlorn Crusaders. There they were welcomed by the Prince and sent forward into Armenia, guided by the posts of the Constable of that harassed kingdom. Everywhere the fame of the Tartars had gone abroad, and with each mile they journeyed the tales became stranger. Conquerers and warriors beyond doubt, but grotesque paladins for the Cross. Men whispered their name with averted faces, and in the eyes of the travelled ones there was the terror of sights remembered outside the mortal pale. Aimery's heart was stout, but he brooded much as the road climbed into the mountains. Far off in Cyprus the Khakan had seemed a humble devotee at Christ's footstool, asking only to serve and learn; but now he had grown to some monstrous Cyclops beyond the stature of man, a portent like a thundercloud brooding over unnumbered miles. Besides, the young lord was homesick, and had long thoughts of Alix his wife and the son she had borne him. As he looked at the stony hills he remembered that it would now be springtide in Picardy, when the young green of the willows fringed every watercourse and the plovers were calling on the windy downs.

The Constable of Armenia dwelt in a castle of hewn stone about which a little city clustered, with mountains on every side to darken the sky, He was as swarthy as a Saracen and had a long nose like a Jew, but he was a good Christian and a wise ruler, though commonly at odds with his cousin of Antioch. From him Aimery had more precise news of the Khakan.

There were two, said the Constable. "One who rules all Western Asia east of the Sultan's principates. Him they call the Ilkhan for title, and Houlagou for name. His armies have eaten up the Chorasmians and the Muscovites and will presently bite their way into Christendom, unless God change their heart. By the Gospels, they are less and more than men. Swinish drinkers and gluttons, they rise from their orgies to sweep the earth like a flame. Here inside our palisade of rock we wait fearfully."

"And the other?" Aimery asked.

"Ah, he is as much the greater as the sun is greater than a star. Kublai they name him, and he is in some sort the lord of Houlagou. I have never met the man who has seen him, for he dwells as far beyond the Ilkhan as the Ilkhan is far from the Pillars of Hercules. But rumour has it that he is a clement and beneficent prince, terrible in battle, but a lover of peace and all good men. They tell wonders about his land of Cathay, where strips of parchment stamped with the King's name take the place of gold among the merchants, so strong is that King's honour. But the journey to Cambaluc, the city of Kublai, would fill a man's lifetime."

One April morning they heard mass after the odd Syrian fashion, and turned their faces eastward. The Constable's guides led them through the mountains, up long sword-cuts of valleys and under frowning snowdrifts, or across stony barrens where wretched beehive huts huddled by the shores of unquiet lakes. Presently they came into summer, and found meadows of young grass and green forests on the hills' skirts, and saw wide plains die into the blueness of morning. There the guides left them, and the little cavalcade moved east into unknown anarchies.

The sky grew like brass over their heads, and the land baked and rutted with the sun's heat. It seemed a country empty of man, though sometimes they came on derelict ploughlands and towns of crumbling brick charred and glazed by fire. In sweltering days they struggled through flats where the grass was often higher than a horse's withers, and forded the tawny streams which brought down the snows of the hills. Now and then they would pass wandering herdsmen, who fled to some earth-burrow at their appearance. The Constable had bidden them make for the rising sun, saying that sooner or later they would foregather with the Khakan's scouts. But days passed into weeks and weeks into months, and still they moved through a tenantless waste. They husbanded jealously the food they had brought, but the store ran low, and there were days of empty stomachs and light heads. Unless, like the King of Babylon, they were to eat grass in the fashion of beasts, it seemed they must soon famish.

But late in summertime they saw before them a wall of mountain, and in three days climbed by its defiles to a pleasant land, where once more they found the dwellings of man. It appeared that they were in a country where the Tartars had been for some time settled and which had for years been free of the ravages of war. The folks were hunters and shepherds who took the strangers for immortal beings and offered food on bent knees like oblations to a god. They knew where the Ilkhan dwelt, and furnished guides for each day's journey. Aimery, who had been sick of a low fever in the plains, and had stumbled on in a stupor torn by flashes of homesickness, found his spirits reviving. He had cursed many times the futility of his errand. While the Franciscans were busied with their punctual offices and asked nothing of each fresh day but that it should be as prayerful as the last, he found a rebellious unbelief rising in his heart. He was travelling roads no Christian had ever trod, on a wild-goose errand, while his comrades were winning fame in the battle-front. Alas! that a bright sword should rust in these barrens!

But with the uplands peace crept into his soul and some of the mystery of his journey. It was a brave venture, whether it failed or no, for he had already gone beyond the pale even of men's dreams. The face of Louis hovered before him. It needed a great king even to conceive such a mission.... He had been sent on a king's errand too. He stood alone for France and the Cross in a dark world. Alone, as kings should stand, for to take all the burden was the mark of kingship. His heart bounded at the thought, for he was young. His father had told him of that old Flanders grandam, who had sworn that his blood came from proud kings.

But chiefly he thought of Louis with a fresh warmth of love. Surely the King loved him, or he would not have chosen him out of many for this fateful work. He had asked of him the ultimate service, as a friend should. Aimery reconstructed in his inner vision all his memories of the King: the close fair hair now thinning about the temples; the small face still contoured like a boy's; the figure strung like a bow; the quick, eager gestures; the blue dove's eyes, kindly and humble, as became one whose proudest title was to be a "sergeant of the Crucified." But those same eyes could also steel and blaze, for his father had been called the Lion, his mother Semiramis, and his grandsire Augustus. In these wilds Aimery was his vicegerent and bore himself proudly as the proxy of such a monarch.

The hour came when they met the Tartar outposts. A cloud of horse swept down on them, each man riding loose with his hand on a taut bowstring. In silence they surrounded the little party, and their leader made signs to Aimery to dismount. The Constable had procured for him a letter in Tartar script, setting out the purpose of his mission. This the outpost could not read, but they recognised some word among the characters, and pointed it out to each other with uncouth murmurings. They were strange folk, with eyes like pebbles and squat frames and short, broad faces, but each horse and man moved in unison like a centaur.

With gestures of respect the Tartars signalled to the Christians to follow, and led them for a day and a night southward down a broad valley, where vines and fruit trees grew and peace dwelt in villages. They passed encampments of riders like themselves, and little scurries of horsemen would ride athwart their road and exchange greetings. On the second morning they reached a city, populous in men but not in houses. For miles stretched lines of skin tents, and in the heart of them by the river's edge stood a great hall of brick, still raw from the builders.

Aimery sat erect on his weary horse with the hum of an outlandish host about him, himself very weary and very sick at heart. For the utter folly of it all had come on him like the waking from a dream. These men were no allies of the West. They were children of the Blue Wolf, as the Constable had said, a monstrous brood, swarming from the unknown to blight the gardens of the world. A Saracen compared to such was a courteous knight.... He thought of Kublai, the greater Khakan. Perhaps in his court might dwell gentlehood and reason. But here was but a wolf pack in the faraway guise of man.

They gave the strangers food and drink, halfcooked fish and a porridge of rye and sour spiced milk, and left them to sleep until sundown. Then the palace guards led them to the presence.

The hall was immense, dim and shapeless like the inside of a hill, not built according to the proportions of mankind. Flambeaux and wicks floating in great basins of mutton fat showed a dense concourse of warriors, and through an aisle of them Aimery approached the throne. In front stood a tree of silver, springing from a pedestal of four lions whose mouths poured streams of wine, syrup, and mead into basins, which were emptied by a host of slaves, the cup-bearers of the assembly. There were two thrones side by side, on one of which sat a figure so motionless that it might have been wrought of jasper. Weighted with a massive head-dress of pearls and a robe of gold brocade, the little grandchild of Prester John seemed like a doll on which some princess had lavished wealth and fancy. The black eyelashes lay quiet on her olive cheeks, and her breathing did not stir her stiff, jewelled bodice.

"I have seen death in life," thought Aimery as he shivered and looked aside.

Houlagou, her husband, was a tall man compared with the others. His face was hairless, and his mouth fine and cruel. His eyes were hard like agates, with no light in them. A passionless power lurked in the low broad forehead, and the mighty head sunk deep between the shoulders; but the power not of a man, but of some abortion of nature, like storm or earthquake. Again Aimery shivered. Had not the prophets foretold that one day Antichrist would be reborn in Babylon?

Among the Ilkhan's scribes was a Greek who spoke a bastard French and acted as interpreter. King Louis' letter was read, and in that hall its devout phrases seemed a mockery. The royal gifts were produced, the tent-chapel with its woven pictures and the sacred utensils. The half-drunk captains fingered them curiously, but the eyes from the throne scarcely regarded them.

"These are your priests," said the Khakan "Let them talk with my priests and then go their own way. I have little concern with priestcraft."

Then Aimery spoke, and the Greek with many haltings translated. He reminded Houlagou of the Tartar envoys who had sought from his King instruction in the Christian faith and had proclaimed his baptism.

"Of that I know nothing," was the answer. "Maybe 'twas some whim of my brother Kublai. I have all the gods I need."

With a heavy heart Aimery touched on the proposed alliance, the advance on Bagdad, and the pinning of the Saracens between two fires. He spoke as he had been ordered, but with a bitter sense of futility, for what kind of ally could be looked for in this proud pagan?

The impassive face showed no flicker of interest.

"I am eating up the Caliphs," he said, "but that food is for my own table. As for allies, I have need of none. The children of the Blue Wolf do not make treaties."

Then he spoke aside to his captains, and fixed Aimery with his agate eyes. It was like listening to a voice from a stone.

"The King of France has sent you to ask for peace. Peace, no doubt, is good, and I will grant it of my favour. A tribute will be fixed in gold and silver, and while it is duly paid your King's lands will be safe from my warriors. Should the tribute fail, France will be ours. I have heard that it is a pleasant place."

The Ilkhan signed that the audience was over. The fountains of liquor ceased to play, and the drunken gathering stood up with a howling like wild beasts to acclaim their King. Aimery went back to his hut, and sat deep in thought far into the night.

He perceived that the shadows were closing in upon him. He must get the friars away, and with them a message to his master. For himself there could be no return, for he could not shame his King who had trusted him. In the bestial twilight of this barbaric court the memory of Louis shone like a star. He must attempt to reach Kublai, of whom men spoke well, though the journey cost him his youth and his life. It might mean years of wandering, but there was a spark of hope in it. There, in the bleak hut, he suffered the extreme of mental anguish. A heavy door seemed to have closed between him and all that he held dear. He fell on his knees and prayed to the saints to support his loneliness. And then he found comfort, for had not God's Son suffered even as he, and left the bright streets of Paradise for loneliness among the lost?

Next morning he faced the world with a clearer eye. It was not difficult to provide for the Franciscans. They, honest men, understood nothing save that the Tartar king had not the love of holy things for which they had hoped. They explained the offices of the Church as well as they could to ribald and uncomprehending auditors, and continued placidly in their devotions. As it chanced, a convoy was about to start for Muscovy, whence by ship they might come to Constantinople. The Tartars made no objection to their journey, for they had some awe of these pale men and were glad to be quit of foreign priestcraft. With them Aimery sent a letter in which he told the King that the immediate errand had been done, but that no good could be looked for from this western Khakan. "I go," he said, "to Kublai the Great, in Cathay, who has a heart more open to God. If I return not, know, Sire, that I am dead in your most loving service, joyfully and pridefully as a Christian knight dies for the Cross, his King, and his lady." He added some prayers on behalf of the little household at Beaumanoir and sealed it with his ring. It was the ring he had got from his father, a thick gold thing in which had been cut his cognisance of three lions' heads.

This done, he sought an audience with the Ilkhan, and told him of his purpose. Houlagou did not speak for a little, and into his set face seemed to creep an ill-boding shadow of a smile. "Who am I," he said at length, "to hinder your going to my brother Kublai? I will give you an escort to my eastern borders."

Aimery bent his knee and thanked him, but from the courtiers rose a hubbub of mirth which chilled his gratitude. He was aware that he sailed on very desperate waters.

Among the Tartars was a recreant Genoese who taught them metal work and had once lived at the court of Cambaluc. The man had glimmerings of honesty, and tried hard to dissuade Aimery from the journey. "It is a matter of years," he told him, "and the road leads through deserts greater than all Europe and over mountains so high and icy that birds are frozen in the crossing. And a word in your ear, my lord. The Ilkhan permits few to cross his eastern marches. Beware of treason, I say. Your companions are the blood-thirstiest of the royal guards."

But from the Genoese he obtained a plan of the first stages of the road, and one morning in autumn he set out from the Tartar city, his squire from the Boulonnais by his side, and at his back a wild motley of horsemen, wearing cuirasses of red leather stamped with the blue wolf of Houlagou's house.

October fell chill and early in those uplands, and on the fourth day they came into a sprinkling of snow. At night round the fires the Tartars made merry, for they had strong drink in many skin bottles, and Aimery was left to his own cold meditations. If he had had any hope, it was gone now, for the escort made it clear that he was their prisoner. Judging from the chart of the Genoese, they were not following any road to Cambaluc, and the sight of the sky told him that they were circling round to the south. The few Tartar words he had learned were not enough to communicate with them, and in any case it was clear that they would take no orders from him. He was trapped like a bird in the fowler's hands. Escape was folly, for in an hour their swift horses would have ridden him down. He had thought he had grown old, but the indignity woke his youth again, and he fretted passionately. If death was his portion, he longed for it to come cleanly in soldier fashion.

One night his squire disappeared. The Tartars, when he tried to question them, only laughed and pointed westward. That was the last he heard of the lad from the Boulonnais.

And then on a frosty dawn, when the sun rose red-rimmed over the barrens, he noted a new trimness in his escort. They rode in line, and they rode before and behind him, so that his captivity was made patent. On a ridge far to the west he saw a great castle, and he knew the palace of Houlagou. His guess had been right; he had been brought back by a circuit to his starting-point.

Presently he was face to face with the Ilkhan, who was hunting. The Greek scribe was with him, so the meeting had been foreseen. The King's face was dark with the weather and his stony eyes had a glow in them.

"O messenger of France," he said, "there is a little custom of our people that I had forgotten. When a stranger warrior visits us it is our fashion to pit him in a bout against one of our own folk, so that if he leaves us alive he may speak well of his entertainment."

"I am willing," said Aimery. "I have but my sword for weapon."

"We have no lack of swordsmen," said the Ilkhan. "I would fain see the Frankish way of it."

A man stepped out from the ring, a great square fellow shorter by a head than Aimery, and with a nose that showed there was Saracen blood in him. He had a heavy German blade, better suited for fighting on horseback than on foot. He had no buckler, and no armour save a headpiece, so the combatants were fairly matched.

It was a contest of speed and deftness against a giant's strength, for a blow from the great weapon would have cut deep into a man's vitals. Aimery was weary and unpractised, but the clash of steel gave life to him. He found that he had a formidable foe, but one who lacked the finer arts of the swordsman. The Tartar wasted his strength in the air against the new French parries and guards, though he drew first blood and gashed his opponent's left arm. Aimery's light blade dazzled his eyes, and presently when breath had grown short claimed its due. A deft cut on the shoulder paralysed the Tartar's sword arm, and a breaststroke brought him to his knees.

"Finish him," said the Ilkhan.

"Nay, sire," said Aimery, "it is not our custom to slay a disabled foe."

Houlagou nodded to one of his guards, who advanced swinging his sword. The defeated man seemed to know his fate, and stretched out his neck. With a single blow his head rolled on the earth.

"You have some skill of the sword, Frenchman," said the Ilkhan. "Hear, now, what I have decreed concerning you. I will have none of this journey to my brother Kublai. I had purposed to slay you, for you have defied my majesty. You sought to travel to Cathay instead of bearing my commands forthwith to your little King. But I am loath to kill so stout a warrior. Swear to me allegiance, and you shall ride with me against the Caliphs."

"And if I refuse?" Aimery asked.

"Then you die ere sundown."

"I am an envoy, sire, from a brother majesty, and of such it is the custom to respect the persons."

"Tush!" said the Ilkhan, "there is no brother majesty save Kublai. Between us we rule the world."

"Hear me, then," said Aimery. The duel had swept all cobwebs from his brain and doubts from his heart. "I am a knight of the Sire Christ and of the most noble King Louis, and I can own no other lord. Do your work, King. I am solitary among your myriads, but you cannot bend me."

"So be it," said Houlagou.

"I ask two boons as one about to die. Let me fall in battle against your warriors. And let me spend the hours till sundown alone, for I would prepare myself for my journey."

"So be it," said Houlagou, and turned to his hounds.

The damoiseau of Beaumanoir sat on a ridge commanding for fifty miles the snow-sprinkled uplands. The hum of the Tartars came faint from a hollow to the west, but where he sat he was in quiet and alone.

He had forgotten the ache of loss which had preyed on him.... His youth had not been squandered. The joy of young manhood which had been always like a tune in his heart had risen to a nobler song. For now, as it seemed to him, he stood beside his King, and had found a throne in the desert. Alone among all Christian men he had carried the Cross to a new world, and had been judged worthy to walk in the footprints of his captain Christ. A great gladness and a great humility possessed him.

He had ridden beyond the ken of his own folk, and no tale of his end would ever be told in that northern hall of his when the hearth-fire flickered on the rafters. That seemed small loss, for they would know that he had ridden the King's path, and that can have but the one ending.... Most clear in his memory now were the grey towers by Canche, where all day long the slow river made a singing among the reeds. He saw Alix his wife, the sun on her hair, playing in the close with his little Philip. Even now in the pleasant autumn weather that curly-pate would be scrambling in the orchard for the ripe apples which his mother rolled to him. He had thought himself born for a high destiny. Well, that destiny had been accomplished. He would not die, but live in the son of his body, and his sacrifice would be eternally a spirit moving in the hearts of his seed. He saw the thing clear and sharp, as if in a magic glass. There was a long road before the house of Beaumanoir, and on the extreme horizon a great brightness.

Now he remembered that he had always known it, known it even when his head had been busy with ardent hopes. He had loved life and had won life everlasting. He had known it when he sought learning from wise books. When he kept watch by his armour in the Abbey church of Corbie and questioned wistfully the darkness, that was the answer he had got. In the morning, when he had knelt in snow-white linen and crimson and steel before the high altar and received back his sword from God, the message had been whispered to his heart. In the June dawn when, barefoot, he was given the pilgrim's staff and entered on his southern journey, he had had a premonition of his goal. But now what had been dim, like a shadow in a mirror, was as clear as the colours in a painted psaltery. "Jerusalem, Jerusalem," he sighed, as his King was wont to sigh. For he was crossing the ramparts of the secret city.

He tried to take the ring from his finger that he might bury it, for it irked him that his father's jewel should fall to his enemies. But the wound had swollen his left hand, and he could not move the ring.

He was looking westward, for that way lay the Holy Places, and likewise Alix and Picardy. His minutes were few now, for he heard the bridles of the guards, as they closed in to carry him to his last fight.... He had with him a fragment of rye-cake and beside him on the ridge was a little spring. In his helmet he filled a draught, and ate a morsel. For, by the grace of the Church to the knight in extremity, he was now sealed of the priesthood, and partook of the mystic body and blood of his Lord....

Somewhere far off there was a grass fire licking the hills, and the sun was setting in fierce scarlet and gold. The hollow of the sky seemed a vast chapel ablaze with lights, like the lifting of the Host at Candlemas.

The tale is not finished. For, as it chanced, one Maffeo of Venice, a merchant who had strayed to the court of Cambaluc and found favour there, was sent by Kublai the next year on a mission to Europe, and his way lay through the camp of Houlagou. He was received with honour, and shown the riches of the Tartar armies. Among other things he heard of a Frankish knight who had fallen in battle with Houlagou's champions, and won much honour, they said, having slain three. He was shown the shrivelled arm of this knight, with a gold ring on the third finger. Maffeo was a man of sentiment, and begged for and was given the poor fragment, meaning to accord it burial in consecrated ground when he should arrive in Europe. He travelled to Bussorah, whence he came by sea to Venice. Now at Venice there presently arrived the Count of St. Pol with a company of Frenchmen, bound on a mission to the Emperor. Maffeo, of whom one may still read in the book of Messer Marco Polo, was become a famous man in the city, and strangers resorted to his house to hear his tales and see his treasures. From him St. Pol learned of the dead knight, and, reading the cognisance on the ring, knew the fate of his friend. On his return journey he bore the relic to Louis at Paris, who venerated it as the limb of a saint; and thereafter took it to Beaumanoir, where the Lady Alix kissed it with proud tears. The arm in a rich casket she buried below the chapel altar, and the ring she wore till her death.

CHAPTER V. THE MAID

The hostel of the Ane Raye poured from its upper and lower windows a flood of light into the gathering August dusk. It stood, a little withdrawn among its beeches, at a cross-roads, where the main route southward from the Valois cut the highway from Paris to Rheims and Champagne. The roads at that hour made ghostly white ribbons, and the fore-court of dusty grasses seemed of a verdure which daylight would disprove. Weary horses nuzzled at a watertrough, and serving-men in a dozen liveries made a bustle around the stables, which formed two sides of the open quadrangle. At the foot of the inn signpost beggars squatted, here a leper whining monotonously, there lustier vagrants dicing for supper. At the main door a knot of young squires stood talking in whispers, impatient, if one judged from the restless clank of metal, but on duty, as appeared when a new-comer sought entrance and was brusquely denied. For in an upper room there was business of great folk, and the commonalty must keep its distance.

That upper room was long and low-ceiled, with a canopied bed in a corner and an oaken table heaped with saddle-bags. A woman sat in a chair by the empty hearth, very bright and clear in the glow of the big iron lantern hung above the chimney. She was a tall girl, exquisitely dressed, from the fine silk of her horned cap to the amethyst buckles on her Spanish shoes. The saddle-bags showed that she was fresh from a journey, but her tirewoman's hands must have been busy, for she bore no marks of the road.

Her chin was in her hands, and the face defined by the slim fingers was small and delicate, pale with the clear pallor of perfect health, and now slowly flushing to some emotion. The little chin was firm, but the mouth was pettish. Her teeth bit on a gold chain, which encircled her neck and held a crystal reliquary. A spoiled pretty child, she looked, and in a mighty ill temper.

The cause of it was a young man who stood disconsolately by a settle a little way out of the lantern's glow. The dust of the white roads lay on his bodyarmour and coated the scabbard of his great sword. He played nervously with the plume of a helmet which lay on the settle, and lifted his face now and then to protest a word. It was an honest face, ruddy with wind and sun and thatched with hair which his mislikers called red but his friends golden.

The girl seemed to have had her say. She turned wearily aside, and drew the chain between her young lips with a gesture of despair.

"Since when have you become Burgundian, Catherine?" the young man asked timidly. The Sieur Guy de Laval was most notable in the field but he had few arts for a lady's chamber.

"I am no Burgundian," she said, "but neither am I Armagnac. What concern have we in these quarrels? Let the Kings who seek thrones do the fighting. What matters it to us whether knock-kneed Charles or fat Philip reign in Paris?"

The young man shuddered as if at a blasphemy "This is our country of France. I would rid it of the English and all foreign bloodsuckers."

"And your way is to foment the quarrel among Frenchmen? You are a fool, Guy. Make peace with Burgundy and in a month there will be no Goddams left in France."

"It is the voice of La Tremouille."

"It is the voice of myself, Catherine of Beaumanoir. And if my kinsman of La Tremouille say the same, the opinion is none the worse for that. You meddle with matters beyond your understanding.... But have done with statecraft, for that is not the heart of my complaint. You have broken your pledged word, sir. Did you not promise me when you set out that you would abide the issue of the Bourbon's battle before you took arms? Yet I have heard of you swashbuckling in that very fight at Rouvray, and only the miracle of God brought you out with an unbroken neck."

"The Bourbon never fought," said de Laval sullenly. "Only Stewart and his Scots stood up against Fastolf's spears. You would not have me stay idle in face of such odds. I was not the only French knight who charged. There was La Hire and de Saintrailles and the Bastard himself."

"Yet you broke your word," was the girl's cold answer. "Your word to me. You are forsworn, sir."

The boy's face flushed deeply. "You do not understand, my sweet Catherine. There have been mighty doings in Touraine, which you have not heard of in Picardy. Miracles have come to pass. Orleans has been saved, and there is now a great army behind Charles. In a little while we shall drive the English from Paris, and presently into the sea. There is hope now and a clear road for us Frenchmen. We have heard the terrible English 'Hurra' grow feeble, and 'St. Denis' swell like a wind in heaven. For God has sent us the Maid...."

The girl had risen and was walking with quick, short steps from hearth to open window.

"Tell me of this maid," she commanded.

"Beyond doubt she is a daughter of God," said de Laval.

"Beyond doubt. But I would hear more of her."

Her tone was ominously soft, and the young man was deceived by it. He launched into a fervid panegyric of Jeanne of Arc. He told of her doings at Orleans, when her standard became the oriflamme of France, and her voice was more stirring than trumpets; of her gentleness and her wisdom. He told of his first meeting with her, when she welcomed him in her chamber. "She sent for wine and said that soon she would drink it with me in Paris. I saw her mount a plunging black horse, herself all in white armour, but unhelmeted. Her eyes were those of a great captain, and yet merciful and mild like God's Mother. The sight of her made the heart sing like a May morning. No man could fear death in her company. They tell how..."

But he got no farther. The girl's face was pale with fury, and she tore at her gold neck-chain till it snapped.

"Enough of your maid!" she cried. "Maid, forsooth! The shame of her has gone throughout the land. She is no maid, but a witch, a light-of-love, a blasphemer. By the Rood, Sir Guy, you choose this instant between me and your foul peasant. A daughter of Beaumanoir does not share her lover with a crack-brained virago."

The young man had also gone pale beneath his sunburn. "I will not listen," he cried. "You blaspheme a holy angel."

"But listen you shall," and her voice quivered with passion. She marched up to him and faced him, her slim figure as stiff as a spear. "This very hour you break this mad allegiance and conduct me home to Beaumanoir. Or, by the Sorrows of Mary, you and I will never meet again."

De Laval did not speak, but stood gazing sadly at the angry loveliness before him. His own face had grown as stubborn as hers.

"You do not know what you ask," he said at length. "You would have me forswear my God, and my King, and my manhood."

"A fig for such manhood," she cried with ringing scorn. "If that is a man's devotion, I will end my days in a nunnery. I will have none of it, I tell you. Choose, my fine lover, choose between me and your peasant."

The young man looked again at the blazing eyes and then without a word turned slowly and left the room. A moment later the sound of horses told that a company had taken the road.

The girl stood listening till the noise died away. Then she sank all limp in a chair and began to cry. There was wrath in her sobs, and bitter self-pity. She had made a fine tragedy scene, but the glory of it was short. She did not regret it, but an immense dreariness had followed on her heroics. Was there ever, she asked herself, a more unfortunate lady?

And she had been so happy. Her lover was the bravest gallant that ever came out of Brittany; rich too, and well beloved, and kin to de Richemont, the Constable. In the happy days at Beaumanoir he was the leader in jousts and valiances, the soul of hunting parties, the lightest foot in the dance. The Beaumanoirs had been a sleepy stock, ever since that Sir Aimery, long ago, who had gone crusading with Saint Louis and ridden out of the ken of mortals. Their wealth had bought them peace, and they had kept on good terms alike with France and Burgundy, and even with the unruly captains of England. Wars might sweep round their marches, but their fields were unravaged. Shrewd, peaceable folk they were, at least the males of the house. The women had been different, for the daughters of Beaumanoir had been notable for beauty and wit and had married proudly, till the family was kin to half the nobleness of Artois and Picardy and Champagne. There was that terrible great-aunt at Coucy, and the aunts at Beaulieu and Avranches, and the endless cousinhood stretching as far south as the Nivernais.... And now the main stock had flowered in her, the sole child of her father, and the best match to be found that side of the Loire.

She sobbed in the chagrin of a new experience. No one in her soft cushioned life had ever dared to gainsay her. At Beaumanoir her word was law. She had loved its rich idleness for the power it gave her. Luxurious as she was, it was no passive luxury that she craved, but the sense of mastery, of being a rare thing set apart. The spirit of the women of Beaumanoir burned fiercely in her... She longed to set her lover in the forefront of the world. Let him crusade if he chose, but not in a beggars' quarrel. And now the palace of glass was shivered, and she was forsaken for a peasant beguine. The thought set her pacing to the window.

There seemed to be a great to-do without. A dozen lanterns lit up the forecourt, and there was a tramping of many horses. A shouting, too, as if a king were on the move. She hurriedly dried her eyes and arranged her dress, tossing the reliquary and its broken chain on the table. Some new guests; and the inn was none too large. She would have the landlord flayed if he dared to intrude on the privacy which she had commanded. Nay, she would summon her people that instant and set off for home, for her company was strong enough to give security in the midnight forests.

She was about to blow a little silver whistle to call her steward when a step at the door halted her. A figure entered, a stranger. It was a tall stripling, half armed like one who is not for battle but expects a brush at any corner of the road. A long surcoat of dark green and crimson fell stiffy as if it covered metal, and the boots were spurred and defended in front with thin plates of steel. The light helm was open and showed a young face. The stranger moved wearily as if from a long journey.

"Good even to you, sister," said the voice, a musical voice with the broad accent of Lorraine. "Help me to get rid of this weariful harness."

Catherine's annoyance was forgotten in amazement. Before she knew what she did her fingers were helping the bold youth to disarm. The helm was removed, the surcoat was stripped, and the steel corslet beneath it. With a merry laugh the stranger kicked off the great boots which were too wide for his slim legs.

He stretched himself, yawning, and then laughed again. "By my staff," he said, "but I am the weary one." He stood now in the full glow of the lantern, and Catherine saw that he wore close-fitting breeches of fine linen, a dark pourpoint, and a tunic of blue. The black hair was cut short like a soldier's, and the small secret face had the clear tan of one much abroad in wind and sun. The eyes were tired and yet merry, great grey eyes as clear and deep as a moorland lake.... Suddenly she understood. It may have been the sight of the full laughing lips, or the small maidenly breasts outlined by the close-fitting linen. At any rate she did not draw back when the stranger kissed her cheek.

"Ah, now I am woman again," said the crooning voice. The unbuckled sword in its leather sheath was laid on the table beside the broken reliquary. "Let us rest side by side, sister, for I long for maids' talk."

But now Catherine started and recoiled. For on the blue tunic she had caught sight of an embroidered white dove bearing in its beak the scroll De par le Roy du ciel. It was a blazon the tale of which had gone through France.

"You are she!" she stammered. "The witch of Lorraine!"

The other looked wonderingly at her. "I am Jeanne of Arc," she said simply. "She whom they call the Pucelle. Do you shrink from me, sister?"

Catherine's face was aflame. She remembered her lost lover, and the tears scarcely dry. "Out upon you!" she cried. "You are that false woman that corrupt men's hearts." And again her fingers sought the silver whistle.

Jeanne looked sadly upon her. Her merry eyes had grown grave.

"I pray you forbear. I do not heed the abuse of men, but a woman's taunts hurt me. They have spoken falsely of me, dear sister. I am no witch, but a poor girl who would fain do the commands of God."

She sank on the settle with the relaxed limbs of utter fatigue. "I was happy when they told me there was a lady here. I bade Louis and Raymond and the Sieur d'Aulon leave me undisturbed till morning, for I would fain rest. Oh, but I am weary of councils! They are all blind. They will not hear the plain wishes of God.... And I have so short a time! Only a year, and now half is gone!"

The figure had lost all its buoyancy, and become that of a sad, overwrought girl. Catherine found her anger ebbing and pity stealing into her heart. Could this tired child be the virago against whom she had sworn vengeance? It had none of a woman's allure, no arts of the light-of-love. Its eyes were as simple as a boy's.... She looked almost kindly at the drooping Maid.

But in a moment the languor seemed to pass from her. Her face lit up, as to the watcher in the darkness a window in a tower suddenly becomes a square of light. She sank on her knees, her head thrown back, her lips parted, the long eyelashes quiet on her cheeks. A sudden stillness seemed to fall on everything. Catherine held her breath, and listened to the beating of her heart.

Jeanne's lips moved, and then her eyes opened. She stood up again, her face entranced and her gaze still dwelling on some hidden world... Never had Catherine seen such happy radiance.

"My Brothers of Paradise spoke with me. They call me sometimes when I am sad. Their voices said to me, 'Daughter of God, go forward. We are at your side.'"

Catherine trembled. She seemed on the edge of a world of which in all her cosseted life she had never dreamed, a world of beautiful and terrible things. There was rapture in it, and a great awe. She had forgotten her grievances in wonder.

"Do not shrink from me," said the voice which seemed to have won an unearthly sweetness. "Let us sit together and tell our thoughts. You are very fair. Have you a lover?"

The word brought the girl to earth. "I had a lover, but this night I dismissed him. He fights in your company, and I see no need for this war."

Jeanne's voice was puzzled. "Can a man fight in a holier cause than to free his country?"

"The country..." But Catherine faltered. Her argument with Guy now seemed only pettishness.

"You are a great lady," said Jeanne, "and to such as you liberty may seem a little thing. You are so rich that you need never feel constraint. But to us poor folk freedom is life itself. It sweetens the hind's pottage, and gives the meanest an assurance of manhood.... Likewise it is God's will. My Holy Ones have told me that sweet France shall be purged from bondage. They have bidden me see the King crowned and lead him to Paris.... After that they have promised me rest."

She laid an arm round Catherine's neck and looked into her eyes.

"You are hungry, sister mine," she said.

The girl started. For the eyes were no longer those of a boy, but of a mother, very wise, very tender. Her own mother had died so long ago that she scarcely remembered her. A rush of longing came over her for something she had never known. She wanted to lay her head on that young breast and weep.

"You are hungry, and yet I think you have been much smiled on by fortune. You are very fair, and for most women to be beautiful is to be happy. But you are not content, and I am glad of it. There is a hunger that is divine...."

She broke off, for the girl was sobbing. Crumpled on the floor, she bent her proud head to the Maid's lap "What must I do?" she cried piteously. "The sight of you makes me feel my rottenness. I have been proud of worthless things and I have cherished that wicked pride that I might forget the doubts knocking on my heart. You say true, I am not content. I shall never be content, I am most malcontent with myself.... Would to God that like you I had been born a peasant!"

The tragic eyes looked up to find the Maid laughing, a kind, gentle merriment. Catherine flushed as Jeanne took her tear-stained face in her hands.

"You are foolish, little sister. I would I had been born to your station. My task would have been easier had I been Yoland of Sicily or that daughter of the King of Scots from whom many looked for the succour of France. Folly, folly! There is no virtue in humble blood. I would I had been a queen! I love fine clothes and rich trappings and the great horse which d'Alencon gave me. God has made a brave world and I would that all His people could get the joy of it. I love it the more because I have only a little time in it."

"But you are happy," said the girl, "and I want such happiness."

"There is no happiness," said the Maid, "save in doing the will of God our Father."

"But I do not know His will.... I am resolved now. I will take the vows and become a religious, and then I shall find peace. I am weary of all this confusing world."

"Foolish one," and Jeanne played with the little curls which strayed around Catherine's ear. "You were not born for a nunnery. Not that way God calls you."

"Show me His way," the girl implored.

"He shows His way privily to each heart, and His ways are many. For some the life of devout contemplation, but not for you, sister. Your blood is too fiery and your heart too passionate.... You have a lover? Tell me his name."

Docilely Catherine whispered it, and Jeanne laughed merrily.

"Sir Guy! My most loyal champion. By my staff, you are the blessed maid. There is no more joyous knight in all the fields of France."

"I do not seek wedlock. Oh, it is well for you who are leading armies and doing the commands of God. Something tells me that in marriage I shall lose my soul."

The girl was on her knees with her hands twined. "Let me follow you," she cried. "I will bring a stout company behind me. Let me ride with you to the freeing of France. I promise to be stalwart."

The Maid shook her head gently.

"Then I take the vows." The obstinate little mouth had shut and there were no tears now in the eyes.

"Listen, child," and Jeanne took the suppliant hands in hers. "It is true that God has called me to a holy task. He has sent His angels to guide me and they talk with me often. The Lady of Fierbois has given me a mystic sword. I think that in a little while this land will be free again.... But I shall not see it, for God's promise is clear, and for me it does not give length of days. I did not seek this errand of mine. I resisted the command, till God was stern with me and I submitted with bitter tears. I shall die a maid, and can never know the blessedness of women. Often at night I weep to think that I shall never hold a babe next my heart."

The face of Jeanne was suddenly strained with a great sadness. It was Catherine's turn to be the comforter. She sat herself beside her and drew her head to her breast.

"For you I see a happier fate, a true man's wife, the mother of sons. Bethink you of the blessedness. Every wife is like the Mother of God, she has the hope of bearing a saviour of mankind. She is the channel of the eternal purpose of Heaven. Could I change, could I change! What fortunate wife would envy a poor maid that dwells in the glare of battle?... Nay, I do not murmur. I do God's will and rejoice in it. But I am very lonely."

For a little there was silence, an ecstatic silence. Something hard within Catherine melted and she felt a gush of pity. No longer self-pity, but compassion for another. Her heart grew suddenly warm. It was as if a window had been opened in a close room to let in air and landscape.

"I must rest, for there is much ado to-morrow. Will you sleep by me, for I have long been starved of a woman's comradeship?"

In the great canopied bed the two girls lay till morning. Once in the darkness Catherine started and found her arms empty. Jeanne was kneeling by the window, her head thrown back and the moonlight on her upturned face. When she woke in the dawn the Maid was already up, trussing the points of her breeches and struggling with her long boots. She was crooning the verse of a ballad:

"Serais je nonette' Crois que non -"

and looking with happy eyes at the cool morning light on the forest.

"Up, sleepy-head," she cried. "Listen to the merry trampling of the horses. I must start, if I would spare the poor things in the noon. Follow me with your prayers, for France rides with me. I love you, sweet sister. Be sure I will hasten to you when my work is done."

So the Maid and her company rode off through the woods to Compiegne, and a brooding and silent Catherine took the north road to Picardy.

The promise was kept. Once again Catherine saw and had speech of Jeanne. It was nearly two years later, when she sat in a May gloaming in the house of Beaumanoir, already three months a bride. Much had happened since she had ridden north from the inn at the forest cross-roads. She had summoned de Laval to her side, and the lovers had been reconciled. Her father had died in the winter and the great fortune and wide manors of the family were now her own. Her lover had fought with Jeanne in the futile battles of the spring, but he had been far away when in the fatal sortie at Compiegne the Maid was taken by her enemies. All the summer of that year he had made desperate efforts at rescue, but Jeanne was tight in English hands, and presently was in prison at Rouen awaiting judgment, while her own king and his false councillors stirred not hand or foot to save her. Sir Guy had hurled himself on Burgundy, and with a picked band made havoc of the eastern roads, but he could not break the iron cordon of Normandy. In February they had been wed, but after that Beaumanoir saw him little, for he was reading Burgundy a lesson in the Santerre.

Catherine sat at home, anxious, tremulous, but happy. A new-made wife lives in a new world, and though at times she grieved for the shame of her land, her mind was too full of housewifely cares, and her heart of her husband, for long repining. But often the thought of Jeanne drove a sword into her contentment.... So when she lifted her eyes from her embroidery and saw the Maid before her, relief and gladness sent her running to greet her.

Long afterwards till she was very old Catherine would tell of that hour. She saw the figure outlined against a window full of the amethyst sky of evening. The white armour and the gay surcoat were gone.

Jeanne was still clad like a boy in a coarse grey tunic and black breeches, but her boots did not show any dust of the summer roads. Her face was very pale, as if from long immurement, and her eyes were no more merry. They shone instead with a grave ardour of happiness, which checked Catherine's embrace and set her heart beating.

She walked with light steps and kissed the young wife's cheek, a kiss like thistledown.

"You are free?" Catherine stammered. Her voice seemed to break unwillingly in a holy quiet.

"I am free," the Maid answered. "I have come again to you as I promised. But I cannot bide long. I am on a journey."

"You go to the King?" said Catherine.

"I go to my King."

The Maid's hand took Catherine's, and her touch was like the fall of gossamer. She fingered the girl's broad ring which had come from distant ancestors, the ring which Sir Aimery of Beaumanoir had worn in the Crusades. She raised it and pressed it to her.

Catherine's limbs would not do her bidding. She would fain have risen in a hospitable bustle, but she seemed to be held motionless. Not by fear, but by an exquisite and happy awe. She remembered afterwards that from the Maid's rough clothes had come a faint savour of wood-smoke, as from one who has been tending a bonfire in the autumn stubble.

"God be with you, lady, and with the good knight, your husband. Remember my word to you, that every wife is like Mary the Blessed and may bear a saviour of mankind. The road is long, but the ways of Heaven are sure."

Catherine stretched out her arms, for a longing so fierce had awoke in her that it gave her power to move again. Never in her life had she felt such a hunger of wistfulness. But Jeanne evaded her embrace. She stood poised as if listening.

"They are calling me. I go. Adieu, sweet sister."

A light shone in her face which did not come from the westering sun. To Catherine there was no sound of voices, but the Maid seemed to hear and answer. She raised her hand as if in blessing and passed out.

Catherine sat long in an entranced silence. Waves of utter longing flowed over her, till she fell on her knees and prayer passionately to her saints, among whom not the least was that grey-tunicked Maid whose eyes seemed doorways into heaven. Her tirewoman found her asleep on her faldstool.

Early next morning there came posts to Beaumanoir, men on weary horses with a tragic message. On the day before, in the market-place of Rouen, the chief among the daughters of God had journeyed through the fire to Paradise.

CHAPTER VI. THE WOOD OF LIFE

The Lady Catherine de Laval, in her own right Countess of Beaumanoir, and mistress of fiefs and manors, rights of chase and warren, mills and hospices, the like of which were not in Picardy, was happy in all things but her family. Her one son had fallen in his youth in an obscure fray in Guienne, leaving two motherless boys who, after her husband's death, were the chief business of life to the Countess Catherine. The elder, Aimery, grew to manhood after the fashion of the men of her own house, a somewhat heavy country gentleman, much set upon rustic sports, slow at learning, and averse alike from camps and cities. The ambition of the grandmother found nothing to feed upon in the young lord of Beaumanoir. He was kind, virtuous and honest, but dull as a pool on a winter's highway.

Catherine would fain have had the one youth a soldier and the other a saint, and of the two ambitions she most cherished the latter. The first made shipwreck on the rustic Aimery, and therefore the second burned more fiercely. She had the promise from the saints that her line had a great destiny, and the form of it she took to be sanctitude. For, all her married days she had ruled her life according to the canons of God, fasting and praying, cherishing the poor, tending the afflicted, giving of her great wealth bountifully to the Church. She had a name for holiness as far as the coasts of Italy. Surely from the blood of Beaumanoir one would arise to be in dark times a defender of the Faith, a champion of Christ whom after death the Church should accept among the beatified. Such a fate she desired for her seed more hungrily than any Emperor's crown.

In the younger, Philip, there was hope. He had been an odd child, slim and pale while Aimery was large and ruddy, shy where his brother was bold and bold where he was shy. He was backward in games and unready in a quarrel, but it was observed that he had no fear of the dark, or of the Green Lady that haunted the river avenue. Father Ambrose, his tutor, reported him of quick and excellent parts, but marred by a dreaminess which might grow into desidia that deadly sin. He had a peculiar grace of body and a silken courtesy of manner which won hearts. His grey eyes, even as a small boy, were serious and wise. But he seemed to dwell aloof, and while his brother's moods were plain for all to read, he had from early days a self-control which presented a mask to his little world. With this stoicism went independence. Philip walked his own way with a gentle obstinacy. "A saint, maybe," Father Ambrose told his grandmother. "But the kind of saint that the Church will ban before it blesses."

To the old dame of Beaumanoir the child was the apple of her eye; and her affection drew from him a tenderness denied to others. But it brought no confidences. The dreaming boy made his own world, which was not, like his grandmother's, one of a dark road visited rarely by angels, with heaven as a shining city at the end of it; or, like his brother's, a green place of earthy jollity. It was as if the Breton blood of the Lavals and Rohans had brought to the solid stock of Beaumanoir the fairy whimsies of their dim ancestors. While the moors and woodlands were to Aimery only places to fly a hawk or follow a stag, to Philip they were a wizard land where dreams grew. And the mysteries of the Church were also food for his gold fancy, which by reshaping them stripped them of all terrors. He was extraordinarily happy, for he had the power to make again each fresh experience in a select inner world in which he walked as king, since he was its creator.

He was a child of many fancies, but one especially stayed with him. When still very small, he slept in a cot in his grandmother's room, the walls of which were hung with tapestry from the Arras looms. One picture caught his eye, for the morning sun struck it, and when he woke early it glowed invitingly before him. It represented a little river twining about a coppice. There was no figure in the piece, which was bounded on one side by a great armoire, and on the other by the jamb of the chimney; but from extreme corner projected the plume of a helmet and the tip of a lance. There was someone there; someone riding towards the trees. It grew upon Philip that that little wood was a happy place, most happy and desirable. He fancied himself the knight, and he longed to be moving up the links of the stream. He followed every step of the way, across the shallow ford, past the sedges of a backwater, between two clumps of willows, and then over smooth green grass to the edge of the wood. But he never tried to picture what lay inside. That was sacred, even from his thoughts.

When he grew older and was allowed to prowl about in the scriptorium of the Abbey of Montmirail which lay by the Canche side, he found his wood again. It was in a Psaltery on which a hundred years before some Flemish monk had lavished his gold and vermilion.

Opposite the verse of Psalm xxiii., "In loco pascuae," was a picture almost the same as that in the bedroom arras. There were the river, the meadows, and the little wood, painted in colours far brighter than the tapestry. Never was such bloom of green or such depth of blue. But there was a difference. No lance or plume projected from the corner. The traveller had emerged from cover, and was walking waist-deep in the lush grasses. He was a thin, nondescript pilgrim, without arms save a great staff like the crozier of a Bishop. Philip was disappointed in him and preferred the invisible knight, but the wood was all he had desired. It was indeed a blessed place, and the old scribe had known it, for a scroll of gold hung above it with the words "Sylva Vitae."

At the age of ten the boy had passed far beyond Father Ambrose, and was sucking the Abbey dry of its learning, like some second Abelard. In the cloisters of Montmirail were men who had a smattering of the New Knowledge, about which Italy had gone mad, and, by the munificence of the Countess Catherine, copies had been made by the Italian stationarii of some of the old books of Rome which the world had long forgotten. In the Abbey library, among a waste of antiphonaries and homilies and monkish chronicles, were to be found texts of Livy and Lucretius and the letters of Cicero. Philip was already a master of Latin, writing it with an elegance worthy of Niccolo the Florentine. At fourteen he entered the college of Robert of Sorbonne, but found little charm in its scholastic pedantry. But in the capital he learned the Greek tongue from a Byzantine, the elder Lascaris, and copied with his own hand a great part of Plato and Aristotle. His thirst grew with every draught of the new vintage. To Pavia he went and sat at the feet of Lorenzo Vallo. The company of Pico della Mirandola at Florence sealed him of the Platonic school, and like his master he dallied with mysteries and had a Jew in his house to teach him Hebrew that he might find a way of reconciling the Scriptures and the classics, the Jew and the Greek. From the verses which he wrote at this time, beautifully turned hexameters with a certain Lucretian cadence, it is clear that his mind was like Pico's, hovering about the borderland of human knowledge, clutching at the eternally evasive. Plato's Banquet was his gospel, where the quest of truth did not lack the warmth of desire. Only a fragment remains now of the best of his poems, that which earned the praise of Ficino and the great Lorenzo, and it is significant that the name of the piece was "The Wood of Life."

At twenty Philip returned to Beaumanoir after long wanderings. He was the perfect scholar who had toiled at books and not less at the study of mankind. But his well-knit body and clear eyes showed no marks of bookishness, and Italy had made him a swordsman. A somewhat austere young man, he had kept himself unspotted in the rotting life of the Italian courts, and though he had learned from them suavity had not lost his simplicity. But he was more aloof than ever. There was little warmth in the grace of his courtesy, and his eyes were graver than before. It seemed that they had found much, but had had no joy of it, and that they were still craving. It was a disease of the time and men called it aegritudo. "No saint," the aged Ambrose told the Countess. "Virtuous, indeed, but not with the virtue of the religious. He will never enter the Church. He has drunk at headier streams." The

Countess was nearing her end. All her days, for a saint, she had been a shrewd observer of life, but with the weakening of her body's strength she had sunk into the ghostly world which the Church devised as an ante-room to immortality. Her chamber was thronged with lean friars like shadows. To her came the Bishop of Beauvais, once a star of the Court, but now in his age a grim watch-dog of the Truth. To him she spoke of her hopes for Philip.

"An Italianate scholar!" cried the old man. "None such shall pollute the Church with my will. They are beguiled by such baubles as the holy Saint Gregory denounced, poetarum figmenta sive deliramenta. If your grandson, madame, is to enter the service of God he must renounce these pagan follies."

The Bishop went, but his words remained. In the hour of her extremity the vision of Catherine was narrowed to a dreadful antagonism of light and darkness, God and Antichrist, the narrow way of salvation and a lost world. She was obsessed by the peril of her darling. Her last act must be to pluck him from his temptress. Her mood was fanned by the monks who surrounded her, narrow men whose honesty made them potent.

The wan face on the bed moved Philip deeply. Tenderness filled his heart, and a great sense of alienation, for the dying woman spoke a tongue he had forgotten. Their two worlds were divided by a gulf which affection could not bridge. She spoke not with her own voice but with that of her confessors when she pled with him to do her wishes.

"I have lived long," she said, "and know that the bread of this world is ashes. There is no peace but in God. You have always been the child of my heart, Philip, and I cannot die at ease till I am assured of your salvation.... I have the prevision that from me a saint shall be born. It is God's plain commandment to you. Obey, and I go to Him with a quiet soul."

For a moment he was tempted. Surely it was a little thing this, to gladden the dying. The rich Abbey of Montmirail was his for the taking, and where would a scholar's life be more happily lived than among its cool cloisters? A year ago, when he had been in the mood of seeing all contraries but as degrees in an ultimate truth, he might have assented. But in that dim chamber, with burning faces around him and the shadow of death overhead, he discovered in himself a new scrupulousness. It was the case of Esau; he was bidden sell his birthright for pottage, and affection could not gloze over the bargain.

"I have no vocation," he said sadly. "I would fain do the will of God, but God must speak His will to each heart, and He does not speak thus to me."

There was that in the words which woke a far-away memory of her girlhood. Once another in a forest inn had spoken thus to her. She stretched out her hand to him, and he covered it with kisses.

But in the night the priests stirred her fears again, and next morning there was another tragic pleading, from which Philip fled almost in tears. Presently he found himself denied her chamber, unless he could give assurance of a changed mind. And so the uneasy days went on, till in a dawn of wind amid a great praying and chanting the soul of the Countess Catherine passed, and Aimery reigned in Beaumanoir.

The place had grown hateful to Philip and he made ready to go. For him in his recalcitrancy there was only a younger son's portion, the little seigneury of Eaucourt, which had been his mother's. The good Aimery would have increased the inheritance, but Philip would have none of it. He had made his choice, and to ease his conscience must abide strictly by the consequences. Those days at Beaumanoir had plucked him from his moorings. For the moment the ardour of his quest for knowledge had burned low. He stifled in the air of the north, which was heavy with the fog of a furious ignorance. But his mind did not turn happily to the trifling of his Italian friends. There was a tragic greatness about such as his grandmother, a salt of nobility which was lacking among the mellow Florentines. Truth, it seemed to him, lay neither with the old Church nor the New Learning, and not by either way could he reach the desire of his heart.

Aimery bade him a reluctant farewell. "If you will not keep me company here, I go to the wars. At Beaumanoir I grow fat. Ugh, this business of dying chills me." And then with a very red face he held out a gold ring. "Take it, Philip. She cherished it, and you were her favourite and should wear it. God knows I have enough."

Likewise he presented him with a little vellum-bound book. "I found this yesterday, and you being the scholar among us should have it. See, the grandmother's name is written within."

It was a bright May morning when Philip, attended by only two lackeys as became a poor man, rode over the bridge of Canche with eyes turned southward. In the green singing world the pall lifted from his spirits. The earth which God had made was assuredly bigger and better than man's philosophies. "It would appear," he told himself, "that like the younger son in the tale, I am setting out to look for fortune."

At an inn in the city of Orleans he examined his brother's gift. It was a volume of careful manuscript, entitled Imago Mundi, and bearing the name of one Pierre d'Ailly, who had been Bishop of Cambray when the Countess Catherine was a child. He opened it and read of many marvels, how that the world was round, as Pythagoras held, so that if a man travelled west he would come in time to Asia where the sun rose. Philip brooded over the queer pages, letting his fancy run free, for he had been so wrapped up in the mysteries of man's soul that he had forgotten the mysteries of the earth which is that soul's place of pilgrimage. He read of cities with silver walls and golden towers waiting on the discoverer, and of a river on whose banks "virescit sylva vitae." And at that phrase he fell to dreaming of his childhood, and a pleasant unrest stirred in his heart. "Aimery has given me a precious viaticum," he said.

He travelled by slow stages into Italy, for he had no cause for haste. At Pavia he wandered listlessly among the lecture halls. What had once seemed to him the fine gold of eloquence was now only leaden rhetoric. In his lodging at Florence he handled once again his treasures, his books from Ficino's press; his manuscripts, some from Byzantium yellow with age, some on clean white vellum new copied by his order; his busts and gems and intaglios. What had become of that fervour with which he had been used to gaze on them? What of that delicious world into which, with drawn curtains and a clear lamp, he could retire at will? The brightness had died in the air.

He found his friends very full of quarrels. There was a mighty feud between two of them on the respective merits of Cicero and Quintilian as lawgivers in grammar, and the air was thick with libels. Another pair wrangled in public over the pre-eminence of Scipio and Julius Caesar; others on narrow points of Latinity. There was a feud among the Platonists on a matter of interpretation, in which already stilettos had been drawn. More bitter still was the strife about mistresses, kitchen-wenches and courtesans, where one scholar stole shamelessly from the other and decked with names like Leshia and Erinna.... Philip sickened at what he had before tolerated, for he had brought back with him from the north a quickened sense of sin. Maybe the Bishop of Beauvais had been right. What virtue was there in this new knowledge if its prophets were apes and satyrs! Not here grew the Wood of Life. Priapus did not haunt its green fringes.

His mind turned towards Venice. There the sea was, and there men dwelt with eyes turned to spacious and honourable quests, not to monkish hells and heavens or inward to unclean hearts. And in Venice in a tavern off the Merceria he spoke with destiny.

It was a warm evening, and, having dined early, he sought the balcony which overlooked the canal. It was empty but for one man who sat at a table with a spread of papers before him on which he was intently engaged. Philip bade him good evening, and a face was raised which promptly took his fancy. The stranger wore a shabby grey doublet, but he had no air of poverty, for round his neck hung a massive chain of gold, and his broad belt held a richly chased dagger. He had unbuckled his sword, and it lay on the table holding down certain vagrant papers which fluttered in the evening wind. His face was hard and red like sandstone, and around his eyes were a multitude of fine wrinkles. It was these eyes that arrested Philip. They were of a pale brown as if bleached by weather and gazing over vast spaces; cool and quiet and friendly, but with a fire burning at the back of them. The man assessed Philip at a glance, and then, as if liking what he found in him, smiled so that white furrows appeared in his tanned cheeks. With a motion of his hand he swept aside his papers and beckoned the other to sit with him. He called on the drawer to bring a flask of Cyprus.

"I was about to have my evening draught," he said. "Will you honour me with your company, sir?"

The voice was so pleasant that Philip, who was in a mood to shun talk, could not refuse. He sat down by the board, and moved aside a paper to make room for the wine. He noticed that it was a map.

The Bishop of Cambray had made him curious about such things. He drew it to him, and saw that it was a copy of Andrea Bianco's chart, drawn nearly half a century before, showing the Atlantic Sea with a maze of islands stretching westwards.

The other shook his head. "A poor thing and out of date. Here," and he plucked a sheet from below the rest, "here is a better, which Fra Mauro of this city drew for the great prince, Henry of Portugal."

Philip looked at the map, which showed a misshapen sprawling Africa, but with a clear ocean way round the south of it. His interest quickened. He peered at the queer shapes in the dimming light.

"Then there is a way to the Indies by sea?"

"Beyond doubt. I myself have turned the butt of Africa.... If these matters interest you? But the thought of that dry land has given me an African thirst. He, drawer!"

He filled his glass from a fresh bottle. "'Twas in June four years back. I was in command of a caravel in the expedition of Diaz. The court of Lisbon had a fit of cold ague and we sailed with little goodwill; therefore it was our business to confound the doubters or perish. Already our seamen had reached the mouth of that mighty river they called the Congo, and clearly the butt of Africa could not be distant. We had the course of Cam and Behaim to guide us thus far, but after that was the darkness."

The man's face had the intent look of one who remembers with passion. He told of the struggle to cross the Guinea Deep instead of hugging the shore; of blue idle days of calm when magic fish flew aboard and Leviathan wallowed so near that the caravels were all but overwhelmed by the wave of him; of a storm which swept the decks and washed away the Virgin on the bows of the Admiral's ship; of landfall at last in a place where the forests were knee deep in a muddy sea, strange forests where the branches twined like snakes; of a going ashore at a river mouth full of toothed serpents and giant apes, and of a fight with Behemoth among the reeds. Then a second storm blowing from the east had flung them seaward, and for weeks they were out of sight of land, steering by strange stars. They had their magnets and astrolabes, but it was a new world they had entered, and they trusted God rather than their wits. At last they turned eastward.

"What distance before the turn?" Philip asked.

"I know not. We were far from land and no man can measure a course on water."

"Nay, but the ancients could," Philip cried, and he explained how the Romans had wheels of a certain diameter fixed to their ships' sides which the water turned in its passing, and which flung for each revolution a pebble into a tally-box.

The other's eyes widened. "A master device! I would hear more of it. What a thing it is to have learning. We had only the hour-glass and guesswork."

Then he told how on a certain day the crews would go no farther, being worn out by storms, for in those seas the tides were like cataracts and the waves were mountains. The admiral, Bartholomew Diaz, was forced to put about with a heavy heart, for he believed that a little way to the east he should find the southern cape of Africa. He steered west by north, looking for no land till Guinea was sighted. "But on the second morning we saw land to the northward, and following it westward came to a mighty cape so high that the top was in the clouds. There was such a gale from the east that we could do no more than gaze on it as we scudded past. Presently, still keeping land in sight, we were able to bend north again, and when we came into calm waters we captains went aboard the admiral's ship and knelt and gave thanks to God for His mercies. For we, the first of mortals, had rounded the butt of Africa and prepared the sea-road to the Indies."

"A vision maybe."

"Nay, it was no vision. I returned there under mild skies, when it was no longer a misty rock, but a green mountain. We landed, and set up a cross and ate the fruits and drank the water of the land. Likewise we changed its name from the Cape of Storms, as Diaz had dubbed it, to the Bona Esperanza, for indeed it seemed to us the hope of the world."

"And beyond it?"

"Beyond it we found a pleasant country, and would doubtless have made the Indies, if our ships had not grown foul and our crews mutinous from fear of the unknown. It is clear to me that we must establish a port of victualling in that southern Africa before we can sail the last stage to Cathay."

The man spoke modestly and simply as if he were talking of a little journey from one village to another. Something in his serious calm powerfully caught Philip's fancy. In all his days he had never met such a one.

"I have not your name, Signor," he said.

"They call me Battista de Cosca, a citizen of Genoa, but these many years a wanderer. And yours?"

Philip gave it and the stranger bowed. The de Lavals were known as a great house far beyond the confines of France.

"You contemplate another voyage?"

The brown man nodded. "I am here on the quest of maps, for these Venetians are the princes of mapmaking. Then I sail again."

"To Cathay?"

A sudden longing had taken Philip. It was as if a bright strange world had been spread before him compared with which the old was tarnished and dingy.

Battista shook his head. "Not Cathay. To go there would be only to make assurance of that which we already know. I have shown the road: let others plan its details and build hostelries. For myself I am for a bolder venture."

The balcony was filling up. A noisy group of young men were chattering at one table, and at others some of the merchants from the Merceria were at wine. But where the two sat it was quiet and dusky, though without on the canal the sky made a golden mirror. Philip could see his companion's face in the reflected light, and it reminded him of the friars who had filled the chamber of his dying grandmother. It was strained with a steadfast ardour.

Battista leaned his elbows on the board and his eyes searched the other's.

"I am minded to open my heart to you," he said. "You are young and of a noble stock. Likewise you are a scholar. I am on a mission, Sir Philip, the loftiest, I think, since Moses led Israel over the deserts. I am seeking a promised land. Not Cathay, but a greater. I sail presently, not the African seas, but the Sea of Darkness, the Mare Atlanticum." He nodded towards Bianco's map. "I am going beyond the Ultimate Islands."

"Listen," he went on, and his voice fell very low and deep. "I take it we live in these latter days of which the prophets spoke. I remember a monk in Genoa who said that the Blessed Trinity ruled in turn, and that the reign of the Father was accomplished and that of the Son nearing its close; and that now the reign of the Spirit was at hand. It may have been heresy, I am no scholar, but he pointed a good moral. For, said he, the old things pass away and the boundaries of the world are shifting. Here in Europe we have come to knowledge of salvation, and brought the soul and mind of man to an edge and brightness like a sword. Having perfected the weapon, it is now God's will that we enter into possession of the new earth which He has kept hidden against this day, and He has sent His Spirit like a wind to blow us into those happy spaces.... Now, mark you, sir, this earth is not a flat plain surrounded by outer darkness, but a sphere hung in the heavens and sustained by God's hand. Therefore if a man travel east or west he will, if God prosper him, return in time to his starting-point."

The speaker looked at Philip as if to invite contradiction, but the other nodded.

"It is the belief of the best sailors," Battista went on; "it is the belief of the great Paolo Toscanelli in this very land of Italy."

"It was the belief of a greater than he. The ancients -"

"Ay, what of your ancients?" Battista asked eagerly.

Philip responded with a scholar's zest. "Four centuries before our Lord's birth Aristotle taught the doctrine, from observing in different places the rise and setting of the heavenly bodies. The sages Eratosthenes, Hipparchus and Ptolemy amplified the teaching. It is found in the poetry of Manilius and Seneca, and it was a common thought in the minds of Virgil and Ovid and Pliny. You will find it in St. Augustine, and St. Isidore and Beda, and in many of the moderns. I myself have little knowledge of such things, but on the appeal to high authority your doctrine succeeds.'

"What a thing is learning!" Battista exclaimed with reverence. "Here have I and such as I been fumbling in the dark when the great ones of old saw clearly!... It follows, then, that a voyage westward will bring a man to Cathay?"

"Assuredly. But how will he return? If the earth is a sphere, his course will be a descent, and on his way back he will have to climb a great steep of waters."

"It is not so," said Battista vigorously. "Though why it is not so I cannot tell. Travelling eastward by land there is no such descent, and in this Mediterranean sea of ours one can sail as easily from Cadiz to Egypt as from Egypt to Cadiz. There is a divine alchemy in it which I cannot fathom, but the fact stands."

"Then you would reach Cathay by the west?"

"Not Cathay." The man's voice was very earnest. "There is a land between us and Cathay, a great islandland beyond the Seven Cities of Antillia."

"Cipango," said Philip, who had read Marco Polo's book in the Latin version published a year or two before.

"Nay, not Cipango. On this side Cipango. Of Cipango the Venetians have told us much, but the land I seek is not Cipango."

He drew closer to Philip and spoke low. "There was a Frenchman, a Rochellois, he is dead these ten years, but I have spoken with him. He was whirled west by storms far beyond Antillia, and was gripped by a great ocean stream and carried to land. What think you it was? No less than Hy-Brasil. There he found men, broad-faced dusky men, with gentle souls, and saw such miracles as have never been vouchsafed to mortals. 'Twas not Cipango or Cathay' for there were no Emperors or cities, but a peaceful race dwelling in innocence. The land was like Eden, bringing forth five harvests in the year, and vines and all manner of fruits grew without tillage. Tortorel was the man's name, and some thought him mad, but I judged differently. I have talked with him and I have copied his charts. I go to find those Fortunate Islands."

"Alone?"

"I have friends. There is a man of my own city, Cristoforo Colombo, they call him. He is a hard man and a bitter, but a master seaman, and there is a fire in him that will not be put out. And there may be others."

His steadfast burning eyes held Philip's.

"And you, what do you seek?" he asked.

Philip was aware that he had come to a cross roads in life. The easy path he had planned for himself was barred by his own nature. Something of his grandmother's blood clamoured within him for a sharper air than the well-warmed chamber of the scholar. This man, chance met in a tavern, had revealed to him his own heart.

"I am looking for the Wood of Life," he said simply and was amazed at his words.

Battista stared at him with open mouth, and then plucked feverishly at his doublet. From an inner pocket he produced a packet rolled in fine leather, and shook papers on the table. One of these was a soiled and worn slip of parchment, covered with an odd design. "Look," he said hoarsely. "Tortorel's map!"

It showed a stretch of country, apparently a broad valley running east to a seashore. Through it twined a river and on both sides were hills dotted with trees. The centre seemed to be meadows, sown with villages and gardens. In one crook of the stream lay a little coppice on which many roads converged, and above it was written the words "Sylva Vitae."

"It is the finger of God," said Battista. "Will you join me and search out this Wood of Life?"

At that moment there was a bustle at the door giving on the main room of the tavern. Lights were being brought in and a new company were entering. They talked in high-pitched affected voices and giggled like bona-robas. There were young men with them, dressed in the height of the fashion; a woman or two, and a man who from the richness of his dress seemed to be one of the princely merchants who played Maecenas to the New Learning. But what caught Philip's sight was a little group of Byzantines who were the guests of honour. They wore fantastic headdresses and long female robes, above which their flowing dyed beards and their painted eyebrows looked like masks of Carnival time. After Battista's gravity their vain eyes and simpering tones seemed an indecent folly. These were the folk he had called friends, this the life he had once cherished. Assuredly he was well rid of it.

He grasped Battista's hand.

"I will go with you," he said, "over the edge of the world."

As it happened Philip de Laval did not sail with Columbus in that first voyage which brought him to San Salvador in the Bahamas. But he and Battista were in the second expedition, when the ship under the command of the latter was separated by a storm from her consorts, and driven on a westerly course when the others had turned south. It was believed to be lost, and for two years nothing was heard of its fate. At the end of that time a tattered little vessel reached Bordeaux, and Philip landed on the soil of Franc. He had a strange story to tell. The ship had been caught up by a current which had borne it north for the space of fifteen days till landfall was made on the coast of what we now call South Carolina. There it had been beached in an estuary, while the crew adventured inland. The land was rich enough, but the tribes were not the gentle race of Battista's imagining. There had been a savage struggle for mastery, till the strangers made alliances and were granted territory between the mountains and the sea. But they were only a handful and Philip was sent back for further colonists and for a cargo of arms and seeds and implements.

The French court was in no humour for his tale, being much involved in its own wars. It may be that he was not believed; anyhow he got no help from his king. At his own cost and with the aid of friends he fitted out his ship for the return. After that the curtain falls. It would appear that the colony did not prosper, for it is on record that Philip in the year 1521 was living at his house at Eaucourt, a married man, occupied with books and the affairs of his little seigneury. A portrait of him still extant by an Italian artist shows a deeply furrowed face and stern brows, as of one who had endured much, but the eyes are happy. It is believed that in his last years he was one of the first of the gentlemen of Picardy to adhere to the Reformed faith.

CHAPTER VII. EAUCOURT BY THE WATERS

The horseman rode down the narrow vennel which led to the St. Denis gate of Paris, holding his nose like a fine lady. Behind him the city reeked in a close August twilight. From every entry came the smell of coarse cooking and unclean humanity, and the heaps of garbage in the gutters sent up a fog of malodorous dust when they were stirred by prowling dogs or hasty passengers.

"Another week of heat and they will have the plague here," he muttered. Oh for Eaucourt, Eaucourt by the waters! I have too delicate a stomach for this Paris."

His thoughts ran on to the country beyond the gates, the fields about St. Denis, the Clermont downs. Soon he would be stretching his bay on good turf.

But the gates were closed, though it was not yet the hour of curfew. The lieutenant of the watch stood squarely before him with a forbidding air, while a file of arquebusiers lounged in the archway.

"There's no going out to-night," was the answer to the impatient rider.

"Tut, man, I am the Sieur de Laval, riding north on urgent affairs. My servants left at noon. Be quick. Open!"

"Who ordered this folly?"

"The Marshal Tavannes. Go argue with him, if your mightiness has the courage."

The horseman was too old a campaigner to waste time in wrangling. He turned his horse's head and retraced his path up the vennel. "Now what in God's name is afoot to-night?" he asked himself, and the bay tossed his dainty head, as if in the same perplexity. He was a fine animal with the deep barrel and great shoulders of the Norman breed, and no more than his master did he love this place of alarums and stenches.

Gaspard de Laval was a figure conspicuous enough even in that city of motley. For one thing he was well over two yards high, and, though somewhat lean for perfect proportions, his long arms and deep chest told of no common strength. He looked more than his thirty years, for his face was burned the colour of teak by hot suns, and a scar just under the hair wrinkled a broad low forehead. His small pointed beard was bleached by weather to the hue of pale honey. He wore a steel back and front over a doublet of dark taffeta, and his riding cloak was blue velvet lined with cherry satin. The man's habit was sombre except for the shine of steel and the occasional flutter of the gay lining. In his velvet bonnet he wore a white plume. The rich clothing became him well, and had just a hint of foreignness, as if commonly he were more roughly garbed. Which was indeed the case, for he was new back from the Western Seas, and had celebrated his home-coming with a brave suit.

As a youth he had fought under Conde in the religious wars, but had followed Jean Ribaut to Florida, and had been one of the few survivors when the Spaniards sacked St. Caroline. With de Gourgues he had sailed west again for vengeance, and had got it. Thereafter he had been with the privateers of Brest and La Rochelle, a hornet to search out and sting the weak places of Spain on the Main and among the islands. But he was not born to live continually in outland parts, loving rather to intercalate fierce adventures between spells of home-keeping. The love of his green Picardy manor drew him back with gentle hands. He had now returned like a child to his playthings, and the chief thoughts in his head were his gardens and fishponds, the spinneys he had planted and the new German dogs he had got for boar-hunting in the forest. He looked forward to days of busy idleness in his modest kingdom.

But first he must see his kinsman the Admiral about certain affairs of the New World which lay near to that great man's heart. Coligny was his godfather, from whom he was named; he was also his kinsman, for the Admiral's wife, Charlotte de Laval, was a cousin once removed. So to Chatillon Gaspard journeyed, and thence to Paris, whither the Huguenot leader had gone for the marriage fetes of the King of Navarre. Reaching the city on the Friday evening, he was met by ill news. That morning the Admiral's life had been attempted on his way back from watching the King at tennis. Happily the wounds were slight, a broken right forefinger and a bullet through the left forearm, but the outrage had taken away men's breath. That the Admiral of France, brought to Paris for those nuptials which were to be a pledge of a new peace, should be the target of assassins shocked the decent and alarmed the timid. The commonwealth was built on the side of a volcano, and the infernal fires were muttering. Friend and foe alike set the thing down to the Guises' credit, and the door of Coligny's lodging in the Rue de Bethisy was thronged by angry Huguenot gentry, clamouring to be permitted to take order with the Italianate murderers.

On the Saturday morning Gaspard was admitted to audience with his kinsman, but found him so weak from Monsieur Ambrose Pare's drastic surgery that he was compelled to postpone his business. "Get you back to Eaucourt," said Coligny, "and cultivate your garden till I send for you. France is too crooked just now for a forthright fellow like you to do her service, and I do not think that the air of Paris is healthy for our house." Gaspard was fain to obey, judging that the Admiral spoke of some delicate state business for which he was aware he had no talent. A word with M. de Teligny reassured him as to the Admiral's safety, for according to him the King now leaned heavily against the Guises.

But lo and behold! the gates of Paris were locked to him, and he found himself interned in the sweltering city.

He did not like it. There was an ugly smack of intrigue in the air, puzzling to a plain soldier. Nor did he like the look of the streets now dim in the twilight. On his way to the gates they had been crammed like a barrel of salt fish, and in the throng there had been as many armed men as if an enemy made a leaguer beyond the walls. There had been, too, a great number of sallow southern faces, as if the Queen-mother had moved bodily thither a city of her countrymen. But now as the dark fell the streets were almost empty. The houses were packed to bursting, a blur of white faces could be seen at the windows, and every entry seemed to be alive with silent men. But in the streets there was scarcely a soul except priests, flitting from door to door, even stumbling against his horse in their preoccupation. Black, brown, and grey crows, they made Paris like Cartagena. The man's face took a very grim set as he watched these birds of ill omen. What in God's name had befallen his honest France?... He was used to danger, but this secret massing chilled even his stout heart. It was like a wood he remembered in Florida where every bush had held an Indian arrow, but without sight or sound of a bowman. There was hell brewing in this foul cauldron of a city.

He stabled his horse in the yard in the Rue du Coq, behind the glover's house where he had lain the night before. Then he set out to find supper. The first tavern served his purpose. Above the door was a wisp of red wool, which he knew for the Guise colours. Inside he looked to find a crowd, but there was but one other guest. Paris that night had business, it seemed, which did not lie in the taverns.

That other guest was a man as big as himself, clad wholly in black, save for a stiff cambric ruff worn rather fuller than the fashion. He was heavily booted, and sat sideways on a settle with his left hand tucked in his belt and a great right elbow on the board. Something in his pose, half rustic, half braggart, seemed familiar to Gaspard. The next second the two were in each other's arms.

"Gawain Champernoun!" cried Gaspard. "When I left you by the Isle of Pines I never hoped to meet you again in a Paris inn? What's your errand, man, in this den of thieves?"

"Business of state," the Englishman laughed. "I have been with Walsingham, her Majesty's Ambassador, and looked to start home to-night. But your city is marvellous unwilling to part with her guests. What's toward, Gaspard?"

"For me, supper," and he fell with zest to the broiled fowl he had ordered. The other sent for another flask of the wine of Anjou, observing that he had a plaguy thirst.

"I think," said Gaspard, at last raising his eyes from his food, "that Paris will be unwholesome to-night for decent folk."

"There's a murrain of friars about," said Champernoun, leisurely picking his teeth.

"The place hums like a bee-hive before swarming. Better get back to your Ambassador, Gawain. There's sanctuary for you under his cloak."

The Englishman made a pellet of bread and flicked it at the other's face. "I may have to box your ears, old friend. Since when have I taken to shirking a fracas? We were together at St. John d'Ulloa, and you should know me better."

"Are you armed?" was Gaspard's next question.

Champernoun patted his sword. "Also there are pistols in my holsters."

"You have a horse, then?"

"Stabled within twenty yards. My rascally groom carried a message to Sir Francis, and as he has been gone over an hour, I fear he may have come to an untimely end."

"Then it will be well this night for us two to hold together. I know our Paris mob and there is nothing crueller out of hell. The pistolling of the Admiral de Coligny has given them a taste of blood, and they may have a fancy for killing Luteranos. Two such as you and I, guarding each other's backs, may see sport before morning, and haply rid the world of a few miscreants. What say you, camerado?"

"Good. But what account shall we give of ourselves if someone questions us?"

"Why, we are Spanish esquires in the train of King Philip's Mission. Our clothes are dark enough for the dons' fashion, and we both speak their tongue freely. Behold in me the Senor Juan Gonzalez de Mendoza, a poor knight of Castile, most earnest in the cause of Holy Church."

"And I," said the Englishman with the gusto of a boy in a game, "am named Rodriguez de Bobadilla. I knew the man, who is dead, and his brother owes me ten crowns.... But if we fall in with the Spanish Ambassador's gentlemen?"

"We will outface them."

"But if they detect the imposture?"

"Why, wring their necks. You are getting as cautious as an apple-wife, Gawain."

"When I set out on a business I like to weigh it, that I may know how much is to be charged to my own wits and how much I must leave to God. To-night it would appear that the Almighty must hold us very tight by the hand. Well, I am ready when I have I drunk another cup of wine." He drew his sword and lovingly fingered its edge, whistling all the while.

Gaspard went to the door and looked into the street. The city was still strangely quiet. No roysterers swaggered home along the pavements, no tramp of cuirassiers told of the passage of a great man. But again he had the sense that hot fires were glowing under these cold ashes. The mist had lifted and the stars were clear, and over the dark mass of the Louvre a great planet burned. The air was warm and stifling, and with a gesture of impatience he slammed the door. By now he ought to have been drinking the cool night on the downs beyond Oise.

The Englishman had called for another bottle, and it was served in the empty tavern by the landlord himself. As the wine was brought in the two fell to talking Spanish, at the sound of which the man visibly started. His furtive sulky face changed to a sly friendliness. "Your excellencies have come to town for the good work," he said, sidling and bowing.

With a more than Spanish gravity Gaspard inclined his head.

"When does it start?" he asked.

"Ah, that we common folk do not know. But there will be a signal. Father Antoine has promised us a signal. But messieurs have not badges. Perhaps they do not need them for their faces will be known. Nevertheless for better security it might be well...." He stopped with the air of a huckster crying his wares.

Gaspard spoke a word to Champernoun in Spanish. Then to the landlord: "We are strangers, so must bow to the custom of your city. Have you a man to send to the Hotel de Guise?"

"Why trouble the Duke, my lord?" was the answer. "See, I will make you badges."

He tore up a napkin, and bound two white strips crosswise on their left arms, and pinned a rag to their bonnets. "There, messieurs, you are now wearing honest colours for all to see. It is well, for presently blood will be hot and eyes blind."

Gaspard flung him a piece of gold, and he bowed himself out. "Bonne fortune, lordships," were his parting words. "'Twill be a great night for our Lord Christ and our Lord King."

"And his lord the Devil," said Champernoun. "What madness has taken your good France? These are Spanish manners, and they sicken me. Cockades and signals and such-like flummery!"

The other's face had grown sober. "For certain hell is afoot to-night. It is the Admiral they seek. The Guisards and their reiters and a pack of 'prentices maddened by sermons. I would to God he were in the Palace with the King of Navarre and the young Conde."

"But he is well guarded. I heard that a hundred Huguenots' swords keep watch by his house."

"Maybe. But we of the religion are too bold and too trustful. We are not match for the Guises and their Italian tricks. I think we will go to Coligny's lodgings. Mounted, for a man on a horse has an advantage if the mob are out!"

The two left the tavern, both sniffing the air as if they found it tainted. The streets were filling now, and men were running as if to a rendezvous, running hot-foot without speech and without lights. Most wore white crosses on their left sleeve. The horses waited, already saddled, in stables not a furlong apart, and it was the work of a minute to bridle and mount. The two as if by a common impulse halted their beasts at the mouth of the Rue du Coq, and listened. The city was quiet on the surface, but there was a low deep undercurrent of sound, like the soft purring of a lion before he roars. The sky was bright with stars. There was no moon, but over the Isle was a faint tremulous glow.

"It is long past midnight," said Gaspard; "in a little it will be dawn."

Suddenly a shot cracked out. It was so sharp a sound among the muffled noises that it stung the ear like a whip-lash. It came from the dark mass of the Louvre, from somewhere beyond the Grand Jardin. It was followed instantly by a hubbub far down the Rue St. Honore and a glare kindled where that street joined the Rue d'Arbre Sec.

"That way lies the Admiral," Gaspard cried. "I go to him," and he clapped spurs to his horse.

But as his beast leapt forward another sound broke out, coming apparently from above their heads. It was the clanging of a great bell.

There is no music so dominant as bells. Their voice occupies sky as well as earth, and they overwhelm the senses, so that a man's blood must keep pace with their beat. They can suit every part, jangling in wild joy, or copying the slow pace of sorrow, or pealing in ordered rhythm, blithe but with a warning of mortality in their cadence. But this bell played dance music. It summoned to an infernal jig. Blood and fever were in its broken fall, hate and madness and death.

Gaspard checked his plunging horse. "By God, it is from St. Germains l'Auxerrois! The Palace church. The King is in it. It is a plot against our faith. They have got the pick of us in their trap and would make an end of us."

From every house and entry men and women and priests were pouring to swell the army that pressed roaring eastwards. No one heeded the two as they sat their horses like rocks in the middle of a torrent.

"The Admiral is gone," said Gaspard with a sob in his voice. "Our few hundred spears cannot stand against the King's army. It remains for us to die with him."

Champernoun was cursing steadily in a mixture of English and Spanish, good mouth-filling oaths delivered without heat. "Die we doubtless shall, but not before we have trounced this bloody rabble."

Still Gaspard did not move. "After to-night there will be no gentlemen left in France, for we of the religion had all the breeding." Then he laughed bitterly. "I mind Ribaut's last words, when Menendez slew him. 'We are of earth,' says he, 'and to earth we must return, and twenty years more or less can matter little!' That is our case to-night, old friend."

"Maybe," said the Englishman. "But why talk of dying? You and I are Spanish caballeros. Walsingham told me that the King hated that nation, and that the Queen-mother loved it not, but it would appear that now we are very popular in Paris."

"Nay, nay, this is no time to play the Nicodemite. It is the hour for public confession. I'm off to the dead Admiral to avenge him on his assassins."

"Softly, Gaspard. You and I are old companions in war, and we do not ride against a stone wall if there be a gate. It was not thus that Gourgues avenged Ribaut at St. John's. Let us thank God that we hold a master card in this game. We are two foxes in a flock of angry roosters, and by the Lord's grace we will take our toll of them. Cunning, my friend. A stratagem of war! We stand outside this welter and, having only the cold passion of revenge, can think coolly. God's truth, man, have we fought the Indian and the Spaniard for nothing? Wily is the word. Are we two gentlemen, who fear God, to be worsted by a rabble of Papegots and Marannes?"

It was the word "Marannes," or, as we say, "halfcastes," which brought conviction to Gaspard. Suddenly he saw his enemies as less formidable, as something contemptible, things of a lower breed, dupers who might themselves be duped.

"Faith, Gawain, you are the true campaigner. Let us forward, and trust to Heaven to show us a road."

They galloped down the Rue St. Honore, finding an open space in the cobbles of the centre, but at the turning into the Rue d'Arbre Sec they met a block. A great throng with torches was coming in on the right from the direction of the Bourbon and d'Alencon hotels. Yet by pressing their horses with whip and spur, and by that awe which the two tall dark cavaliers inspired even in a mob which had lost its wits, they managed to make their way to the entrance of the Rue de Bethisy. There they came suddenly upon quiet.

The crowd was held back by mounted men who made a ring around the gate of a high dark building. Inside its courtyard there were cries and the rumour of fighting, but out in the street there was silence. Every eye was turned to the archway, which was bright as day with the glare of fifty lanterns.

The two rode straight to the ring of soldiers.

"Make way," Gaspard commanded, speaking with a foreign accent.

"For whom, monsieur?" one asked who seemed to be of a higher standing than the rest.

"For the Ambassador of the King of Spain."

The man touched his bonnet and opened up a road by striking the adjacent horses with the flat of his sword, and the two rode into the ring so that they faced the archway. They could see a little way inside the courtyard, where the light gleamed on armour. The men there were no rabble, but Guise's Swiss.

A priest came out, wearing the Jacobin habit, one of those preaching friars who had been fevering the blood of Paris. The crowd behind the men-at-arms knew him, for even in its absorption it sent up shouts of greeting. He flitted like a bat towards Gaspard and Champernoun and peered up at them. His face was lean and wolfish, with cruel arrogant eyes.

"Hail, father!" said Gaspard in Spanish. "How goes the good work?"

He replied in the same tongue. "Bravely, my children. But this is but the beginning. Are you girt and ready for the harvesting?"

"We are ready," said Gaspard. His voice shook with fury, but the Jacobin took it for enthusiasm. He held up his hand in blessing and fluttered back to the archway.

From inside the courtyard came the sound of something falling, and then a great shout. The mob had jumped to a conclusion. "That is the end of old Toothpick," a voice cried, using the Admiral's nickname. There was a wild surge round the horsemen, but the ring held. A body of soldiers poured out of the gate, with blood on their bare swords. Among them was one tall fellow all in armour, with a broken plume on his bonnet. His face was torn and disfigured and he was laughing horribly. The Jacobin rushed to embrace him, and the man dropped on his knees to receive a blessing.

"Behold our hero," the friar cried. "His good blade has rid us of the arch-heretic," and the mob took up the shout.

Gaspard was cool now. His fury had become a cold thing like a glacier.

"I know him!" he whispered to Champernoun. "He is the Italian Petrucci. He is our first quarry."

"The second will be that damned friar," was the Englishman's answer.

Suddenly the ring of men-at-arms drew inward as a horseman rode out of the gate followed by half a dozen attendants. He was a tall young man, very noble to look upon, with a flushed face like a boy warm from the game of paume. His long satin coat was richly embroidered, and round his neck hung the thick gold collar of some Order. He was wiping a stain from his sleeve with a fine lawn handkerchief.

"What is that thing gilt like a chalice?" whispered Champernoun.

"Henry of Guise," said Gaspard.

The Duke caught sight of the two men in the centre of the ring. The lanterns made the whole place bright and he could see every detail of their dress and bearing. He saluted them courteously.

"We make your Grace our compliments," said Gaspard. "We are of the household of the Ambassador of Spain, and could not rest indoors when great deeds were being done in the city."

The young man smiled pleasantly. There was a boyish grace in his gesture.

"You are welcome, gentlemen. I would have every good Catholic in Europe see with his own eyes the good work of this Bartholomew's day. I would ask you to ride with me, but I leave the city in pursuit of the Count of Montgomery, who is rumoured to have escaped. There will be much for you to see on this happy Sunday. But stay! You are not attended, and our streets are none too safe for strangers. Presently the Huguenots will counterfeit our white cross, and blunders may be made by the overzealous."

He unclasped the jewel which hung at the end of his chain. It was a little Agnus of gold and enamel, surmounting a lozenge-shaped shield charged with an eagle.

"Take this," he said, "and return it to me when the work is over. Show it if any man dares to question you. It is a passport from Henry of Guise.... And now forward," he cried to his followers. "Forward for Montgomery and the Vidame."

The two looked after the splendid figure. "That bird is in fine feather," said Champernoun.

Gaspard's jaw was very grim. "Someday he will lie huddled under the assassin's knife. He will die as he has made my chief die, and his body will be cast to the dog's.... But he has given me a plan," and he spoke in his companion's ear.

The Englishman laughed. His stolidity had been slow to quicken, but his eyes were now hot and he had altogether ceased to swear.

"First let me get back to Walsingham's lodging. I have a young kinsman there, they call him Walter Raleigh, who would dearly love this venture."

"Tut, man, be serious. We play a desperate game, and there is no place for boys in it. We have Guise's jewel, and by the living God we will use it. My mark is Petrucci."

"And the priest," said Champernoun.

The crowd in the Rue de Bethisy was thinning, as bands of soldiers, each with its tail of rabble, moved off to draw other coverts. There was fighting still in many houses, and on the roof-tops as the pale dawn spread could be seen the hunt for fugitives. Torches and lanterns still flickered obscenely, and the blood in the gutters shone sometimes golden in their glare and sometimes spread drab and horrid in the waxing daylight.

The Jacobin stood at their elbow. "Follow me, my lords of Spain," he cried. "No friends of God and the Duke dare be idle this happy morn. Follow, and I will show you wonders."

He led them east to where a broader street ran to the river.

"Somewhere here lies Teligny," he croaked. "Once he is dead the second head is lopped from the dragon of Babylon. Oh that God would show us where Conde and Navarre are hid, for without them our task is incomplete."

There was a great crowd about the door of one house, and into it the Jacobin fought his way with prayers and threats. Some Huguenot, Teligny it might be, was cornered there, but in the narrow place only a few could join in the hunt, and the hunters, not to be impeded by the multitude, presently set a guard at the street door. The mob below was already drunk with blood, and found waiting intolerable; but it had no leader and foamed aimlessly about the causeway. There were women in it with flying hair like Maenads, who shrilled obscenities, and drunken butchers and watermen and grooms who had started out for loot and ended in sheer lust of slaying, and dozens of broken desperadoes and led-captains who looked on the day as their carnival. But to the mob had come one of those moments of indecision when it halted and eddied like a whirlpool.

Suddenly in its midst appeared two tall horsemen.

"Men of Paris," cried Gaspard with that masterful voice which is born of the deep seas. "You see this jewel. It was given me an hour back by Henry of Guise."

A ruffian examined it. "Ay," he murmured with reverence, "it is our Duke's. I saw it on his breast before Coligny's house."

The mob was all ears. "I have the Duke's command," Gaspard went on. "He pursues Montgomery and the Vidame of Chartres. Coligny is dead. Teligny in there is about to die. But where are all the others? Where is La Rochefoucault? Where is Rosny? Where is Grammont? Where, above all, are the young Conde and the King of Navarre?"

The names set the rabble howling. Every eye was on the speaker.

Gaspard commanded silence. "I will tell you. The Huguenots are cunning as foxes. They planned this very day to seize the King and make themselves masters of France. They have copied your badge," and he glanced towards his left arm. "Thousands of them are waiting for revenge, and before it is full day they will be on you. You will not know them, you will take them for your friends, and you will have your throats cut before you find out your error."

A crowd may be wolves one moment and chickens the next, for cruelty and fear are cousins. A shiver of apprehension went through the soberer part. One drunkard who shouted was clubbed on the head by his neighbour. Gaspard saw his chance.

"My word to you, the Duke's word, is to forestall this devilry. Follow me, and strike down every band of white-badged Huguenots. For among them be sure is the cub of Navarre."

It was the leadership which the masterless men wanted. Fifty swords were raised, and a shout went up which shook the windows of that lodging where even now Teligny was being done to death. With the two horsemen at their head the rabble poured westwards towards the Rue d'Arbre Sec and the Louvre, for there in the vicinity of the Palace were the likeliest coverts.

"Now Heaven send us Petrucci," said Gaspard. "Would that the Little Man had been alive and with us! This would have been a ruse after his own heart."

"I think the great Conde would have specially misliked yon monk," said the Englishman.

"Patience, Gawain. One foe at a time. My heart tells me that you will get your priest."

The streets, still dim in the dawn, were thickly carpeted with dead. The mob kicked and befouled the bodies, and the bravos in sheer wantonness spiked them with their swords. There were women there, and children, lying twisted on the causeway. Once a fugitive darted out of an entry, to be brought down by a butcher's axe.

"I have never seen worse in the Indies," and Champernoun shivered. "My stomach turns. For heaven's sake let us ride down this rabble!"

"Patience," said Gaspard, his eyes hard as stones. "Cursed be he that putteth his hand to the plough and then turns back."

They passed several small bodies of Catholic horse, which they greeted with cheers. That was in the Rue des Poulies; and at the corner where it abutted on the quay before the Hotel de Bourbon, a ferret-faced man ran blindly into them. Gaspard caught him and drew him to his horse's side, for he recognised the landlord of the tavern where he had supped.

"What news, friend?" he asked.

The man was in an anguish of terror, but he recognised his former guest.

"There is a band on the quay," he stammered. "They are mad and do not know a Catholic when they see him. They would have killed me, had not the good Father Antoine held them till I made off."

"Who leads them?" Gaspard asked, having a premonition.

"A tall man in crimson with a broken plume."

"How many?"

"Maybe a hundred, and at least half are men-at-arms."

Gaspard turned to Champernoun.

"We have found our quarry," he said.

Then he spoke to his following, and noted with comfort that it was now some hundred strong, and numbered many swords. "There is a Huguenot band before us," he cried. "They wear our crosses, and this honest fellow has barely escaped from them. They are less than three score. On them, my gallant lads, before they increase their strength, and mark specially the long man in red, for he is the Devil. It may be Navarre is with them."

The mob needed no second bidding. Their chance had come, and they swept along with a hoarse mutter more fearful than any shouting.

"Knee to knee, Gawain," said Gaspard, "as at St. John d'Ulloa. Remember, Petrucci is for me."

The Italian's band, crazy with drink and easy slaying, straggled across the wide quay and had no thought of danger till the two horsemen were upon them. The songs died on their lips as they saw bearing down on them an avenging army. The scared cries of "The Huguenots!" "Montgomery!" were to Gaspard's following a confirmation of their treachery. The swords of the bravos and the axes and knives of the Parisian mob made havoc with the civilian rabble, but the men-at-arms recovered themselves and in knots fought a stout battle. But the band was broken at the start by the two grim horsemen who rode through it as through meadow grass, their blades falling terribly, and then turned and cut their way back. Yet a third time they turned, and in that last mowing they found their desire. A tall man in crimson appeared before them. Gaspard flung his reins to Champernoun and in a second was on the ground, fighting with a fury that these long hours had been stifled. Before his blade the Italian gave ground till he was pinned against the wall of the Bourbon hotel. His eyes were staring with amazement and dawning fear. "I am a friend," he stammered in broken French and was answered in curt Spanish. Presently his guard weakened and Gaspard gave him the point in his heart. As he drooped to the ground, his conqueror bent over him. "The Admiral is avenged," he said. "Tell your master in hell that you died at the hands of Coligny's kinsman."

Gaspard remounted, and, since the fight had now gone eastward, they rode on to the main gate of the Louvre, where they met a company of the royal Guards coming out to discover the cause of an uproar so close to the Palace. He told his tale of the Spanish Embassy and showed Guise's jewel. "The streets are full of Huguenots badged as Catholics. His Majesty will be well advised to quiet the rabble or he will lose some trusty servants."

In the Rue du Coq, now almost empty, the two horsemen halted.

"We had better be journeying, Gawain. Guise's jewel will open the gates. In an hour's time all Paris will be on our trail."

"There is still that priest," said Champernoun doggedly. He was breathing heavily, and his eyes were light and daring. Like all his countrymen, he was slow to kindle but slower to cool.

"In an hour, if we linger here, we shall be at his mercy. Let us head for the St. Antoine gate."

The jewel made their way easy, for through that gate Henry of Guise himself had passed in the small hours. "Half an hour ago," the lieutenant of the watch told them, "I opened to another party which bore the Duke's credentials. They were for Amiens to spread the good news."

"Had they a priest with them?"

"Ay, a Jacobin monk, who cried on them to hasten and not spare their horses. He said there was much to do in the north."

"I think the holy man spoke truth," said Gaspard, and they rode into open country.

They broke their fast on black bread and a cup of wine at the first inn, where a crowd of frightened countrymen were looking in the direction of Paris. It was now about seven o'clock, and a faint haze, which promised heat, cloaked the ground. From it rose the towers and high-peaked roofs of the city, insubstantial as a dream.

"Eaucourt by the waters!" sighed Gaspard. "That the same land should hold that treasure and this foul city!"

Their horses, rested and fed, carried them well on the north road, but by ten o'clock they had overtaken no travellers, save a couple of servants, on sorry nags, who wore the Vidame of Amiens' livery. They were well beyond Oise ere they saw in the bottom of a grassy vale a little knot of men.

"I make out six," said Champernoun, who had a falcon's eye. "Two priests and four men-at-arms. Reasonable odds, such as I love. Faith, that monk travels fast!"

"I do not think there will be much fighting," said Gaspard.

Twenty minutes later they rode abreast of the party, which at first had wheeled round on guard, and then had resumed its course at the sight of the white armlets. It was as Champernoun had said. Four lusty arquebusiers escorted the Jacobin. But the sixth man was no priest. He was a Huguenot minister whom Gaspard remembered with Conde's army, an elderly frail man bound with cruel thongs to a horse's back and his legs tethered beneath its belly.

Recognition awoke in the Jacobin's eye. "Ah, my lords of Spain! What brings you northward?"

Gaspard was by his side, while Champernoun a pace behind was abreast the minister.

"To see the completion of the good work begun this morning."

"You have come the right road. I go to kindle the north to a holy emulation. That heretic dog behind is a Picard, and I bring him to Amiens that he may perish there as a warning to his countrymen."

"So?" said Gaspard, and at the word the Huguenot's horse, pricked stealthily by Champernoun's sword, leaped forward and dashed in fright up the hill, its rider sitting stiff as a doll in his bonds. The Jacobin cried out and the soldiers made as if to follow, but Gaspard's voice checked them. "Let be. The beast will not go far. I have matters of importance to discuss with this reverend father."

The priest's face sharpened with a sudden suspicion. "Your manners are somewhat peremptory, sir Spaniard. But speak and let us get on."

"I have only the one word. I told you we had come north to see the fruition of the good work, and you approved. We do not mean the same. By good work I mean that about sunrise I slew with this sword the man Petrucci, who slew the Admiral. By its fruition I mean that I have come to settle with you."

"You...?" the other stammered.

"I am Gaspard de Laval, a kinsman and humble follower of Goligny."

The Jacobin was no coward. "Treason!" he cried. "A Huguenot! Cut them down, my men," and he drew a knife from beneath his robe.

But Gaspard's eye and voice checked the troopers. He held in his hand the gold trinket. "I have no quarrel with you. This is the passport of your leader, the Duke. I show it to you, and if you are questioned about this day's work you can reply that you took your orders from him who carried Guise's jewel. Go your ways back to Paris if you would avoid trouble."

Two of the men seemed to waver, but the maddened cry of the priest detained them. "They seek to murder me," he screamed. "Would you desert God's Church and burn in torment for ever?" He hurled himself on Gaspard, who caught his wrist so that the knife tinkled on the high road while the man overbalanced himself and fell. The next second the mellay had begun.

It did not last long. The troopers were heavy fellows, cumbrously armed, who, even with numbers on their side, stood little chance against two swift swordsmen, who had been trained to fight together against odds. One Gaspard pulled from the saddle so that he lay senseless on the ground. One Champernoun felled with a sword cut of which no morion could break the force. The two others turned tail and fled, and the last seen of them was a dust cloud on the road to Paris.

Gaspard had not drawn his sword. They stood by the bridge of a little river, and he flung Guise's jewel far into its lilied waters.

"A useful bauble," he smiled, "but its purpose is served."

The priest stood in the dust, with furious eyes burning in an ashen face.

"What will you do with me?"

"This has been your day of triumph, father. I would round it off worthily by helping you to a martyr's crown. Gawain," and he turned to his companion, "go up the road and fetch me the rope which binds the minister."

The runaway was feeding peaceably by the highway. Champernoun cut the old man's bonds, and laid him fainting on the grass. He brought back with him a length of stout cord.

"Let the brute live," he said. "Duck him and truss him up, but don't dirty your hands with him. I'd as lief kill a woman as a monk."

But Gaspard's smiling face was a rock. "This is no Englishman's concern. To-day's shame is France's and a Frenchman alone can judge it. Innocent blood is on this man's hands, and it is for me to pay the first instalment of justice. The rest I leave to God."

So when an hour later the stunned troopers recovered their senses they found a sight which sent them to their knees to patter prayers. For over the arch of the bridge dangled the corpse of the Jacobin. And on its breast it bore a paper setting forth that this deed had been done by Gaspard de Laval, and the Latin words "O si sic omnes!"

Meantime far up in the folds of the Santerre a little party was moving through the hot afternoon. The old Huguenot, shaken still by his rough handling, rode as if in a trance. Once he roused himself and asked about the monk.

"I hanged him like a mad dog," said Gaspard.

The minister shook his head. "Violence will not cure violence."

"Nay, but justice may follow crime. I am no Nicodemite. This day I have made public confession of my faith, and abide the consequences. From this day I am an exile from France so long as it pleases God to make His Church an anvil for the blows of His enemies."

"I, too, am an exile," said the old man. "If I come safe to Calais I shall take ship for Holland and find shelter with the brethren there. You have preserved my life for a few more years in my master's vineyard. You say truly, young sir, that God's Church is now an anvil, but remember for your consolation that it is an anvil which has worn out many hammers."

Late in the evening they came over a ridge and looked down on a shallow valley all green and gold in the last light. A slender river twined by alder and willow through the meadows. Gaspard reined in his horse and gazed on the place with a hand shading his eyes.

"I have slain a man to my hurt," he said. "See, there are my new fishponds half made, and the herb garden, and the terrace that gets the morning sun. There is the lawn which I called my quarter-deck, the place to walk of an evening. Farewell, my little grey dwelling."

Champernoun laid a kindly hand on his shoulder.

"We will find you the mate of it in Devon, old friend," he said.

But Gaspard was not listening. "Eaucourt by the waters," he repeated like the refrain of a song, and his eyes were full of tears.

CHAPTER VIII. THE HIDDEN CITY

The two ports of the cabin were discs of scarlet, that pure translucent colour which comes from the reflection of sunset in leagues of still water. The ship lay at anchor under the high green scarp of an island, but on the side of the ports no land was visible, only a circle in which sea and sky melted into the quintessence of light. The air was very hot and very quiet. Inside a lamp had been lit, for in those latitudes night descends like a thunderclap. Its yellow glow joined with the red evening to cast orange shadows. On the wall opposite the ports was a small stand of arms, and beside it a picture of the Magdalen, one of two presented to the ship by Lord Huntingdon; the other had been given to the wife of the Governor of Gomera in the Canaries when she sent fruit and sugar to the voyagers. Underneath on a couch heaped with deerskins lay the Admiral.

The fantastic light revealed every line of the man as cruelly as spring sunshine. It showed a long lean face cast in a high mould of pride. The jaw and cheekbones were delicate and hard; the straight nose and the strong arch of the brows had the authority of one who all his days had been used to command. But age had descended on this pride, age and sickness. The peaked beard was snowy white, and the crisp hair had thinned from the forehead. The forehead itself was high and broad, crossed with an infinity of small furrows. The cheeks were sallow, with a patch of faint colour showing as if from a fever. The heavy eyelids were grey like a parrot's. It was the face of a man ailing both in mind and body. But in two features youth still lingered. The lips under their thatch of white moustache were full and red, and the eyes, of some colour between blue and grey, had for all their sadness a perpetual flicker of quick fire.

He shivered, for he was recovering from the fifth fever he had had since he left Plymouth. The ailment was influenza, and he called it a calenture. He was richly dressed, as was his custom even in outlandish places, and the furred robe which he drew closer round his shoulders hid a doublet of fine maroon velvet. For comfort he wore a loose collar and band instead of his usual cut ruff. He stretched out his hand to the table at his elbow where lay the Latin version of his Discovery of Guiana, of which he had been turning the pages, and beside it a glass of whisky, almost the last of the thirty-two gallon cask which Lord Boyle had given him in Cork on his way out. He replenished his glass with water from a silver carafe, and sipped it, for it checked his cold rigours. As he set it down he looked up to greet a man who had just entered.

The new-comer was not more than forty years old, like the Admiral, but he was lame of his left leg, and held himself with a stoop. His left arm, too hung limp and withered by his side. The skin of his face was gnarled like the bark of a tree, and seamed with a white scar which drooped over the corner of one eye and so narrowed it to half the size of the other. He was the captain of Raleigh's flagship, the Destiny, an old seafarer, who in twenty years had lived a century of adventure.

"I wish you good evening, Sir Walter," he said in his deep voice. "They tell me the fever is abating."

The Admiral smiled wanly, and in his smile there was still a trace of the golden charm which had once won all men's hearts.

"My fever will never abate this side the grave," he said. "Jasper, old friend, I would have you sit with me tonight. I am like King Saul, the sport of devils. Be you my David to exorcise them. I have evil news. Tom Keymis is dead."

The other nodded. Tom Keymis had been dead for ten days, since before they left Trinidad. He was aware of the obsession of the Admiral, which made the tragedy seem fresh news daily.

"Dead," said Raleigh. "I slew him by my harshness. I see him stumbling off to his cabin, an old bent man, though younger than me. But he failed me. He betrayed his trust.... Trust, what does that matter? We are all dying. Old Tom has only gone on a little way before the rest. And many went before him."

The voice had become shrill and hard. He was speaking to himself.

"The best, the very best. My brave young Walter, and Cosmor and Piggot and John Talbot and Ned Coffyn.... Ned was your kinsman, Jasper?"

"My cousin, the son of my mother's brother." The man spoke, like Raleigh, in a Devon accent, with the creamy slur in the voice and the sing-song fall of West England.

"Ah, I remember. Your mother was Cecily Coffyn, from Combas on the Moor at the back of Lustleigh. A pretty girl, I mind her long ago. I would I were on the Moor now, where it is always fresh and blowing.... And your father, the big Frenchman who settled on one of Gawain Champernoun's manors. I loved his jolly laugh. But Cecily sobered him, for the Coffyns were always a grave and pious race. Gawain is dead these many years. Where is your father?

"He died in '82 with Sir Humfrey Gilbert."

Raleigh bowed his head. "He went to God with brother Humfrey! Happy fate! Happy company! But he left a brave son behind him, and I have lost mine. Have you a boy, Jasper?"

"But the one. My wife died ten years ago come Martinmas. The child is with his grandmother on the Moor."

"A promising child?"

"A good lad, so far as I have observed him, and that is not once a twelvemonth."

"You are a hungry old sea-dog. That was not the Coffyn fashion. Ned was for ever homesick out of sight of Devon. They worshipped their bleak acres and their fireside pieties. Ah, but I forget. You are de Laval on one side, and that is strong blood. There is not much in England to vie with it. You were great nobles when our Cecils were husbandmen."

He turned on a new tack. "You know that Whitney and Wollaston have deserted me. They would have had me turn pirate, and when I refused they sailed off and left me. This morning I saw the last of their topsails. Did I right?" he asked fiercely.

"In my judgment you did right."

"But why, why?" Raleigh demanded. "I have the commission of the King of France. What hindered me to use my remnant like hounds to cut off the stragglers of the Plate Fleet? That way lies much gold, and gold will buy pardon for all offences. What hindered me, I say?"

"Yourself, Sir Walter."

Raleigh let his head fall back on the couch and smiled bitterly.

"You say truly, myself. 'Tis not a question of morals, mark ye. A better man than I might turn pirate with a clear conscience. But for Walter Raleigh it would be black sin. He has walked too brazenly in all weathers to seek common ports in a storm.... It becomes not the fortune in which he once lived to go journeys of picory.... And there is another reason. I have suddenly grown desperate old. I think I can still endure, but I cannot institute. My action is by and over and my passion has come."

"You are a sick man," said the captain with pity in his voice.

"Sick! Why, yes. But the disease goes very deep. The virtue has gone out of me, old comrade. I no longer hate or love, and once I loved and hated extremely. I am become like a frail woman for tolerance. Spain has worsted me, but I bear her no ill will, though she has slain my son. Yet once I held all Spaniards the devil's spawn."

"You spoke kindly of them in your History," said the other, "when you praised their patient virtue."

"Did I? I have forgot. Nay, I remember. When I wrote that sentence I was thinking of Berreo. I loved him, though I took his city. He was a valiant and liberal gentleman, and of a great heart. I mind how I combated his melancholy, for he was most melancholic. But now I have grown like him. Perhaps Sir Edward Coke was right and I have a Spanish heat. I think a man cannot strive whole-heartedly with an enemy unless he have much in common with him, and as the strife goes on he gets liker.... Ah, Jasper, once I had such ambitions that they made a fire all around me. Once I was like Kit Marlowe's Tamburlaine:

'Threatening the world with high astounding terms,
And scourging kingdoms with his conquering sword.'

But now the flame has died and the ashes are cold. And I would not revive them if I could. There is nothing under heaven that I desire."

The seaman's face was grave and kindly.

"I think you have flown too high, Sir Walter. You have aimed at the moon and forgotten the merits of our earthly hills."

"True, true!" Raleigh's mien was for a moment more lively. "That is a shrewd comment. After three-score years I know my own heart. I have been cursed with a devil of pride,

Jasper.... Man, I have never had a friend. Followers and allies and companions, if you please, but no friend. Others, simple folk, would be set singing by a May morning, or a warm tavern fire, or a woman's face. I have known fellows to whom the earth was so full of little pleasures that after the worst clouts they rose like larks from a furrow. A wise philosophy, but I had none of it. I saw always the little pageant of man's life like a child's peep-show beside the dark wastes of eternity. Ah, I know well I struggled like the rest for gauds and honours, but they were only tools for my ambition. For themselves I never valued them. I aimed at a master-fabric, and since I have failed I have now no terrestrial cover."

The night had fallen black, but the cabin windows were marvellously patined by stars. Raleigh's voice had sunk to the hoarse whisper of a man still fevered. He let his head recline again on the skins and closed his eyelids. Instantly it became the face of an old and very weary man.

The sailor Jasper Lauval, for so he now spelled his name on the rare occasions when he wrote it, thought he was about to sleep and was rising to withdraw, when Raleigh's eyes opened.

"Stay with me," he commanded. "Your silence cheers me. If you leave me I have thoughts that might set me following Tom Keymis. Kit Marlowe again! I cannot get rid of his accursed jingles. How do they go?

"'Hell hath no limite, nor is circumscribed
In one self-place, for where we are is hell
And where hell is there must we ever be.'"

Lauval stretched out a cool hand and laid it on the Admiral's hot forehead. He had a curiously steadfast gaze for all his drooping left eye. Raleigh caught sight of the withered arm.

"Tell me of your life, Jasper. How came you by such a mauling? Let the tale of it be like David's harping and scatter my demons."

The seaman sat himself in a chair. "That was my purpose, Sir Walter. For the tale is in some manner a commentary on your late words."

"Nay, I want no moral. Let me do the moralising. The tale's the thing. See, fill a glass of this Irish cordial. Twill keep off the chill from the night air. When and where did you get so woefully battered?"

"'Twas six years back when I was with Bovill."

Raleigh whistled. "You were with Robert Bovill' What in Heaven's name did one of Coffyn blood with Robert? If ever man had a devil, 'twas he. I mind his sullen black face and his beard in two prongs. I have heard he is dead on a Panama gibbet?"

"He is dead; but not as he lived. I was present when he died. He went to God a good Christian, praying and praising. Next day I was to follow him, but I broke prison in the night with the help of an Indian, and went down the coast in a stolen patache to a place where thick forests lined the sea. There I lay hid till my wounds healed, and by and by I was picked up by a Bristol ship that had put in to water."

"But your wounds, how got you them?"

"At the hands of the priests. They would have made a martyr of me, and used their engines to bend my mind. Being obstinate by nature I mocked them till they wearied of the play. But they left their marks on this arm and leg. The scar I had got some months before in a clean battle."

"Tell me all. What did Robert Bovill seek? And where?"

"We sought the Mountain of God," said the seaman reverently.

"I never heard o't. My own Manoa, maybe, where gold is quarried like stone."

"Nay, not Manoa. The road to it is from the shore of the Mexican gulf. There was much gold."

"You found it?"

"I found it and handled it. Enough, could we have brought it off, to freight a dozen ships. Likewise jewels beyond the imagining of kings."

Raleigh had raised himself on his elbow, his face sharp and eager.

"I cannot doubt you, for you could not lie were it to win salvation. But, heavens! man, what a tale! Why did I not know of this before I broke my fortune on Tom Keymis' mine?"

"I alone know of it, the others being dead."

"Who first told you of it?"

"Captain Bovill had the rumour from a dying Frenchman who was landed in his last hours at Falmouth. The man mentioned no names, but the tale set the captain inquiring and he picked up the clue in Bristol. But 'twas in north Ireland that he had the whole truth and a chart of the road."

"These charts!" sighed Raleigh. "I think the fairies have the making of them, for they bewitch sober men. A scrap of discoloured paper and a rag of canvas; some quaint lines drawn often in a man's blood, and a cross in a corner marking 'much gold.' We mortals are eternally babes, and our heads are turned by toys."

"This chart was no toy, and he who owned it bought it with his life. Nay, Sir Walter, I am of your mind. Most charts are playthings from the devil. But this was in manner of speaking sent from God. Only we did not read it right. We were blind men that thought only of treasure."

"It is the common story," said Raleigh. "Go on, Jasper."

"We landed in the Gulf, at the point marked. It was at the mouth of a wide river so split up by sand bars that no ship could enter. But by portage and hard rowing we got our boats beyond the shoals and found deep water. We had learned beforehand that there were no Spanish posts within fifty miles, for the land was barren and empty even of Indians. So for ten days we rowed and poled through a flat plain, sweating mightily, till we came in sight of mountains. At that we looked for more comfort, for the road on our chart now led away from the river up a side valley. There we hoped for fruits, since it was their season, and for deer; and 'twas time, for our blood was thick with rotten victuals."

The man shivered, as if the recollection had still terrors for him.

"If ever the Almighty permitted hell on earth 'twas that valley. There was no stream in it and no verdure. Oathsome fleshy shrubs, the colour of mouldy copper, dotted the slopes, and a wilderness of rocks through which we could scarce find a road. There was no living thing in it but carrion birds. And serpents. They dwelt in every cranny of stone, and the noise of them was like bees humming. We lost two stout fellows from their poison. The sky was brass above us and our tongues were dry sticks, and by the foul vapours of the place our scanty food was corrupted. Never have men been nearer death. I think we would have retreated but for our captain; who had a honest heart. He would point out to us the track in the chart running through that accursed valley, and at the end the place lettered 'Mountain of God.' I mind how his hand shook as he pointed, for he was as sick as any. He was very gentle too, though for usual a choleric man."

"Choleric, verily," said Raleigh. "It must have been no common sufferings that tamed Robert Bovill. How long were you in the valley?"

"The better part of three days. 'Twas like sword-cut in a great mountain plain, and on the third day we came to a wall of rock which was the head of it. This we scaled, how I do not know, by cracks and fissures, the stronger dragging up the weaker by means of the tow-rope which by the mercy of God we carried with us. There we lost Francis Derrick, who fell a great way and crushed his skull on a boulder. You knew the man?"

"He sailed with me in '95. So that was the end of Francis?"

"We were now eleven, and two of them dying. Above the rocks on the plain we looked for ease, but found none. 'Twas like the bottom of a dry sea, all sand and great clefts, and in every hollow monstrous crabs that scattered the sand like spindrift as they fled from us.

Some of the beasts we slew, and the blood of them was green as ooze, and their stench like a charnel house. Likewise there were everywhere fat vultures that dropped so close they fanned us with their wings. And in some parts there were cracks in the ground through which rose the fumes of sulphur that set a man's head reeling."

Raleigh shivered. "Madre de Dios, you portray the very floor of hell."

"Beyond doubt the floor of hell. There was but one thing that could get us across that devil's land, for our bones were molten with fear. At the end rose further hills, and we could see with our eyes they were green.... Captain Bovill was like one transfigured. 'See,' he cried, 'the Mountain of God! Paradise is before you, and the way to Paradise, as is well known, lies through the devil's country. A little longer, brave hearts, and we shall be in port.' And so fierce was the spirit of that man that it lifted our weary shanks and fevered bodies through another two days of torment. I have no clear memory of those hours. Assuredly we were all mad and spoke with strange voices. My eyes were so gummed together that I had often to tear the lids apart to see. But hourly that green hill came nearer, and towards dusk of the second day it hung above us. Also we found sweet water, and a multitude of creeping vines bearing a wholesome berry. Then as we lay down to sleep, the priest came to us."

Raleigh exclaimed. "What did a priest in those outlands? A Spaniard?"

"Ay. But not such as you and I have ever known elsewhere. Papegot or no, he was a priest of the Most High. He was white and dry as a bone, and his eyes burned glassily. Captain Bovill, who liked not the dark brothers, would have made him prisoner, for he thought him a forerunner of a Spanish force, but he held up a ghostly hand and all of us were struck with a palsy of silence. For the man was on the very edge of death.

"'Moriturus te saluto,' he says, and then he fell to babbling in Spanish, which we understood the better. Food, such as we had, he would not touch, nor the sweet well-water. 'I will drink no cup,' he said, 'till I drink the new wine with Christ in His Father's Kingdom. For I have seen what mortal eyes have not seen, and I have spoken with God's ministers, and am anointed into a new priesthood.'

"I mind how he sat on the grass, his voice drifting faint and small like a babe's crying. He told us nothing of what he was or whence he came, for his soul was possessed of a revelation. 'These be the hills of God,' he cried. 'In a little you will come to a city of the old kings where gold is as plentiful as sand of the sea. There they sit frozen in metal waiting the judgment. Yet they are already judged, and, I take it, justified, for the dead men sit as warders of a greater treasurehouse.

"I think that we eleven, and two of us near death, were already half out of the body, for weariness and longing shift the mind from its moorings. I can hear yet Captain Bovill asking very gently of this greater treasure-house, and I can hear the priest, like one in a trance, speaking high and strange. 'It is the Mountain of God, he said, 'which lies a little way further. There may be seen the heavenly angels ascending and descending.'"

Raleigh shook his head. "Madness, Jasper, the madness begot of too much toil... I know it... And yet I do not know. 'Tis not for me to set limits to the marvels that are hid in that western land. What next, man?"

"In the small hours of the morning the priest died. Likewise our two sick. We dug graves for them, and the Captain bade me say prayers over them. The nine of us left were shaking with a great awe. We felt lifted up in bodily strength, as if for a holy labour. Captain Bovill's stout countenance wore an air of humility. 'We be dedicate,' he said, 'to some high fortune. Let us go humbly and praise God.' The first steps we took that morning we walked like men going into church. Up a green valley we journeyed, where every fruit grew and choirs of birds sang, up a crystal river to a cup in the hills. And I think there was no one of us but had his mind more on the angels whom the priest had told of than on the golden kings."

Raleigh had raised himself from the couch, and sat with both elbows on the table, staring hard at the speaker. "You found them? The gold kings?"

"We found them. Before noon we came into a city of tombs. Grass grew in the streets and courts, and the bronze doors hung broken on their hinges. But no wild things had laired there. The place was clean and swept and silent. In each dwelling the roof was of beaten gold, and the square pillars were covered with gold plates, and where the dead sat was a wilderness of jewels.... I tell you, all the riches that Spain has drawn from all her Indies since the first conquistador set foot in them would not vie with the preciousness of a single one among those dead kings' houses."

"And the kings?" Raleigh interjected.

"They sat stiff in gold on their thrones, their bodies fashioned in the likeness of men. But they had no faces only golden plates set with gems."

"What fortune! What fortune! And what did you then?"

"We went mad." The seaman's voice was slow and melancholy. "We, who an hour before had been filled with high contemplations, went mad like common bravos at the sight of plunder. No man thought of the greater treasure which these gold things warded. We laughed and cried like children, and tore at the plated dead.... I mind how I wrenched off one jewelled face with the haft of my dagger, and a thin trickle of bones fell inside.... And yet, as we ravened and plundered we would fall into fits of shivering, for the thing was not of this world. Often a man would stop and fall to weeping. But the lust of gold consumed us, and presently we only sorrowed because we had no sumpter mules to aid its transit, and had a terror of the infernal plain and valley we had travelled...."

"Captain Bovill made camp in a mead outside the city, and one of us shot a deer, so that we supped full. He unfolded his purpose, which was that we should pack about our persons such jewels as were the smallest and most precious, and some gold likewise as an earnest, and by striking northward through the mountains seek to reach at a higher point in its course the river by which we had entered from the sea. I mistrusted the plan, for the chart had shown but the one way, but the terror of the road we had come was strong on me and I made no protest. So we packed our treasure, so that each man staggered under it, and before noon left the place of the kings."

"And then? Was the road desperate?" Raleigh's pale eyes had the ardour of a boy's.

"Desperate beyond all telling. An escalade of sheer mountains and a battling through vales choked with unbelievable thorns. Yet there was water and food, and the hardships were not beyond mortal endurance. 'Twas not a haunted hell like the way up. Wherefore I knew it would lead us to disaster, for 'twas not ordained as the path in the chart had been."

Raleigh laughed. "Faith, you show your mother's race. All Coffyns have in their souls the sour milk of Jean Calvin."

"Judge if I speak not the truth. Bit by bit we had to cast our burdens till only the jewels remained. And on the seventh day, when we were in sight of the river, we met a Spanish party, a convoy from their northern mines. We marched loosely and blindly, and they came on us unawares. We had all but reached the river's brink, so had the stream for a defence on one side, but before we knew they had taken us on flank and rear."

"Many?"

"A matter of three score, fresh and well armed, against nine weary men mortally short of powder. That marked the end of our madness and we became again sober Christians. Most notable was Captain Bovill. 'We have seen what we have seen,' he told us, as we cast up our defences under Spanish bullets, 'and none shall wrest the secret from us. If God wills that we perish, 'twill perish too. The odds are something heavier than I like, and if the worst befall I trust every man to fling into the river what jewels he carries sooner than let them become spoil of war. For if they see such preciousness they will be fired to inquiry and may haply stumble on our city. Such of us as live will someday return there....' I have said we had little powder, but for half a day we withstood the assault, and time and again when the enemy leapt inside our lines we beat him back. At the end, when hope was gone, you would hear little splashes in the waters as this man or that put his treasures into eternal hiding. A Spanish sword was like to have cleft my skull, but before I lost my senses I noted Captain Bovill tearing the chart in shreds and using them to hold down the last charges for his matchlock. He was crying, too, in English that some day we would return the road we had come."

"And you returned?"

The seaman shook his head. "Not with earthly feet. Two of us they slew outright, and two more died on the way coastwards. For long I was between death and life, and knew little till I woke in the Almirante's cell at Panama.... The rest you have heard. Captain Bovill died praising God, and with him three stout lads out of Somerset. I escaped and tell you the tale."

Raleigh had sunk his brow on his hands as if in meditation. With a sudden motion he rose to his feet and stared through the port, which was now tremulous with the foreglow of the tropic dawn. He put his head out and sniffed the sweet cold air. Then he turned to his companion.

"You know the road back to the city?"

The other nodded. "I alone of men."

"What hinders, Jasper?" Raleigh's face was sharp and eager, and his eyes had the hunger of an old hound on a trail. "They are all deserting me and look but to save their throats. Most are scum and have no stomach for great enterprises. I can send Herbert home with three shiploads of faint hearts, while you and I take the Destiny and steer for fortune. Ned King will come, ay, and Pommerol. What hinders, old friend?"

The seaman shook his head. "Not for me, Sir Walter."

"Why, man, will you let that great marvel lie hid till the hills crumble and bury it?"

"I will return, but not yet. When I have seen my son a man, I go back, but I go alone."

"To the city of the gold kings?"

"Nay, to the Mount of the Angels, of which the priest told."

There was silence for a minute. The light dawn wind sent a surge of little waves against the ship's side, so that it seemed as if the now flaming sky was making its song of morning. Raleigh blew out the flickering lamp, and the cabin was filled with a clear green dusk like palest emerald. The air from the sea flapped the pages of the book upon the table. He flung off his furred gown, and stretched his long arms to the ceiling.

"I think the fever has left me.... You said your tale was a commentary on my confessions. Wherefore, O Ulysses?"

"We had the chance of immortal joys, but we forsook them for lesser things. For that we were thoroughly punished and failed even in our baseness. You, too, Sir Walter, have glanced aside after gauds."

"For certain I have," and Raleigh laughed.

"Yet not for long. You have cherished most resolutely an elect purpose and in that you cannot fail."

"I know not. I know not. I have had great dreams and I have striven to walk in the light of them. But most men call them will o' the wisps, Jasper. What have they brought me? I am an old sick man, penniless and disgraced. His slobbering Majesty will give me a harsh welcome. For me the Mount of the Angels is like to be a scaflold."

"Even so. A man does not return from those heights. When I find my celestial hill I will lay my bones there. But what matters the fate of these twisted limbs or even of your comely head? All's one in the end, Sir Walter. We shall not die. You have lit a fire among Englishmen which will kindle a hundred thousand hearths in a cleaner world."

Raleigh smiled, sadly yet with a kind of wistful pride.

"God send it! And you?"

"I have a son of my body. That which I have sowed he may reap. He or his son, or his son's son."

The morning had grown bright in the little room. Of the two the Admiral now looked the younger. The fresh light showed the other like a wrinkled piece of driftwood. He rose stiffly and moved towards the door.

"You have proved my David in good truth," said Raleigh. "This night has gone far to heal me in soul and body. Faith, I have a mind to breakfast.... What a miracle is our ancient England! French sire or no, Jasper, you have that slow English patience that is like the patience of God."

CHAPTER IX. THE REGICIDE

There was a sharp grue of ice in the air, as Mr. Nicholas Lovel climbed the rickety wooden stairs to his lodgings in Chancery Lane hard by Lincoln's Inn. That morning he had ridden in from his manor in the Chilterns, and still wore his heavy horseman's cloak and the long boots splashed with the mud of the Colne fords. He had been busy all day with legal matters, conveyances on which his opinion was sought, for, though it was the Christmas vacation, his fame among the City merchants kept him busy in term and out of it. Rarely, he thought, had he known London in so strange a temper. Men scarcely dared to speak above their breath of public things, and eyed him fearfully, even the attorneys who licked his boots, as if a careless word spoken in his presence might be their ruin. For it was known that this careful lawyer stood very near Cromwell, had indeed been his comrade at bed and board from Marston to Dunbar, and, though no Commons man, had more weight than any ten in Parliament. Mr. Lovel could not but be conscious of the tension among his acquaintances, and had he missed to note it there he would have found it in the streets. Pride's troopers were everywhere, riding in grim posses or off duty and sombrely puffing tobacco, vast, silent men, lean from the wars. The citizens on the causeway hurried on their errand, eager to find sanctuary from the biting air and the menace of unknown perils. Never had London seen such a Christmastide. Every man was moody and careworn, and the bell of Paul's as it tolled the hours seemed a sullen prophet of woe.

His servant met him on the stair.

"He is here," he said. "I waited for him in the Bell Yard and brought him in secretly."

Lovel nodded, and stripped off his cloak, giving it to the man. "Watch the door like a dragon, Matthew," he told him. "For an hour we must be alone. Forbid anyone, though it were Sir Harry himself."

The little chamber was bright with the glow of a coal fire. The red curtains had been drawn and one lamp lit. The single occupant sprawled in a winged leather chair, his stretched-out legs in the firelight, but his head and shoulders in shadow. A man entering could not see the face, and Lovel, whose eyes had been weakened by study, peered a second before he closed the door behind him.

"I have come to you, Nick, as always when my mind is in tribulation."

The speaker had a harsh voice, like a bellman's which has been ruined by shouting against crowds. He had got to his feet and seemed an elderly man, heavy in body, with legs too short for the proportions of his trunk. He wore a soldier's coat and belt, but no sword. His age might have been fifty, but his face was so reddened by weather that it was hard to judge. The thick straight black locks had little silver in them, but the hair that sprouted from a mole on the chin was grey. His cheeks were full and the heavy mouth was pursed like that of a man in constant painful meditation. He looked at first sight a grazier from the shires or some new-made squire of a moderate estate. But the eyes forbade that conclusion. There was something that brooded and commanded in those eyes, something that might lock the jaw like iron and make their possessor a hammer to break or bend the world.

Mr. Lovel stirred the fire very deliberately and sat himself in the second of the two winged chairs.

"The King?" he queried. "You were in two minds when we last spoke on the matter. I hoped I had persuaded you. Has some new perplexity arisen?"

The other shook his big head, so that for a moment he had the look of a great bull that paws the ground before charging.

"I have no clearness," he said, and the words had such passion behind them that they were almost a groan.

Lovel lay back in his chair with his finger tips joined, like a jurisconsult in the presence of a client. "Clearness in such matters is not for us mortals," he said. "You are walking dark corridors which the lamp of the law does not light. You are not summoned to do justice, being no judge, but to consider the well-being of the State. Policy, Oliver. Policy, first and last."

The other nodded. "But policy is two-faced, and I know not which to choose."

"Is it still the business of the trial?" Lovel asked sharply. "We argued that a fortnight since, and I thought I had convinced you. The case has not changed. Let me recapitulate. Imprimis, the law of England knows no court which can bring the King of England before it."

"Tchut, man. Do not repeat that. Vane has been clacking it in my ear. I tell you, as I told young Sidney, that we are beyond courts and lawyer's quibbles, and that if England requires it I will cut off the King's head with the crown on it."

Lovel smiled. "That is my argument. You speak of a trial, but in justice there can be no trial where there is neither constituted court nor valid law. If you judge the King, 'tis on grounds of policy. Can you defend that policy, Oliver? You yourself have no clearness. Who has? Not Vane. Not Fairfax. Not Whitelocke, or Widdrington, or Lenthall. Certes, not your old comrade Nick Lovel."

"The Army desires it, notably those in it who are most earnest in God's cause."

"Since when have you found a politic judgment in raw soldiers? Consider, my friend. If you set the King on his trial it can have but the one end. You have no written law by which to judge him, so your canon will be your view of the public weal, against which he has most grievously offended. It is conceded your verdict must be guilty and your sentence death. Once put him on trial and you unloose a great stone in a hill-side which will gather speed with every yard it journeys. You will put your King to death, and in whose name?"

Cromwell raised his head which he had sunk between his hands. "In the name of the Commons of Parliament and all the good people of England."

"Folly, man. Your Commons are a disconsidered rump of which already you have made a laughingstock. As for your good people of England, you know well that ten out of any dozen are against you. The deed will be done in your own name and that of the hoteads of the Army. 'Twill be an act of war. Think you that by making an end of the King you will end the Kings party? Nay, you will give it a martyr. You will create for every woman in England a new saint. You will outrage all sober folk that love order and at the very moment when you seek to lay down the sword you make it the sole arbitrament. Whatsay you to that?"

"There is no need to speak of his death. What if the Court depose him only?"

"You deceive yourself. Once put him on trial and you must go through with it to the end. A deposed king will be like a keg of gunpowder set by your hearth. You cannot hide him so that he ceases to be a peril. You cannot bind him to terms."

"That is naked truth," said Cromwell grimly. "The man is filled with a devil of pride. When Denbigh and the other lords went to him he shut the door in their face. I will have no more of ruining hypocritical agreements. If God's poor people are to be secure we must draw his fangs and destroy his power for ill. But how to do it?" And he made a gesture of despair.

"A way must be found. And let it not be that easy way which will most utterly defeat your honest purpose. The knots of the State are to be unravelled, not cut with the sword."

Cromwell smiled sadly, and his long face had for the moment a curious look of a puzzled child.

"I believe you to be a godly man, friend Nicholas. But I fear your soul is much overlaid with worldly things, and you lean too much on frail understanding. I, too, am without clearness. I assent to your wisdom, but I cannot think it concludes the matter. In truth, we have come in this dark hour to the end of fleshly reasonings. It cannot be that the great marvels which the Lord has shown us can end in barrenness. His glorious dispensations must have an honest fruition, for His arm is not shortened."

He rose to his feet and tightened the belt which he had unbuckled. "I await a sign," he said. "Pray for me, friend, for I am a man in sore perplexity. I lie o' nights at Whitehall in one of the King's rich beds, but my eyes do not close. From you I have got the ripeness of human wisdom, but my heart is not satisfied. I am a seeker, with my ear intent to hear God's command, and I doubt not that by some providence He will yet show me His blessed way."

Lovel stood as if in a muse while the heavy feet tramped down the staircase. He heard a whispering below and then the soft closing of a door. For maybe five minutes he was motionless: then he spoke to himself after the habit he had. "The danger is not over," he said, "but I think policy will prevail. If only Vane will cease his juridical chatter.... Oliver is still at the cross-roads, but he inclines to the right one.... I must see to it that Hugh Peters and his crew manufacture no false providences. Thank God, if our great man is one-third dreamer, he is two-thirds doer, and can weigh his counsellors."

Whereupon, feeling sharp-set with the cold and the day's labour, he replenished the fire with a beech faggot, resumed the riding cloak he had undone and, after giving his servant some instructions, went forth to sup in a tavern. He went unattended, as was his custom. The city was too sunk in depression to be unruly.

He crossed Chancery Lane and struck through the narrow courts which lay between Fleet Street and Holborn. His goal was Gilpin's in Fetter Lane, a quiet place much in favour with those of the long robe. The streets seemed curiously quiet. It was freezing hard and threatening snow, so he flung a fold of his cloak round his neck, muffling his ears. This deadened his hearing, and his mind also was busy with its own thoughts, so that he did not observe that soft steps dogged him. At the corner of an alley he was tripped up, and a heavy garment flung over his head. He struggled to regain his feet, but an old lameness, got at

Naseby, impeded him. The cobbles, too, were like glass, and he fell again, this time backward. His head struck the ground, and though he did not lose consciousness, his senses were dazed. He felt his legs and arms being deftly tied, and yards of some soft stuff enveloping his head. He ceased to struggle as soon as he felt the odds against him, and waited on fortune. Voices came to his ears, and it seemed that one of them was a woman's.

The crack on the causeway must have been harder than it appeared, for Mr. Lovel fell into a doze. When he woke he had some trouble in collecting his wits. He felt no bodily discomfort except a little soreness at the back of his scalp. His captors had trussed him tenderly, for his bonds did not hurt, though a few experiments convinced him that they were sufficiently secure. His chief grievance was a sharp recollection that he had not supped; but, being a philosopher, he reflected that, though hungry, he was warm. He was in a glass coach driven rapidly on a rough road, and outside the weather seemed to be wild, for the snow was crusted on the window. There were riders in attendance; he could hear the click-clack of ridden horses. Sometimes a lantern flashed on the pane, and a face peered dimly through the frost. It seemed a face that he had seen before.

Presently Mr. Lovel began to consider his position. Clearly he had been kidnapped, but by whom and to what intent? He reflected with pain that it might be his son's doing, for that gentleman had long been forbidden his door. A rakehell of the Temple and married to a cast-off mistress of Goring's, his son was certainly capable of any evil, but he reminded himself that Jasper was not a fool and would scarcely see his profit in such an escapade. Besides, he had not the funds to compass an enterprise which must have cost money. He thought of the King's party, and dismissed the thought. His opponents had a certain regard for him, and he had the name of moderate. No, if politics touched the business, it was Ireton's doing. Ireton feared his influence with Cromwell. But that sober man of God was no bravo. He confessed himself at a loss.

Mr. Lovel had reached this point in his meditations when the coach suddenly stopped. The door opened, and as he peered into the semicircle of wavering lamp light he observed a tall young lady in a riding coat white with snowflakes. She had dismounted from her horse, and the beast's smoking nostrils were thawing the ice on her sleeve. She wore a mask, but she did not deceive her father.

"Cecily," he cried, astounded out of his calm. "What madcap trick is this?"

The girl for answer flung her bridle to a servant and climbed into the coach beside him. Once more the wheels moved.

"Oh, father, dearest father, pray forgive me. I have been so anxious. When you fell I begged Tony to give up the plan, but he assured me you had taken no hurt. Tell me you are none the worse."

Mr. Lovel began to laugh, and there was relief in his laugh, for he had been more disquieted than he would have confessed.

"I am very greatly the worse!" He nodded to his bonds. "I do not like your endearments, Cis."

"Promise me not to try to escape, and I will cut them." The girl was very grave as she drew from a reticule beneath her cloak a pair of housewife's scissors.

Mr. Lovel laughed louder. "I promise to bide where I am in this foul weather."

Neatly and swiftly she cut the cords and he stretched arms and legs in growing comfort.

"Also I have not supped."

"My poor father. But in two hours' time you will have supper. We sleep at - but that I must not say."

"Where does this journey end? Am I to have no news at all, my dear?"

"You promised, remember, so I will tell you. Tony and I are taking you to Chastlecote."

Mr. Lovel whistled. "A long road and an ill. The wind blows bitter on Cotswold in December. I would be happier in my own house."

"But not safe." The girl's voice was very earnest. "Believe me, dearest father, we have thought only of you. Tony says that London streets will soon be running blood. He has it from secret and sure sources. There is a King's faction in the Army and already it is in league with the Scots and our own party to compass the fall of Cromwell. He says it will be rough work and the innocent will die with the guilty.... When he told me that, I feared for your life, and Tony, too, for he loves you. So we carry you to Chastlecote till January is past, for by then Tony says there will be peace in England."

"I thank you, Cis, and Tony also, who loves me. But if your news be right, I have a duty to do. I am of Cromwell's party, as you and Tony are of the King's. You would not have me run from danger."

She primmed her pretty mouth. "You do not run, you are carried off. Remember your promise."

"But a promise given under duress is not valid in law."

"You are a gentleman, sir, before you are a lawyer. Besides, there are six of Tony's men with us, and all armed."

Mr. Lovel subsided with a chuckle. This daughter of his should have been a man. Would that Heaven had seen fit to grant him such a son!

"Two hours to supper," was what he said. "By the slow pace of our cattle I judge we are on Denham hill. Permit me to doze, my dear. 'Tis the best antidote to hunger. Whew, but it is cold! If you catch a quinsy, blame that foolish Tony of yours."

But, though he closed his eyes, he did not sleep. All his life he had been something of a fatalist, and this temper had endeared him to Cromwell, who held that no man travelled so far as he who did not know the road he was going. But while in Oliver's case the belief came from an ever-present sense of a directing God, in him it was more of a pagan philosophy. Mr. Lovel was devout after his fashion, but he had a critical mind and stood a little apart from enthusiasm. He saw man's life as a thing foreordained, yet to be conducted under a pretence of freedom, and while a defender of liberty his admiration inclined more naturally to the rigour of law. He would oppose all mundane tyrannies, but bow to the celestial bondage.

Now it seemed that fate had taken charge of him through the medium of two green lovers. He was to be spared the toil of decision and dwell in an enforced seclusion. He was not averse to it. He was not Cromwell with Cromwell's heavy burden; he was not even a Parliment man; only a private citizen who wished greatly for peace. He had laboured for peace both in field and council, and that very evening he had striven to guide the ruler of England. Assuredly he had done a citizen's duty and might now rest.

His thoughts turned to his family, the brave girl and the worthless boy. He believed he had expunged Jasper from his mind, but the recollection had still power to pain him. That was the stuff of which the King's faction was made, half-witted rakes who were arrogant without pride and volcanic without courage.... Not all, perhaps. The good Tony was a welcome enough son-in-law, though Cecily would always be the better man. The young Oxfordshire squire was true to his own royalties, and a mortal could be no more. He liked the flaxen poll of him, which contrasted well with Cecily's dark beauty, and his jolly laugh and the noble carriage of his head. Yet what wisdom did that head contain which could benefit the realm of England?

This story of a new plot! Mr. Lovel did not reject it. It was of a piece with a dozen crazy devices of the King. The man was no Englishman, but an Italian priest who loved dark ways. A little good sense, a little honesty, and long ago there would have been a settlement. But to treat with Charles was to lay foundations on rotten peat.

Oddly enough, now that he was perforce quit of any share in the business, he found his wrath rising against the King. A few hours back he had spoken for him. Had he after all been wrong? He wondered. Oliver's puzzled face rose before him. He had learned to revere that strange man's perplexities. No brain was keener to grasp an argument, for the general was as quick at a legal point as any lawyer. When, therefore, he still hesitated before what seemed a final case, it was well to search for hidden flaws. Above all when he gave no reason it was wise to hasten to him, for often his mind flew ahead of logic, and at such times he was inspired. Lovel himself and Vane and Fairfax had put the politic plea which seemed unanswerable, and yet Oliver halted and asked for a sign. Was it possible that the other course, the wild course, Ireton's course, was the right one?

Mr. Lovel had bowed to fate and his captors, and conscious that no action could follow on any conclusion he might reach, felt free to indulge his thoughts. He discovered these growing sterner. He reviewed is argument against the King's trial. Its gravamen lay in the certainty that trial meant death. The plea against death was that it would antagonise three-fourths of England, and make a martyr out of a fool. Would it do no more? Were there no gains to set against that loss? To his surprise he found himself confessing a gain.

He had suddenly become impatient with folly. It was Cromwell's mood, as one who, living under the eye of God, scorned the vapourings of pedestalled mortals. Mr. Lovel by a different road reached the same goal. An abiding sense of fate ordering the universe made him intolerant of trivial claims of prerogative and blood. Kingship for him had no sanctity save in so far as it was truly kingly. Were honest folk to be harried because of the whims of a man whose remote ancestor had been a fortunate bandit? Charles had time and again broke faith with his people and soaked the land in blood. In law he could do no wrong, but, unless God slept, punishment should follow the crime, and if the law gave no aid the law must be dispensed with. Man was not made for it, but it for man.

The jurist in him pulled up with a start. He was arguing against all his training.... But was the plea false? He had urged on Cromwell that the matter was one of policy. Agreed. But which was the politic road? If the King lost his head, there would beyond doubt be a sullen struggle ahead. Sooner or later the regicides would fall, of that he had no doubt. But what of the ultimate fate of England? They would have struck a blow against privilege which would never be forgotten. In future all kings would walk warily. In time the plain man might come to his own. In the long run was not this politic?

"'Tis a good thing my mouth is shut for some weeks," he told himself. "I am coming round to Ireton. I am no fit company for Oliver."

He mused a little on his inconstancy. It had not been a frequent occurrence in his life. But now he seemed to have got a sudden illumination, such as visited Cromwell in his prayers. He realised how it had come about. Hitherto he had ridden his thoughts unconsciously on the curb of caution, for a conclusion reached meant deeds to follow. But, with the possibility of deeds removed, his mind had been freed. What had been cloudy before now showed very bright, and the little lamp of reason he had once used was put out by an intolerable sunlight. He felt himself quickened to an unwonted poetry.... His whole outlook had changed, but the change brought no impulse to action. He submitted to be idle, since it was so fated. He was rather glad of it, for he felt weary and giddy in mind.

But the new thoughts once awakened ranged on their courses. To destroy the false kingship would open the way for the true. He was no leveller; he believed in kings who were kings in deed. The world could not do without its leaders. Oliver was such a one, and others would rise up. Why reverence a brocaded puppet larded by a priest with oil, when there were men who needed no robes or sacring to make them kingly? Teach the Lord's Anointed his mortality, and there would be hope in the years to come of a true anointing.

He turned to his daughter.

"I believe your night's work, Cis, has been a fortunate thing for our family."

She smiled and patted his hand, and at the moment with a great jolting the coach pulled up. Presently lanterns showed at the window, the door was opened, and Sir Anthony Colledge stood revealed in the driving snow. In the Chilterns it must have been falling for hours, for the road was a foot deep, and the wind had made great drifts among the beech boles. The lover looked somewhat sheepish as he swept a bow to his prisoner.

"You are a noted horse-doctor, sir," he said. "The off leader has gotten a colic. Will you treat him? Then I purpose to leave him with a servant in some near-by farm, and put a ridden horse in his place."

Mr. Lovel leaped from the coach as nimbly as his old wound permitted. It was true that the doctoring of horses was his hobby. He loved them and had a way with them.

The medicine box was got out of the locker and the party grouped round the grey Flemish horses, which stood smoking in the yellow slush. The one with the colic had its legs stretched wide; its flanks heaved and spasms shook its hindquarters. Mr. Lovel set to work and mixed a dose of spiced oil and spirits which he coaxed down its throat. Then he very gently massaged certain corded sinews in its belly. "Get him under cover now, Tony," he said "and tell your man to bed him warm and give him a bucket of hot water strained from oatmeal and laced with this phial. In an hour he will be easy."

The beast was led off, another put in its place, and the postilions were cracking their whips, when out of the darkness a knot of mounted men rode into the lamplight. There were at least a dozen of them, and at their head rode a man who at the sight of Lovel pulled up sharp.

"Mr. Lovel!" he cried. "What brings you into these wilds in such weather? Can I be of service? My house is not a mile off."

"I thank you, Colonel Flowerdue, but I think the mischief is now righted. I go on a journey into Oxfordshire with my daughter, and the snow has delayed us."

He presented the young Parliament soldier, a cousin of Fairfax, to Cecily and Tony, the latter of whom eyed with disfavour the posse of grave Ironside troopers.

"You will never get to Wendover this night," said Flowerdue. "The road higher up is smothered four feet deep. See, I will show you a woodland road which the wind has kept clear, and I protest that your company sleep the night with me at Downing."

He would take no denial, and indeed in the face of his news to proceed would have been folly. Even Sir Anthony Colledge confessed it wryly. One of Flowerdue's men mounted to the postilion's place, and the coach was guided through a belt of beeches, and over a strip of heath to the gates of a park.

Cecily seized her father's hand. "You have promised, remember."

"I have promised," he replied. "To-morrow, if the weather clears, I will go with you to Chastlecote."

He spoke no more till they were at the house door, for the sense of fate hung over him like a cloud. His cool equable soul was stirred to its depths. There was surely a grim fore-ordering in this chain of incidents. But for the horse's colic there would have been no halt. But for his skill in horse doctoring the sick beast would have been cut loose, and Colonel Flowerdue's party would have met only a coach laboring through the snow and would not have halted to discover its occupants.... He was a prisoner bound by a promise, but this meeting with Flowerdue had opened up a channel to communicate with London and that was not forbidden. It flashed on him suddenly that the change of mind which he had suffered was no longer a private matter. He had now the power to act upon it.

He was extraordinarily averse to the prospect. Was it mere petulance that had swung round his opinions so violently during the journey? He examined himself and found his new convictions unshaken. It was what the hot-gospellers would call a "Holy Ghost conversion." Well, let it rest there. Why spread the news beyond his own home? There were doctors enough inspecting the health of the State. Let his part be to stand aside.

With something like fear he recognised that that part was no longer possible. He had been too directly guided by destiny to refuse the last stage. Cromwell was waiting on a providence, and of that providence it was clear that fate had made him the channel. In the coach he had surrendered himself willingly to an unseen direction, and now he dared not refuse the same docility. He, who for usual was ripe, balanced, mellow in judgment, felt at the moment the gloomy impulsion of the fanatic. He was only a pipe for the Almighty to sound through.

In the hall at Downing the logs were stirred to a blaze, and food and drink brought in a hospitable stir.

"I have a letter to write before I sleep," Mr. Lovel told his daughter. "I will pray from Colonel Flowerdue the use of his cabinet."

Cecily looked at him inquiringly, and he laughed.

"The posts at Chastlecote are infrequent, Cis, and I may well take the chance when it offers. I assure you I look forward happily to a month of idleness stalking Tony's mallards and following Tony's hounds."

In the cabinet he wrote half a dozen lines setting out simply the change in his views. "If I know Oliver," he told himself, "I have given him the sign he seeks. I am clear it is God's will, but Heaven help the land, Heaven help us all." Having written, he lay back in his chair and mused.

When Colonel Flowerdue entered he found a brisk and smiling gentleman, sealing a letter.

"Can you spare a man to ride express with this missive to town? It is for General Cromwell's private hand."

"Assuredly. He will start at once lest the storm worsens. It is business of State?"

"High business of State, and I think the last I am likely to meddle with."

Mr. Lovel had taken from his finger a thick gold ring carved with a much-worn cognisance. He held it up in the light of the candle.

"This thing was once a king's," he said. "As the letter touches the affairs of his Majesty, I think it fitting to seal it with a king's signet."

CHAPTER X. THE MARPLOT

At a little after six o'clock on the evening of Saturday, 12th October, in the year 1678, the man known commonly as Edward Copshaw came to a halt opposite the narrow entry of the Savoy, just west of the Queen's palace of Somerset House. He was a personage of many names. In the register of the Benedictine lay-brothers he had been entered as James Singleton. Sundry Paris tradesmen had known him as Captain Edwards, and at the moment were longing to know more of him. In a certain secret and tortuous correspondence he figured as Octavius, and you may still read his sprawling script in the Record Office. His true name, which was Nicholas Lovel, was known at Weld House, at the White Horse Tavern, and the town lodgings of my lords Powis and Bellasis, but had you asked for him by that name at these quarters you would have been met by a denial of all knowledge. For it was a name which for good reasons he and his patrons desired to have forgotten.

He was a man of not yet forty, furtive, ill-looking and lean to emaciation. In complexion he was as swarthy as the King, and his feverish black eyes were set deep under his bushy brows. A badly dressed peruke concealed his hair. His clothes were the remnants of old finery, well cut and of good stuff, but patched and threadbare. He wore a sword, and carried a stout rustic staff. The weather was warm for October, and the man had been walking fast, for, as he peered through the autumn brume into the dark entry, he mopped his face with a dirty handkerchief.

The exercise had brought back his ailment and he shivered violently. Punctually as autumn came round he had these fevers, the legacy of a year once spent in the Pisan marshes. He had doped himself with Jesuits' powder got from a woman of Madame Carwell's, so that he was half deaf and blind. Yet in spite of the drug the fever went on burning.

But to anyone looking close it would have seemed that he had more to trouble him than a malarial bout. The man was patently in an extreme terror. His lantern-jaw hung as loose as if it had been broken. His lips moved incessantly. He gripped savagely at his staff, and next moment dropped it. He fussed with the hilt of his sword.... He was a coward, and yet had come out to do murder.

It had taken real panic to bring him to the point. Throughout his tattered life he had run many risks, but never a peril so instant as this. As he had followed his quarry that afternoon his mind had been full of broken memories. Bitter thoughts they were, for luck had not been kind to him. A childhood in cheap lodgings in London and a dozen French towns, wherever there was a gaming-table and pigeons for his father to pluck. Then drunken father and draggletailed mother had faded from the scene, and the boy had been left to a life of odd jobs and fleeting patrons. His name was against him, for long before he reached manhood the King had come back to his own, and his grandfather's bones had jangled on a Tyburn gibbet. There was no hope for one of his family, though Heaven knew his father had been a stout enough Royalist. At eighteen the boy had joined the Roman Church, and at twenty relapsed to the fold of Canterbury. But his bread-and-butter lay with Rome, and in his trade few questions were asked about creed provided the work were done. He had had streaks of fortune, for there had been times when he lay soft and ate delicately and scattered money. But nothing lasted. He had no sooner made purchase with a great man and climbed a little than the scaffolding fell from his feet. He thought meanly of human nature for in his profess he must cringe or snarl, always the undermost dog. Yet he had some liking for the priests, who had been kind to him, and there was always a glow in his heart for the pale wife who dwelt with his child in the attic in Billingsgate. Under happier circumstances Mr. Nicholas Lovel might have shone with the domestic virtues.

Business had been good of late, if that could ever be called good which was undertaken under perpetual fear. He had been given orders which took him into Whig circles, and had made progress among the group of the King's Head Tavern. He had even won an entrance into my Lord Shaftesbury's great house in Aldersgate Street. He was there under false colours, being a spy of the other camp, but something in him found itself at home among the patriots. A resolve had been growing to cut loose from his old employers and settle down among the Whigs in comparative honesty. It was the winning cause, he thought, and he longed to get his head out of the kennels.... But that had happened yesterday which scattered his fine dreams and brought him face to face with terror. God's curse on that ferrety Justice, Sir Edmund Berry Godfrey.

He had for some time had his eye on the man. The year before he had run across him in Montpelier, being then engaged in a very crooked business, and had fancied that the magistrate had also his eye on him. Taught by long experience to watch potential enemies, he had taken some trouble over the lean high-beaked dignitary. Presently he had found out curious things. The austere Protestant was a friend of the Duke's man, Ned Coleman, and used to meet him at Colonel Weldon's house. This hinted at blackmailable stuff in the magistrate, so Lovel took to haunting his premises in Hartshorn Lane by Charing Cross, but found no evidence which pointed to anything but a prosperous trade in wood and sea-coal. Faggots, but not the treasonable kind! Try as he might, he could-get no farther with that pillar of the magistracy, my Lord Danly's friend, the beloved of Aldermen. He hated his solemn face, his prim mouth, his condescending stoop. Such a man was encased in proof armour of public esteem, and he heeded Mr. Lovel no more than the rats in the gutter.

But the day before had come a rude awakening. All this talk of a Popish plot, discovered by the Salamanca Doctor, promised a good harvest to Mr. Lovel. He himself had much to tell and more to invent. Could he but manage it discreetly, he might assure his fortune with the Whigs and get to his feet at last. God knew it was time, for the household in the Billingsgate attic was pretty threadbare. His busy brain had worked happily on the plan. He would be the innocent, cursed from childhood with undesired companions, who would suddenly awaken in horror to the guilt of things he had not understood. There would be a welcome for a well-informed penitent.... But he must move slowly and at his own time.... And now he was being himself hustled into the dock, perhaps soon to the gallows.

For the afternoon before he had been sent for by Godfrey and most searchingly examined. He had thought himself the spy, when all the while he had been the spied upon. The accursed Justice knew everything. He knew a dozen episodes each enough to hang a poor man. He knew of Mr. Lovel's dealings with the Jesuits Walsh and Phayre, and of a certain little hovel in Battersea whose annals were not for the public ear. Above all, he knew of the great Jesuit consult in April at the Duke of York's house. That would have mattered little, indeed the revelation of it was part of Mr. Lovel's plans, but he knew Mr. Lovel's precise connection with it, and had damning evidence to boot. The spy shivered when he remembered the scene in Hartshorn Lane. He had blundered and stuttered and confessed his alarm by his confusion, while the Justice recited what he had fondly believed was known only to the Almighty and some few whose mortal interest it was to be silent.... He had been amazed that he had not been there and then committed to Newgate. He had not gone home that night, but wandered the streets and slept cold under a Marylebone hedge. At first he had thought of flight, but the recollection of his household detained him. He would not go under. One pompous fool alone stood between him and safety, perhaps fortune. Long before morning he had resolved that Godfrey should die.

He had expected a difficult task, but lo! it was unbelievably easy. About ten o'clock that day he had found Sir Edmund in the Strand. He walked hurriedly as if on urgent business, and Lovel had followed him up through Covent Garden, across the Oxford road, and into the Marylebone fields. There the magistrate's pace had slackened, and he had loitered like a truant schoolboy among the furze and briars. His stoop had deepened, his head was sunk on his breast, his hands twined behind him.

Now was the chance for the murderer lurking in the brambles. It would be easy to slip behind and give him the sword-point. But Mr. Lovel tarried. It may have been compunction, but more likely it was fear. It was also curiosity, for the magistrate's face, as he passed Lovel's hiding-place, was distraught and melancholy. Here was another man with bitter thoughts, perhaps with a deadly secret. For a moment the spy felt a certain kinship.

Whatever the reason he let the morning go by. About two in the afternoon Godfrey left the fields and struck westward by a bridle-path that led through the Paddington Woods to the marshes north of Kensington. He walked slowly, but with an apparent purpose. Lovel stopped for a moment at the White House, a dirty little hedge tavern, to swallow a mouthful of ale, and tell a convincing lie to John Rawson, the innkeeper, in case it should come in handy some day. Then occurred a diversion. Young Mr. Forset's harriers swept past, a dozen riders attended by a ragged foot following. They checked by the path, and in the confusion of the halt Godfrey seemed to vanish. It was not till close on Paddington village that Mr. Lovel picked him up again. He was waiting for the darkness, for he knew that he could never do what he purposed in cold daylight. He hoped that the magistrate would make for Kensington, for that was a lonely path.

But Sir Edmund seemed to be possessed of a freakish devil. No sooner was he in Paddington than, after buying a glass of milk from a milk-woman, he set off citywards again by the Oxford road. Here there were many people, foot travellers and coaches, and Mr. Lovel began to fear for his chance. But at Tyburn Godfrey struck into the fields and presently was in the narrow lane called St. Martin's Hedges, which led to Charing Cross. Now was the occasion. The dusk was falling, and a light mist was creeping up from Westminster. Lovel quickened his steps, for the magistrate was striding at a round pace. Then came mischance. First one, then another of the Marylebone cow-keepers blocked the lane with their driven beasts. The place became as public as Bartholomew's Fair. Before he knew it he was at Charing Cross.

He was now in a foul temper. He cursed his weakness in the morning, when fate had given him every opportunity. He was in despair too. His case was hopeless unless he struck soon. If Godfrey returned to Hartshorn Lane he himself would be in Newgate on the morrow.... Fortunately the strange man did not seem to want to go home. He moved east along the Strand, Lovel a dozen yards behind him.

Out from the dark Savoy entry ran a woman, screaming, and with her hair flying. She seized on Godfrey and clutched his knees. There was a bloody fray inside, in which her husband fought against odds. The watch was not to be found. Would he, the great magistrate, intervene? The very sight of his famous face would quell riot.

Sir Edmund looked up and down the street, pinched his chin and peered down the precipitous Savoy causeway. Whatever the burden on his soul he did not forget his duty.

"Show me," he said, and followed her into the gloom.

Lovel outside stood for a second hesitating. His chance had come. His foe had gone of his own will into the place in all England where murder could be most safely done. But now that the moment had come at last, he was all of a tremble and his breath choked. Only the picture, always horribly clear in his mind, of a gallows dark against a pale sky and the little fire beneath where the entrails of traitors were burned, a nightmare which had long ridden him, nerved him to the next step. "His life or mine," he told himself, as he groped his way into a lane as steep, dank, and black as the sides of a well.

For some twenty yards he stumbled in an air thick with offal and garlic. He heard steps ahead, the boots of the doomed magistrate and the slipshod pattens of the woman. Then they stopped; his quarry seemed to be ascending a stair on the right. It was a wretched tenement of wood, two hundred years old, once a garden house attached to the Savoy palace. Lovel scrambled up some rickety steps and found himself on the rotten planks of a long passage, which was lit by a small window giving to the west. He heard the sound of a man slipping at the other end, and something like an oath. Then a door slammed violently, and the place shook. After that it was quiet. Where was the bloody fight that Godfrey had been brought to settle?

It was very dark there; the window in the passage was only a square of misty grey. Lovel felt eerie, a strange mood for an assassin. Magistrate and woman seemed to have been spirited away.... He plucked up courage and continued, one hand on the wall on his left. Then a sound broke the silence, a scuffle, and the long grate of something heavy dragged on a rough floor. Presently his fingers felt a door. The noise was inside that door. There were big cracks in the panelling through which an eye could look, but all was dark within. There were human beings moving there, and speaking softly. Very gingerly he tried the hasp, but it was fastened firm inside.

Suddenly someone in the room struck a flint and lit a lantern. Lovel set his eyes to a crack and stood very still. The woman had gone, and the room held three men. One lay on the floor with a coarse kerchief, such as grooms wear, knotted round his throat. Over him bent a man in a long coat with a cape, a man in a dark peruke, whose face was clear in the lantern's light. Lovel knew him for one Bedloe, a led-captain and cardsharper, whom he had himself employed on occasion. The third man stood apart and appeared from his gesticulations to be speaking rapidly. He wore his own sandy hair, and every line of his mean freckled face told of excitement and fear. Him also Lovel recognised, Carstairs, a Scotch informer who had once made a handsome living through spying on conventicles, but had now fallen into poverty owing to conducting an affair of Buckingham's with a brutality which that fastidious nobleman had not bargained for.... Lovel rubbed his eyes and looked again. He knew likewise the man on the floor. It was Sir Edmund Godfrey, and Sir Edmund Godfrey was dead.

The men were talking. "No blood-letting," said Bedloe. "This must be a dry job. Though, by God, I wish I could stick my knife into him, once for Trelawney, once for Frewen, and a dozen times for myself. Through this swine I have festered a twelvemonth in Little Ease."

Lovel's first thought, as he stared, was an immense relief. His business had been done for him, and he had escaped the guilt of it. His second, that here lay a chance of fair profit. Godfrey was a great man, and Bedloe and Carstairs were the seediest of rogues. He might make favor for himself with the Government if he had them caught red-handed. It would help his status in Aldersgate Street.... But he must act at once or the murderers would be gone. He tiptoed back along the passage, tumbled down the crazy steps, and ran up the steep entry to where he saw a glimmer of light from the Strand.

At the gate he all but fell into the arms of a man, a powerful fellow, for it was like running against a brick wall. Two strong arms gripped Lovel by the shoulder, and a face looked into his. There was little light in the street, but the glow from the window of a Court perruquier was sufficient to reveal the features. Lovel saw a gigantic face, with a chin so long that the mouth seemed to be only half-way down it. Small eyes, red and fiery, were set deep under a beetling forehead. The skin was a dark purple, and the wig framing it was so white and fleecy that the man had the appearance of a malevolent black-faced sheep.

Lovel gasped, as he recognised the celebrated Salamanca Doctor. He was the man above all others whom he most wished to see.

"Dr. Oates!" he cried. "There's bloody work in the Savoy. I was passing through a minute agone and I saw that noble Justice, Sir Edmund Berry Godfrey, lie dead, and his murderers beside the body. Quick, let us get the watch and take them red-handed."

The big paws, like a gorilla's, were withdrawn from his shoulders. The purple complexion seemed to go nearly black, and the wide mouth opened as if to bellow. But the sound which emerged was only a whisper.

"By the maircy of Gaad we will have 'em!... A maist haarrid and unnaitural craime. I will take 'em with my own haands. Here is one who will help." And he turned to a man who had come up and who looked like a city tradesman. "Lead on, honest fellow, and we will see justice done. 'Tis pairt of the bloody Plaat.... I foresaw it. I warned Sir Edmund, but he flouted me. Ah, poor soul, he has paid for his unbelief."

Lovel, followed by Oates and the other whom he called Prance, dived again into the darkness. Now he had no fears. He saw himself acclaimed with the Doctor as the saviour of the nation, and the door of Aldersgate Street open at his knocking. The man Prance produced a lantern, and lighted them up the steps and into the tumbledown passage. Fired with a sudden valour, Lovel drew his sword and led the way to the sinister room. The door was open, and the place lay empty, save for the dead body.

Oates stood beside it, looking, with his bandy legs great shoulders, and bull neck, like some forest baboon.

"Oh, maist haunourable and noble victim!" he cried. "England will maarn you, and the spawn of Raam will maarn you, for by this deed they have rigged for thaimselves the gallows. Maark ye, Sir Edmund is the proto-martyr of this new fight for the Praatestant faith. He has died that the people may live, and by his death Gaad has given England the sign she required.... Ah, Prance, how little Tony Shaston will exult in our news! 'Twill be to him like a bone to a cur-dog to take his ainemies thus red-haanded."

"By your leave, sir," said Lovel, "those same enemies have escaped us. I saw them here five minutes since, but they have gone to earth. What say you to a hue-and-cry, though this Savoy is a snug warren to hide vermin."

Oates seemed to be in no hurry. He took the lantern from Prance and scrutinised Lovel's face with savage intensity.

"Ye saw them, ye say.... I think, friend, I have seen ye before, and I doubt in no good quaarter. There's a Paapist air about you."

"If you have seen me, 'twas in the house of my Lord Shaftesbury, whom I have the honour to serve," said Lovel stoutly.

"Whoy, that is an haanest house enough. Whaat like were the villains, then? Jaisuits, I'll warrant? Foxes from St. Omer's airth?"

"They were two common cutthroats whose names I know."

"Tools, belike. Fingers of the Paape's hand.... Ye seem to have a good acquaintance among rogues, Mr. Whaat's-you-name."

The man Prance had disappeared, and Lovel suddenly saw his prospects less bright. The murderers were being given a chance to escape, and to his surprise he found himself in a fret to get after them. Oates had clearly no desire for their capture, and the reason flashed on his mind. The murder had come most opportunely for him, and he sought to lay it at Jesuit doors. It would ill suit his plans if only two common rascals were to swing for it. Far better let it remain a mystery open to awful guesses. Omne ignotum pro horrifico.... Lovel's temper was getting the better of his prudence, and the sight of this monstrous baboon with his mincing speech stirred in him a strange abhorrence.

"I can bear witness that the men who did the deed were no more Jesuits than you. One is just out of Newgate, and the other is a blackguard Scot late dismissed the Duke of Buckingham's service."

"Ye lie," and Oates' rasping voice was close to his ear. "'Tis an incraidible tale. Will ye outface me, who alone discovered the Plaat, and dispute with me on high poalicy?... Now I come to look at it, ye have a true Jaisuit face. I maind of ye at St. Omer. I judge ye an accoamplice..."

At that moment Prance returned and with him another, a man in a dark peruke, wearing a long coat with a cape. Lovel's breath went from him as he recognised Bedloe.

"There is the murderer," he cried in a sudden fury "I saw him handle the body. I charge you to hold him."

Bedloe halted and looked at Oates, who nodded. Then he strode up to Lovel and took him by the throat.

"Withdraw your words, you dog," he said, "or I will cut your throat. I have but this moment landed at the river stairs and heard of this horrid business. If you say you have ever seen me before you lie most foully. Quick, you ferret. Will Bedloe suffers no man to charge his honour."

The strong hands on his neck, the fierce eyes of the bravo, brought back Lovel's fear and with it his prudence. He saw very plainly the game, and he realised that he must assent to it. His contrition was deep and voluble.

"I withdraw," he stammered, "and humbly crave pardon. I have never seen this honest gentleman before."

"But ye saw this foul murder, and though the laight was dim ye saw the murderers, and they had the Jaisuitical air?"

Oates' menacing voice had more terror for Lovel than Bedloe's truculence. "Beyond doubt," he replied.

"Whoy, that is so far good," and the Doctor laughed. "Ye will be helped later to remember the names for the benefit of his Maajesty's Court.... 'Tis time we set to work. Is the place quiet?"

"As the grave, doctor," said Prance.

"Then I will unfold to you my pairpose. This noble magistrate is foully murdered by pairsons unknown as yet, but whom this haanest man will swear to have been disguised Jaisuits. Now in the sairvice of Goad and the King 'tis raight to pretermit no aiffort to bring the guilty to justice. The paiple of England are already roused to a holy fairvour, and this haarrid craime will be as the paistol flash to the powder caask. But that the craime may have its full effaict on the paapulace 'tis raight to take some trouble with the staging. 'Tis raight so to dispose of the boady that the complaicity of the Paapists will be clear to every doubting fool. I, Taitus Oates, take upon myself this responsibility, seeing that under Goad I am the chosen ainstrument for the paiple's salvation. To Soamersait Haase with it, say I, which is known for a haaunt of the paapistically-minded.... The postern ye know of is open, Mr. Prance?"

"I have seen to it," said the man, who seemed to conduct himself in this wild business with the decorum of a merchant in his shop.

"Up with him, then," said Oates.

Prance and Bedloe swung the corpse on their shoulders and moved out, while the doctor, gripping Lovel's arm like a vice, followed at a little distance.

The Savoy was very quiet that night, and very dark. The few loiterers who observed the procession must have shrugged their shoulders and turned aside, zealous only to keep out of trouble. Such sights were not uncommon in the Savoy. They entered a high ruinous house on the east side, and after threading various passages reached a door which opened on a flight of broken steps where it was hard for more than one to pass at a time. Lovel heard the carriers of the dead grunting as they squeezed up with their burden. At the top another door gave on an outhouse in the yard of Somerset House between the stables and the west water-gate.... Lovel, as he stumbled after them with Oates' bulk dragging at his arm, was in a confusion of mind such as his mean time-serving life had never known.

He was in mortal fear, and yet his quaking heart would suddenly be braced by a gust of anger. He knew he was a rogue, but there were limits to roguery, and something in him, conscience, maybe, or forgotten gentility, sickened at this outrage. He had an impulse to defy them, to gain the street and give the alarm to honest men. These fellows were going to construct a crime in their own way which would bring death to the innocent.... Mr. Lovel trembled at himself, and had to think hard on his family in the Billingsgate attic to get back to his common-sense. He would not be believed if he spoke out. Oates would only swear that he was the culprit, and Oates had the ear of the courts and the mob. Besides, he had too many dark patches in his past. It was not for such as he to be finicking.

The body was pushed under an old truckle-bed which stood in the corner, and a mass of frails, such as gardeners use, flung over it for concealment. Oates rubbed his hands.

"The good work goes merrily," he said. "Sir Edmund dead, and for a week the good fawk of London are a-fevered. Then the haarrid discovery, and such a Praatestant uprising as will shake the maightiest from his pairch. Wonderful are Goad's ways and surprising His jaidgements! Every step must be weighed, since it is the Laard's business. Five days we must give this city to grow uneasy, and then ... The boady will be safe here?"

"I alone have the keys," said Prance.

The doctor counted on his thick fingers. "Monday - Tuesday - Waidnesday - aye, Waidneday's the day. Captain Bedloe, ye have chairge of the removal. Before dawn by the water-gate, and then a chair and a trusty man to cairry it to the plaace of discovery. Ye have appainted the spoat?"

"Any ditch in the Marylebone fields," said Bedloe.

"And before ye remove it, on the Tuesday naight haply, ye will run the boady through with his swaard, Sir Edmund's swaard."

"So you tell me," said Bedloe gruffly, "but I see no reason in it. The foolishest apothecary will be able tell how the man met his death."

Oates grinned and laid his finger to his nose. "Ye laack subtelty, fraiend. The priests of Baal must be met with their own waipons. Look ye. This poor man is found with his swaard in his braist. He has killed himself, says the fool. Not so, say the apothecaries. Then why the swaard, asks the coroner. Because of the daivilish cunning of his murderers, says Doctor Taitus Oates. A clear proof that the Jaisuits are in it, says every honest Praatistant. D'ye take me?"

Bedloe declared with oaths his admiration of the Doctor's wit, and good humour filled the hovel; All but Lovel, who once again was wrestling with something elemental in him that threatened to ruin everything. He remembered the bowed stumbling figure that had gone before him in the Marylebone meadows. Then he had been its enemy; now by a queer contortion of the mind he thought of himself as the only protector of that cold clay under the bed, honoured in life, but in death a poor pawn in a rogue's cause. He stood a little apart from the others near the door, and his eyes sought it furtively. He was not in the plot, and yet the plotters did not trouble about him. They assumed his complaisance. Doubtless they knew his shabby past.

He was roused by Oates' voice. The Doctor was arranging his plan of campaign with gusto. Bedloe was to disappear to the West Country till the time came for him to offer his evidence. Prance was to go about his peaceful trade till Bedloe gave him the cue. It was a masterly stratagem, Bedloe to start the ball, Prance to be accused as accomplice and then on his own account to give the other scoundrel corroboration.

"Attend, you sir," the doctor shouted to Lovel. "Ye will be called to swear to the murderers whom this haanest man will name. If ye be a true Praatestant ye will repeat the laisson I taich you. If not, ye will be set down as one of the villains and the good fawk of this city will tear the limbs from ye at my nod. Be well advaised, my friend, for I hold ye in my haand." And Oates raised a great paw and opened and shut it.

Lovel mumbled assent. Fear had again descended on him. He heard dimly the Doctor going over the names of those to be accused.

"Ye must bring in one of the sairvants of this place," he said. "Some common paarter, who has no friends."

"Trust me," said Prance. "I will find a likely fellow among the Queen's household. I have several in my mind for the honour."

"Truly the plaace is a nest of Paapists," said Oates. "And not such as you, Mr. Prance, who putt England before the Paape. Ye are worth a score of Praatestants to the good caause, and it will be remaimbered. Be assured it will be remaimbered.... Ye are clear about the main villains? Walsh, you say, and Pritchard and the man called Le Fevre?"

"The last most of all. But they are sharp-nosed as hounds, and unless we go warily they will give us the slip, and we must fall back on lesser game."

"Le Fevre." Oates mouthed the name. "The Queen's confessor. I was spit upon by him at St. Omer, and would waipe out the affront. A dog of a Frainch priest! A man I have long abhaarred."

"So also have I." Prance had venom in his level voice. "But he is no Frenchman. He is English as you, a Phayre out of Huntingdon."

The name penetrated Lovel's dulled wits. Phayre! It was the one man who in his father's life had shown him unselfish kindness. Long ago in Paris this Phayre had been his teacher, had saved him from starvation, had treated him with a gentleman's courtesy. Even his crimes had not estranged this friend. Phayre had baptized his child, and tended his wife when he was in hiding. But a week ago he had spoken a kindly word in the Mall to one who had rarely a kind word from an honest man.

That day had been to the spy a revelation of odd corners in his soul. He had mustered in the morning the resolution to kill one man. Now he discovered a scruple which bade him at all risks avert the killing of another. He perceived very clearly what the decision meant, desperate peril, perhaps ruin and death. He dare not delay, for in a little he would be too deep in the toils. He must escape and be first with the news of Godfrey's death in some potent quarter. Buckingham, who was a great prince. Or Danby. Or the King himself....

The cunning of a lifetime failed him in that moment. He slipped through the door, but his coat caught in a splinter of wood, and the rending of it gave the alarm. As with quaking heart he ran up the silent stable-yard towards the Strand gate he felt close on him the wind of the pursuit. In the dark he slipped on a patch of horse-dung and was down. Something heavy fell atop of him, and the next second a gross agony tore the breath from him.

Five minutes later Bedloe was unknotting a coarse kerchief and stuffing it into his pocket. It was the same that had strangled Godfrey.

"A good riddance," said Oates. "The fool had seen too much and would have proved but a saarry witness. Now by the mairciful dispensation of Goad he has ceased to trouble us. Ye know him, Captain Bedloe?"

"A Papistical cur, and white-livered at that," the bravo answered.

"And his boady? It must be praamptly disposed of."

"An easy task. There is the Savoy water-gate and in an hour the tide will run. He has no friends to inquire after him."

Oates rubbed his hands and cast his eyes upward. "Great are the doings of the Laard," he said, "and wonderful in our saight!"

CHAPTER XI. THE LIT CHAMBER

He was hoisted on his horse by an ostler and two local sots from the tap-room, his valise was strapped none too securely before him, and with a farewell, which was meant to be gracious but was only foolish, he tittuped into the rain. He was as drunk as an owl, though he did not know it. All afternoon he had been mixing strong Cumberland ale with the brandy he had got from the Solway free-traders, and by five o'clock had reached that state when he saw the world all gilt and rosy and himself as an applauded actor on a splendid stage. He had talked grandly to his fellow topers, and opened to their rustic wits a glimpse of the great world. They had bowed to a master, even those slow Cumbrians who admired little but fat cattle and blood horses. He had made a sensation, had seen wonder and respect in dull eyes, and tasted for a moment that esteem which he had singularly failed to find elsewhere.

But he had been prudent. The Mr. Gilbert Craster who had been travelling on secret business in Nithsdale and the Ayrshire moorlands had not been revealed in the change-house of Newbigging. There he had passed by the name, long since disused, of Gabriel Lovel, which happened to be his true one. It was a needful precaution, for the times were crooked. Even in a Border hamlet the name of Craster might be known and since for the present it had a Whig complexion it was well to go warily in a place where feeling ran high and at an hour when the Jacobites were on the march. But that other name of Lovel was buried deep in the forgotten scandal of London by-streets.

The gentleman late re-christened Lovel had for the moment no grudge against life. He was in the pay of a great man, no less than the lord Duke of Marlborough, and he considered that he was earning his wages. A soldier of fortune, he accepted the hire of the best paymaster; only he sold not a sword, but wits. A pedant might have called it honour, but Mr. Lovel was no pedant. He had served a dozen chiefs on different sides. For Blingbroke he had scoured France and twice imperilled his life in Highland bogs. For Somers he had travelled to Spain, and for Wharton had passed unquiet months on the Welsh marches. After his fashion he was an honest servant and reported the truth so far as his ingenuity could discern it. But, once quit of a great man's service, he sold his knowledge readily to an opponent, and had been like to be out of employment, since unless his masters gave him an engagement for life he was certain some day to carry the goods they had paid for to their rivals. But Marlborough had seen his uses, for the great Duke sat loose to parties and earnestly desired to know the facts. So for Marlborough he went into the conclaves of both Whig and Jacobite, making his complexion suit his company.

He was new come from the Scottish south-west, for the Duke was eager to know if the malcontent moorland Whigs were about to fling their blue bonnets for King James. A mission of such discomfort Mr. Lovel had never known, not even when he was a go-between for Ormonde in the Irish bogs. He had posed as an emissary from the Dutch brethren, son of an exiled Brownist, and for the first time in his life had found his regicide great-grandfather useful. The jargon of the godly fell smoothly from his tongue, and with its aid and that of certain secret letters he had found his way to the heart of the sectaries. He had sat through weary sermons in Cameronian sheilings, and been present at the childish parades of the Hebronite remnant. There was nothing to be feared in that quarter, for to them all in authority were idolaters and George no worse than James. In those moorland sojournings, too, he had got light on other matters, for he had the numbers of Kenmure's levies in his head, had visited my lord Stair at his grim Galloway castle, and had had a long midnight colloquy with Roxburghe on Tweedside. He had a pretty tale for his master, once he could get to him. But with Northumberland up and the Highlanders at Jedburgh and Kenmure coming from the west, it had been a ticklish business to cross the Border. Yet by cunning and a good horse it had been accomplished, and he found himself in Cumberland with the road open southward to the safe Lowther country. Wherefore Mr. Lovel had relaxed, and taken his ease in an inn.

He would not have admitted that he was drunk, but he presently confessed that he was not clear about his road. He had meant to lie at Brampton, and had been advised at the tavern of a short cut, a moorland bridle-path. Who had told him of it? The landlord, he thought, or the merry fellow in brown who had stood brandy to the company? Anyhow, it was to save him five miles, and that was something in this accursed weather. The path was clear, he could see it squelching below him, pale in the last wet daylight, but where the devil did it lead? Into the heart of a moss, it seemed, and yet Brampton lay out of the moors in the tilled valley.

At first the fumes in his head raised him above the uncertainty of his road and the eternal downpour. His mind was far away in a select world of his own imagining. He saw himself in a privy chamber, to which he had been conducted by reverent lackeys, the door closed, the lamp lit, and the Duke's masterful eyes bright with expectation. He saw the fine thin lips, like a woman's, primmed in satisfaction. He heard words of compliment - "none so swift and certain as you" - "in truth, a master-hand" - "I know not where to look for your like." Delicious speeches seemed to soothe his ear. And gold, too, bags of it, the tale of which would never appear in any accompt-book. Nay, his fancy soared higher. He saw himself presented to Ministers as one of the country's saviours, and kissing the hand of Majesty. What Majesty and what Ministers he knew not, and did not greatly care, that was not his business. The rotundity of the Hanoverian and the lean darkness of the Stuart were one to him. Both could reward an adroit servant.... His vanity, terribly starved and cribbed in his normal existence, now blossomed like a flower. His muddled head was fairly ravished with delectable pictures. He seemed to be set at a great height above mundane troubles, and to look down on men like a benignant God. His soul glowed with a happy warmth.

But somewhere he was devilish cold. His wretched body was beginning to cry out with discomfort. A loop of his hat was broken and the loose flap was a conduit for the rain down his back. His old ridingcoat was like a dish-clout, and he felt icy about the middle. Separate streams of water entered the tops of his ridingboots, they were a borrowed pair and too big for him, and his feet were in puddles. It was only by degrees that he realised this misery. Then in the boggy track his horse began to stumble. The fourth or fifth peck woke irritation, and he jerked savagely at the bridle, and struck the beast's dripping flanks with his whip. The result was a jib and a flounder, and the shock squeezed out the water from his garments as from a sponge. Mr. Lovel descended from the heights of fancy to prosaic fact, and cursed.

The dregs of strong drink were still in him, and so soon as exhilaration ebbed they gave edge to his natural fears. He perceived that it had grown very dark and lonely. The rain, falling sheer, seemed to shut him into a queer wintry world. All around the land echoed with the steady drum of it, and the rumour of swollen runnels. A wild bird wailed out of the mist and startled Mr. Lovel like a ghost. He heard the sound of men talking and drew rein; it was only a larger burn foaming by the wayside. The sky was black above him, yet a faint grey light seemed to linger, for water glimmered and he passed what seemed to be the edge of a loch.... At another time the London-bred citizen would have been only peevish, for Heaven knew he had faced ill weather before in ill places. But the fiery stuff he had swallowed had woke a feverish fancy. Exaltation suddenly changed to foreboding.

He halted and listened. Nothing but the noise of the weather, and the night dark around him like a shell. For a moment he fancied he caught the sound of horses, but it was not repeated. Where did this accursed track mean to lead him? Long ago he should have been in the valley and nearing Brampton. He was as wet as if he had wallowed in a pool, cold, and very weary. A sudden disgust at his condition drove away his fears and he swore lustily at fortune. He longed for the warmth and the smells of his favourite haunts, Gilpin's with oysters frizzling in a dozen pans, and noble odours stealing from the tap-room, the Green Man with its tripe-suppers, Wanless's Coffee House, noted for its cuts of beef and its white puddings. He would give much to be in a chair by one of those hearths and in the thick of that blowsy fragrance. Now his nostrils were filled with rain and bog water and a sodden world. It smelt sour, like stale beer in a mouldy cellar. And cold! He crushed down his hat on his head and precipitated a new deluge.

A bird skirled again in his ear, and his fright returned. He felt small and alone in a vast inhospitable universe. And mingled with it all was self-pity, for drink had made him maudlin. He wanted so little, only a modest comfort, a little ease. He had forgotten that half an hour before he had been figuring in princes' cabinets. He would give up this business and be quit of danger and the high road. The Duke must give him a reasonable reward, and with it he and his child might dwell happily in some country place. He remembered a cottage at Guildford all hung with roses.... But the Duke was reputed a miserly patron, and at the thought Mr. Lovel's eyes overflowed. There was that damned bird again, wailing like a lost soul. The eeriness of it struck a chill to his heart, so that if he had been able to think of any refuge he would have set spurs to his horse and galloped for it in blind terror. He was in the mood in which men compose poetry, for he felt himself a midget in the grip of immensities. He knew no poetry, save a few tavern songs; but in his youth he had had the Scriptures drubbed into him. He remembered ill-omened texts, one especially about wandering through dry places seeking rest. Would to Heaven he were in a dry place now!...

The horse sprang aside and nearly threw him. It had blundered against the stone pillar of a gateway. It was now clear even to Mr. Lovel's confused wits that he was lost. This might be the road to Tophet, but it was no road to Brampton. He felt with numbed hands the face of the gateposts. Here was an entrance to some dwelling, and it stood open. The path led through it, and if he left the path he would without doubt perish in a bog-hole. In his desolation he longed for a human face. He might find a good fellow who would house him; at the worst he would get direction about the road. So he passed the gateway and entered an avenue.

It ran between trees which took the force of the downpour, so that it seemed a very sanctuary after the open moor. His spirits lightened. The infernal birds had stopped crying, but again he heard the thud of hooves. That was right, and proved the place was tenanted. Presently he turned a corner and faced a light which shone through the wet, rayed like a heraldic star.

The sight gave him confidence, for it brought him back to a familiar world. He rode straight to it, crossing a patch of rough turf, where a fallen log all but brought him down. As he neared it the light grew till he saw its cause. He stood before the main door of a house and it was wide open. A great lantern, hung from a beam just inside, showed a doorway of some size and magnificence. And below it stood a servant, an old man, who at the sight of the stranger advanced to hold his stirrup.

"Welcome, my lord," said the man. "All is ready for you."

The last hour had partially sobered the traveller, but, having now come safe to port, his drunkenness revived. He saw nothing odd in the open door or the servant's greeting. As he scrambled to the ground he was back in his first exhilaration. "My lord!" Well, why not? This was an honest man who knew quality when he met it.

Humming a tune and making a chain of little pools on the stone flags of the hall, Mr. Lovel followed his guide, who bore his shabby valise, another servant having led away the horse. The hall was dim with flickering shadows cast by the lamp in the doorway, and smelt raw and cold as if the house had been little dwelt in. Beyond it was a stone passage where a second lamp burned and lit up a forest of monstrous deer horns on the wall. The butler flung open a door.

"I trust your lordship will approve the preparations," he said. "Supper awaits you, and when you have done I will show you your chamber. There are dry shoes by the hearth." He took from the traveller his sopping overcoat and drew from his legs the pulpy riding-boots. With a bow which might have graced a court he closed the door, leaving Mr. Lovel alone to his entertainment.

It was a small square room panelled to the ceiling in dark oak, and lit by a curious magnificence of candles. They burned in sconces on the walls and in tall candlesticks on the table, while a log fire on the great stone hearth so added to the glow that the place was as bright as day. The windows were heavily shuttered and curtained, and in the far corner was a second door. On the polished table food had been laid, a noble ham, two virgin pies, a dish of fruits, and a group of shining decanters. To one coming out of the wild night it was a transformation like a dream, but Mr. Lovel, half drunk, accepted it as no more than his due. His feather brain had been fired by the butler's "my lord," and he did not puzzle his head with questions. From a slim bottle he filled himself a glass of brandy, but on second thoughts set it down untasted. He would sample the wine first and top off with the spirit. Meantime he would get warm.

He stripped off his coat, which was dampish, and revealed a dirty shirt and the dilapidated tops of his small clothes. His stockings were torn and soaking, so he took them off, and stuck his naked feet into the furred slippers which stood waiting by the hearth. Then he sat himself in a great brocaded arm-chair and luxuriously stretched his legs to the blaze.

But his head was too much afire to sit still. The comfort soaked into his being through every nerve and excited rather than soothed him. He did not want to sleep now, though little before he had been crushed by weariness.... There was a mirror beside the fireplace, the glass painted at the edge with slender flowers and cupids in the Caroline fashion. He saw his reflection and it pleased him. The long face with the pointed chin, the deep-set dark eyes, the skin brown with weather, he seemed to detect a resemblance to Wharton. Or was it Beaufort? Anyhow, now that the shabby coat was off, he might well be a great man in undress. "My lord!" Why not? His father had always told him he came of an old high family. Kings, he had said, of France, or somewhere... A gold ring he wore on his left hand slipped from his finger and jingled on the hearthstone. It was too big for him, and when his fingers grew small with cold or wet it was apt to fall off. He picked it up and laid it beside the decanters on the table. That had been his father's ring, and he congratulated himself that in all his necessities he had never parted from it. It was said to have come down from ancient kings.

He turned to the table and cut himself a slice of ham. But he found he had no appetite. He filled himself a bumper of claret. It was a ripe velvety liquor and cooled his hot mouth. That was the drink for gentlemen. Brandy in good time, but for the present this soft wine which was in keeping with the warmth and light and sheen of silver.... His excitement was dying now into complacence. He felt himself in the environment for which Providence had fitted him. His whole being expanded in the glow of it. He understood how able he was, how truly virtuous, a master of intrigue, but one whose eye was always fixed on the star of honour. And then his thoughts wandered to his son in the mean London lodgings. The boy should have his chance and walk some day in silks and laces. Curse his aliases! He should be Lovel, and carry his head as high as any Villiers or Talbot.

The reflection sent his hand to an inner pocket of the coat now drying by the hearth. He took from it a thin packet of papers wrapped in oil-cloth. These were the fruits of his journey, together with certain news too secret to commit to writing which he carried in his head. He ran his eye over them, approved them, and laid them before him on the table. They started a train of thought which brought him to the question of his present quarters.... A shadow of doubt flickered over his mind. Whose house was this and why this entertainment? He had been expected, or someone like him. An old campaigner took what gifts the gods sent, but there might be questions to follow. There was a coat of arms on the plate, but so dim that he could not read it. The one picture in the room showed an old man in a conventional suit of armour. He did not recognise the face or remember any like it.... He filled himself another bumper of claret, and followed it with a little brandy. This latter was noble stuff, by which he would abide. His sense of ease and security returned. He pushed the papers farther over, sweeping the ring with them, and set his elbows on the table, a gentleman warm, dry, and content, but much befogged in the brain.

He raised his eyes to see the far door open and three men enter. The sight brought him to his feet with a start, and his chair clattered on the oak boards. He made an attempt at a bow, backing steadily towards the fireplace and his old coat.

The faces of the new-comers exhibited the most lively surprise. All three were young, and bore marks of travel, for though they had doffed their riding coats, they were splashed to the knees with mud and their unpowdered hair lay damp on their shoulders. One was a very dark man who might have been a Spaniard but for his blue eyes. The second was a mere boy with a ruddy face and eyes full of dancing merriment. The third was tall and red-haired, tanned of countenance and lean as a greyhound. He wore trews of a tartan which Mr. Lovel, trained in such matters, recognised as that of the house of Atholl.

Of the three he only recognised the leader, and the recognition sobered him. This was that Talbot, commonly known from his swarthiness as the Crow, who was Ormonde's most trusted lieutenant. He had once worked with him; he knew his fierce temper, his intractable honesty. His bemused wits turned desperately to concocting a conciliatory tale.

But he seemed to be unrecognised. The three stared at him in wild-eyed amazement.

"Who the devil are you, sir?" the Highlander stammered.

Mr. Lovel this time brought off his bow. "A stormstayed traveller," he said, his eyes fawning, "who has stumbled on this princely hospitality. My name at your honour's service is Gabriel Lovel."

There was a second of dead silence and then the boy laughed. It was merry laughter and broke in strangely on the tense air of the room.

"Lovel," he cried, and there was an Irish burr in his speech. "Lovel! And that fool Jobson mistook it for Lovat! I mistrusted the tale, for Simon is too discreet even in his cups to confess his name in a changehouse. It seems we have been stalking the cailzie-cock and found a common thrush."

The dark man Talbot did not smile. "We had good reason to look for Lovat. Widrington had word from London that he was on his way to the north by the west marches. Had we found him we had found a prize, for he will play hell with Mar if he crosses the Highland line. What say you, Lord Charles?"

The Highlander nodded. "I would give my sporran filled ten times with gold to have my hand on Simon. What devil's luck to be marching south with that old fox in our rear!"

The boy pulled up a chair to the table. "Since we have missed the big game, let us follow the less. I'm for supper, if this gentleman will permit us to share a feast destined for another. Sit down, sir, and fill your glass. You are not to be blamed for not being a certain Scots lord. Lovel, I dare say, is an honester name than Lovat!"

But Talbot was regarding the traveller with hard eyes. "You called him a thrush, Nick, but I have a notion he is more of a knavish jackdaw. I have seen this gentleman before. You were with Ormonde?"

"I had once the honour to serve his Grace," said Lovel, still feverishly trying to devise a watertight tale.

"Ah, I remember now. You thought his star descending and carried your wares to the other side. And who is your new employer, Mr. Lovel? His present Majesty?"

His glance caught the papers on the table and he swept them towards him.

"What have we here?" and his quick eye scanned the too legible handwriting. Much was in cipher and contractions, but some names stood out damningly. In that month of October in that year 1715 "Ke" could only stand for "Kenmure" and "Ni" for "Nithsdale."

Mr. Lovel made an attempt at dignity.

"These are my papers, sir," he blustered. "I know not by what authority you examine them." But his protest failed because of the instability of his legs, on which his potations early and recent had suddenly a fatal effect. He was compelled to collapse heavily in the arm-chair by the hearth.

"I observe that the gentleman has lately been powdering his hair," said the boy whom they called Nick.

Mr. Lovel was wroth. He started upon the usual drunkard's protestations, but was harshly cut short by Talbot.

"You ask me my warrant 'Tis the commission of his Majesty King James in whose army I have the honour to hold a command."

He read on, nodding now and then, pursing his mouth at a word, once copying something on to his own tablets. Suddenly he raised his head.

"When did his Grace dismiss you?" he asked.

Now Ormonde had been the Duke last spoken of, but Mr. Lovel's precarious wits fell into the trap. He denied indignantly that he had fallen from his master's favour.

A grim smile played round Talbot's mouth.

"You have confessed," he said. Then to the others: "This fellow is one of Malbrouck's pack. He has been nosing in the Scotch westlands. Here are the numbers of Kenmure and Nithsdale to enable the great Duke to make up his halting mind. See, he has been with Roxburghe too.... We have a spy before us, gentlemen, delivered to our hands by a happy incident. Whig among the sectaries and with Stair and Roxburghe, and Jacobite among our poor honest folk, and wheedling the secrets out of both sides to sell to one who disposes of them at a profit in higher quarters. Faug! I know the vermin. An honest Whig like John Argyll I can respect and fight, but for such rats as this. What shall we do with it now that we have trapped it?"

"Let it go," said the boy, Nick Wogan. "The land crawls with them and we cannot go rat-hunting when we are aiming at a throne." He picked up Lovel's ring and spun it on a finger tip. "The gentleman has found more than news in the north. He has acquired a solid lump of gold."

The implication roused Mr. Lovel out of his embarrassment. "I wear the ring by right. I had it from my father." His voice was tearful with offended pride

"The creature claims gentility," said Talbot, as he examined the trinket. "Lovel you call yourself. But Lovel bears barry nebuly or chevronels. This coat has three plain charges. Can you read them, Nick, for my eyes are weak! I am curious to know from whom he stole it."

The boy scanned it closely. "Three of something I think they are fleur-de-lys, which would spell Montgomery. Or lions' heads, maybe, for Buchan?"

He passed it to Lord Charles, who held it to a candle's light. "Nay, I think they are Cummin garbs. Some poor fellow dirked and spoiled."

Mr. Lovel was outraged and forgot his fears. He forgot, indeed, most things which he should have remembered. He longed only to establish his gentility in the eyes of those three proud gentlemen. The liquor was ebbing in him and with it had flown all his complacence. He felt small and mean and despised, and the talents he had been pluming himself on an hour before had now shrunk to windlestraws.

"I do assure you, sirs," he faltered, "the ring is mine own. I had it from my father, who had it from his. I am of an ancient house, though somewhat decayed."

His eyes sought those of his inquisitors with the pathos of a dog. But he saw only hostile faces, Talbot's grave and grim, Lord Charles' contemptuous, the boy's smiling ironically.

"Decayed, indeed," said the dark man, "pitifully decayed. If you be gentle the more shame on you."

Mr. Lovel was almost whining. "I swear I am honest. I do my master's commissions and report what I learn."

"Aye, sir, but how do you learn it? By playing the imposter and winning your way into an unsuspecting confidence. To you friendship is a tool and honour a convenience. You cheat in every breath you draw. And what a man gives you in his innocence may bring him to the gallows. By God! I'd rather slit throats on a highway for a purse or two than cozen men to their death by such arts as yours."

In other circumstances Mr. Lovel might have put up a brazen defence, but now he seemed to have lost assurance. "I do no ill," was all he could stammer, "for I have no bias. I am for no side in politics."

"So much the worse. A man who spies for a cause in which he believes may redeem by that faith a dirty trade. But in cold blood you practise infamy."

The night was growing wilder, and even in that sheltered room its echoes were felt. Wind shook the curtains and blew gusts of ashes from the fire. The place had become bleak and tragic and Mr. Lovel felt the forlornness in his bones. Something had woke in him which shivered the fabric of a lifetime. The three faces, worn, anxious, yet of a noble hardihood, stirred in him a strange emotion. Hopes and dreams, long forgotten, flitted like spectres across his memory. He had something to say, something which demanded utterance, and his voice grew bold.

"What do you know of my straits?" he cried. "Men of fortune like you! My race is old, but I never had the benefit of it. I was bred in a garret and have all my days been on nodding terms with starvation.... What should I know about your parties? What should I care for Whig and Tory or what king has his hinderend on the throne? Tell me in God's name how should such as I learn loyalty except to the man who gives me gold to buy food and shelter? Heaven knows I have never betrayed a master while I served him."

The shabby man with the lean face had secured an advantage. For a moment the passion in his voice dominated the room.

"Cursed if this does not sound like truth," said the boy, and his eyes were almost friendly.

But Talbot did not relax.

"By your own confession you are outside the pale of gentility. I do not trouble to blame you, but I take leave to despise you. By your grace, sir, we will dispense with your company."

The ice of his scorn did not chill the strange emotion which seemed to have entered the air. The scarecrow by the fire had won a kind of dignity.

"I am going," he said. "Will you have the goodness to send for my horse?... If you care to know, gentleman, you have cut short a promising career.... To much of what you say I submit. You have spoken truth, not all the truth, but sufficient to unman me. I am a rogue by your reckoning, for I think only of my wages. Pray tell me what moves you to ride out on what at the best is a desperate venture?"

There was nothing but sincerity in the voice, and Talbot answered.

"I fight for the King ordained by God and for a land which cannot flourish under the usurper. My loyalty to throne, Church, and fatherland constrains me."

Lovel's eye passed to Lord Charles. The Highlander whistled very softly a bar or two of a wild melody with longing and a poignant sorrow in it.

"That," he said. "I fight for the old ways and the old days that are passing."

Nick Wogan smiled. "And I for neither, wholly. I have a little of Talbot in me and more of Charles. But I strike my blow for romance, the little against the big, the noble few against the base many. I am for youth against all dull huckstering things."

Mr. Lovel bowed. "I am answered. I congratulate you, gentlemen, on your good fortune. It is my grief that I do not share it. I have not Mr. Talbot's politics, nor am I a great Scotch lord, nor have I the felicity to be young.... I would beg you not to judge me harshly."

By this time he had struggled into his coat and boots He stepped to the table and picked up the papers.

"By your leave," he said, and flung them into the fire.

"You were welcome to them," said Talbot. "Long ere they got to Marlborough they would be useless."

"That is scarcely the point," said Lovel "I am somewhat dissatisfied with my calling and contemplate a change."

"You may sleep here if you wish," said Lord Charles.

"I thank you, but I am no fit company for you. I am better on the road."

Talbot took a guinea from his purse "Here's to help your journey," he was saying, when Nick Wogan flushing darkly, intervened. "Damn you, James don't be a boor," he said.

The boy picked up the ring and offered it to Mr. Lovel as he passed through the door. He also gave him his hand.

The traveller spurred his horse into the driving rain, but he was oblivious of the weather. When he came to Brampton he discovered to his surprise that he had been sobbing. Except in liquor, he had not wept since he was a child.

CHAPTER XII. IN THE DARK LAND

The fire was so cunningly laid that only on one side did it cast a glow, and there the light was absorbed by a dark thicket of laurels. It was built under an overhang of limestone so that the smoke in the moonlight would be lost against the grey face of the rock. But, though the moon was only two days past the full, there was no sign of it, for the rain had come and the world was muffled in it. That morning the Kentucky vales, as seen from the ridge where the camp lay, had been like a furnace with the gold and scarlet of autumn, and the air had been heavy with sweet October smells. Then the wind had suddenly shifted, the sky had grown leaden, and in a queer dank chill the advance-guard of winter had appeared, that winter which to men with hundreds of pathless miles between them and their homes was like a venture into an uncharted continent.

One of the three hunters slipped from his buffalo robe and dived into the laurel thicket to replenish the fire from the stock of dry fuel. His figure revealed itself fitfully in the firelight, a tall slim man with a curious lightness of movement like a cat's. When he had done his work he snuggled down in his skins in the glow, and his two companions shifted their positions to be near him. The fire-tender was the leader of the little party The light showed a face very dark with weather. He had the appearance of wearing an untidy perruque, which was a tight-fitting skin-cap with the pelt hanging behind. Below its fringe straggled a selvedge of coarse black hair. But his eyes were blue and very bright, and his eyebrows and lashes were flaxen, and the contrast of light and dark had the effect of something peculiarly bold and masterful. Of the others one was clearly his brother, heavier in build, but with the same eyes and the same hard pointed chin and lean jaws. The third man was shorter and broader, and wore a newer hunting shirt than his fellows and a broad belt of wool and leather.

This last stretched his moccasins to the blaze and sent thin rings of smoke from his lips into the steam made by the falling rain.

He bitterly and compendiously cursed the weather. The little party had some reason for ill-temper. There had been an accident in the creek with the powder supply, and for the moment there were only two charges left in the whole outfit. Hitherto they had been living on ample supplies of meat, though they were on short rations of journey-cake, for their stock of meal was low. But that night they had supped poorly, for one of them had gone out to perch a turkey, since powder could not be wasted, and had not come back.

"I reckon we're the first as ever concluded to winter in Kaintuckee," he said between his puffs. "Howard and Salling went in in June, I've heerd. And Finley? What about Finley, Dan'l?"

"He never stopped beyond the fall, though he was once near gripped by the snow. But there ain't no reason why winter should be worse on the O-hio than on the Yadkin. It's a good hunting time, and snow'll keep the redskins quiet. What's bad for us is wuss for them, says I.... I won't worry about winter nor redskins, if old Jim Lovelle 'ud fetch up. It beats me whar the man has got to."

"Wandered, maybe?" suggested the first speaker, whose name was Neely.

"I reckon not. Ye'd as soon wander a painter. There ain't no sech hunter as Jim ever came out of Virginny, no, nor out of Caroliny, neither. It was him that fust telled me of Kaintuck'. 'The dark and bloody land, the Shawnees calls it,' he says, speakin' in his eddicated way, and dark and bloody it is, but that's man's doing and not the Almighty's. The land flows with milk and honey, he says, clear water and miles of clover and sweet grass, enough to feed all the herds of Basham, and mighty forests with trees that thick ye could cut a hole in their trunks and drive a waggon through, and sugar-maples and plums and cherries like you won't see in no set orchard, and black soil fair crying for crops. And the game, Jim says, wasn't to be told about without ye wanted to be called a liar, big black-nosed buffaloes that packed together so the whole placed seemed moving, and elk and deer and bar past counting.... Wal, neighbours, ye've seen it with your own eyes and can jedge if Jim was a true prophet. I'm Moses, he used to say, chosen to lead the Children of Israel into a promised land, but I reckon I'll leave my old bones on some Pisgah-top on the borders. He was a sad man, Jim, and didn't look for much comfort this side Jordan.... I wish I know'd whar he'd gotten to."

Squire Boone, the speaker's brother, sniffed the air dolefully. "It's weather that 'ud wander a good hunter."

"I tell ye, ye couldn't wander Jim," said his brother fiercely. "He come into Kaintuckee alone in '52, and that was two years before Finley. He was on the Ewslip all the winter of '58. He was allus springing out of a bush when ye didn't expect him. When we was fighting the Cherokees with Montgomery in '61 he turned up as guide to the Scotsmen, and I reckon if they'd attended to him there'ud be more of them alive this day. He was like a lone wolf, old Jim, and preferred to hunt by hisself, but you never knowed that he wouldn't come walking in and say 'Howdy' while you was reckoning you was the fust white man to make that trace. Wander Jim? Ye might as well speak of wandering a hakk."

"Maybe the Indians have got his sculp," said Neely.

"I reckon not," said Boone. "Leastways if they have, he must ha' struck a new breed of redskin. Jim was better nor any redskin in Kaintuck', and they knowed it. I told ye, neighbours, of our doings before you come west through the Gap. The Shawnees cotched me and Jim in a cane-brake, and hit our trace back to camp, so that they cotched Finley too, and his three Yadkiners with him. Likewise they took our hosses, and guns and traps and the furs we had gotten from three months' hunting. Their chief made a speech saying we had no right in Kaintuckee and if they cotched us again our lives'ud pay for it. They'd ha' sculped us if it hadn't been for Jim, but you could see they knew him, and was feared of him. Wal, Finley reckoned the game was up, and started back with the Yadkiners. Cooley and Joe Holden and Mooneyiye mind them, Squire! But I was feeling kinder cross and wanted my property back, and old Jim, why, he wasn't going to be worsted by no redskins. So we trailed the Shawnees, us two, and come up with them one night encamped beside a salt-lick. Jim got into their camp while I was lying shivering in the cane, and blessed if he didn't snake back four of our hosses and our three best Deckards. Tha's craft for ye. By sunrise we was riding south on the Warriors' Path but the hosses was plumb tired, and afore midday them pizonous Shawnees had cotched up with us. I can tell ye, neighbours, the hair riz on my head, for I expected nothing better than a bloody sculp and six feet of earth.... But them redskins didn't hurt us. And why, says ye? 'Cos they was scared of Jim. It seemed they had a name for him in Shawnee which meant the 'old wolf that hunts by night. They started out to take us way north of the Ohio to their Scioto villages, whar they said we would be punished.

Jim told me to keep up my heart, for he reckoned we wasn't going north of no river. Then he started to make friends with them redskins, and in two days he was the most popilar fellow in that company. He was a quiet man and for general melancholious, but I guess he could be amusing when he wanted to. You know the way an Indian laughs grunts in his stomach and looks at the ground. Wal, Jim had them grunting all day, and, seeing he could speak all their tongues, he would talk serious too. Ye could see them savages listening, like he was their own sachem."

Boone reached for another faggot and tossed it on the fire. The downpour was slacking, but the wind had risen high and was wailing in the sycamores.

"Consekince was," he went on, "for prisoners we wasn't proper guarded. By the fourth day we was sleeping round the fire among the Shawnees and marching with them as we pleased, though we wasn't allowed to go near the hosses. On the seventh night we saw the Ohio rolling in the hollow, and Jim says to me it was about time to get quit of the redskins. It was a wet night with a wind, which suited his plan, and about one in the morning, when Indians sleep soundest, I was woke by Jim's hand pressing my wrist. Wal, I've trailed a bit in my day, but I never did such mighty careful hunting as that night. An inch at a time we crawled out of the circle, we was lying well back on purpose, and got into the canes. I lay there while Jim went back and fetched guns and powder. The Lord knows how he done it without startling the hosses. Then we quit like ghosts, and legged it for the hills. We was aiming for the Gap, but it took us thirteen days to make it, travelling mostly by night, and living on berries, for we durstn't risk a shot. Then we made up with you. I reckon we didn't look too pretty when ye see'd us first."

"Ye looked," said his brother soberly, "Like two scare-crows that had took to walkin'. There was more naked skin than shirt about you Dan'l. But Lovelle wasn't complaining, except about his empty belly."

"He was harder nor me, though twenty years older. He did the leading, too, for he had forgotten more about woodcraft than I ever know'd...."

The man Neely, who was from Virginia, consumed tobacco as steadily as a dry soil takes in water.

"I've heerd of this Lovelle," he said. "I've seed him too, I guess. A long man with black eyebrows and hollow eyes like as he was hungry. He used ter live near my folks in Palmer Country. What was he looking for in those travels of his?"

"Hunting maybe," said Boone. "He was the skilfullest hunter, I reckon, between the Potomac and the Cherokee. He brought in mighty fine pelts, but he didn't seem to want money. Just so much as would buy him powder and shot and food for the next venture, ye understand.... He wasn't looking for land to settle on, neighber, for one time he telled me he had had all the settling he wanted in this world.... But he was looking for something else. He never talked about it, but he'd sit often with his knees hunched up and his eyes staring out at nothing like a bird's. I never know'd who he was or whar he come from. You say it was Virginny?"

"Aye, Palmer County. I mind his old dad, who farmed a bit of land by Nelson's Cross Roads, when he wasn't drunk in Nelson's tavern. The boys used to follow him to laugh at his queer clothes, and hear his fine London speech when he cursed us. By thunder, he was the one to swear. Jim Lovelle used to clear us off with a whip, and give the old man his arm into the shack. Jim too was a queer one, but it didn't do to make free with him, unless ye was lookin' for a broken head. They was come of high family, I've heerd."

"Aye, Jim was a gentleman and no mistake," said Boone. "The way he held his head and looked straight through the man that angered him. I reckon it was that air of his and them glowering eyes that made him powerful with the redskins. But he was mighty quiet always. I've seen Cap'n Evan Shelby roaring at him like a bull and Jim just staring back at him, as gentle as a girl, till the Cap'n began to stutter and dried up. But, Lordy, he had a pluck in a fight, for I've seen him with Montgomery.... He was eddicated too, and could tell you things out of books. I've knowed him sit up all night talking law with Mr. Robertson.... He was always thinking. Queer thoughts they was sometimes."

"Whatten kind of thoughts, Dan'l?" his brother asked.

Boone rubbed his chin as if he found it hard to explain. "About this country of Ameriky," he replied. "He reckoned it would soon have to cut loose from England, and him knowing so much about England I used ter believe him. He allowed there 'ud be bloody battles before it happened, but he held that the country had grown up and couldn't be kept much longer in short clothes. He had a power of larning about things that happened to folks long ago called Creeks and Rewmans that pinted that way, he said. But he held that when we had fought our way quit of England, we was in for a bigger and bloodier fight among ourselves. I mind his very words. 'Dan'l,' he says, 'this is the biggest and best slice of the world which we Americans has struck, and for fifty years or more, maybe, we'll be that busy finding out what we've got that we'll have no time to quarrel. But there's going to come a day, if Ameriky s to be a great nation, when she'll have to sit down and think and make up her mind about one or two things. It won't be easy, for she won't have the eddication or patience to think deep, and there'll be plenty selfish and short-sighted folk that won't think at all. I reckon she'll have to set her house in order with a hickory stick. But if she wins through that all right, she'll be a country for our children to be proud of and happy in.'"

"Children? Has he any belongings?" Squire Boone

Daniel looked puzzled. "I've heerd it said he had a wife, though he never telled nie of her."

"I've seed her," Neely put in. "She was one of Jake Early's daughters up to Walsing Springs. She didn't live no more than a couple of years after they was wed. She left a gal behind her, a mighty finelooking gal. They tell me she's married on young Abe Hanks, I did hear that Abe was thinking of coming west, but them as told me allowed that Abe hadn't got the right kinder wife for the Border. Polly Hanker they called her, along of her being Polly Hanks, and likewise wantin' more than other folks had to get along with. See?"

This piece of news woke Daniel Boone to attention. "Tell me about Jim's gal," he demanded.

"Pretty as a peach," said Neely "Small, not higher nor Abe's shoulder, and as light on her feet as a deer. She had a softish laughing look in her eyes that made the lads wild for her. But she wasn't for them and I reckon she wasn't for Abe neither. She was nicely eddicated, though she had jest had field-schooling like the rest, for her dad used to read books and tell her about 'em. One time he took her to Richmond for the better part of a winter, where she larned dancing and music. The neighbours allowed that turned her head. Ye couldn't please her with clothes, for she wouldn't look at the sun-bonnets and nettle-linen that other gals wore. She must have a neat little bonnet and send to town for pretty dresses.... The women couldn't abide her, for she had a high way of looking at 'em and talking at 'em as if they was jest black trash. But the men 'ud walk miles to see her on a Sunday.... I never could jest understand why she took Abe Hanks. 'Twasn't for lack of better offers."

"I reckon that's women's ways," said Boone meditatively. "She must ha' favoured Jim, though he wasn't partickler about his clothes. Discontented, ye say she was?"

"Aye. Discontented. She was meant for a fine lady, I reckon. I dunno what she wanted, but anyhow it was something that Abe Hanks ain't likely to give her. I can't jest picture her in Kaintuck'!"

Squire Boone was asleep, and Daniel drew the flap of his buffalo robe over his head and prepared to follow suit. His last act was to sniff the air. "Please God the weather mends," he muttered. "I've got to find old Jim."

Very early next morning there was a consultation. Lovelle had not appeared and hunting was impossible on two shoots of powder. It was arranged that two of them should keep camp that day by the limestone cliff while Daniel Boone went in search of the missing man, for it was possible that Jim Lovelle had gone to seek ammunition from friendly Indians. If he did not turn up or if he returned without powder, there would be nothing for it but to send a messenger back through the Gap for supplies.

The dawn was blue and cloudless and the air had the freshness of a second spring. The autumn colour glowed once more, only a little tarnished; the gold was now copper, the scarlet and vermilion were dulling to crimson. Boone took the road at the earliest light and made for the place where the day before he had parted from Lovelle. When alone he had the habit of talking to himself in an undertone. "Jim was hunting down the west bank of that there crick, and I heard a shot about noon beyond them big oaks, so I reckon he'd left the water and gotten on the ridge." He picked up the trail and followed it with difficulty, for the rain had flattened out the prints. At one point he halted and considered. "That's queer," he muttered. "Jim was running here. It wasn't game, neither, for there's no sign of their tracks." He pointed to the zig-zag of moccasin prints in a patch of gravel. "That's the way a man sets his feet when he's in a hurry."

A little later he stood and sniffed, with his brows wrinkled. He made an epic figure as he leaned forward, every sense strained, every muscle alert, slim and shapely as a Greek, the eternal pathfinder. Very gently he smelled the branches of a mulberry thicket.

"There's been an Indian here," he meditated. "I kinder smell the grease on them twigs. In a hurry, too, or he wouldn't have left his stink behind.... In war trim, I reckon." And he took a tiny wisp of scarlet feather from a fork.

Like a hound he nosed about the ground till he found something. "Here's his print;" he said "He was a-followin' Jim, for see! he has his foot in Jim's track. I don't like it. I'm fear'd of what's comin'."

Slowly and painfully he traced the footing, which led through the thicket towards a long ridge running northward. In an open grassy place he almost cried out. "The redskin and Jim was friends. See, here's their prints side by side, going slow. What in thunder was old Jim up to?"

The trail was plainer now, and led along the scarp of the ridge to a little promontory which gave a great prospect over the flaming forests and yellow glades. Boone found a crinkle of rock where he flung himself down. "It's plain enough," he said. "They come up here to spy. They were fear'd of something, and whatever it was it was coming from the west. See, they kep' under the east side of this ridge so as not to be seen, and they settled down to spy whar they couldn't be observed from below. I reckon Jim and the redskin had a pretty good eye for cover."

He examined every inch of the eyrie, sniffing like a pointer dog. "I'm plumb puzzled about this redskin," he confessed. "Shawnee, Cherokee, Chickasaw, it ain't likely Jim would have dealings with 'em. It might be one of them Far Indians."

It appeared as if Lovelle had spent most of the previous afternoon on the ridge, for he found the remains of his night's fire half way down the north side in a hollow thatched with vines. It was now about three o'clock. Boone, stepping delicately, examined the ashes, and then sat himself on the ground and brooded.

When at last he lifted his eyes his face was perplexed.

"I can't make it out nohow. Jim and this Indian was good friends. They were feelin' pretty safe, for they made a mighty careless fire and didn't stop to tidy it up. But likewise they was restless, for they started out long before morning.... I read it this way. Jim met a redskin that he knowed before and thought he could trust anyhow, and he's gone off with him seeking powder. It'd be like Jim to dash off alone and play his hand like that. He figured he'd come back to us with what we needed and that we'd have the sense to wait for him. I guess that's right. But I'm uneasy about the redskin. If he's from north of the river, there's a Mingo camp somewhere about and they've gone there.... I never had much notion of Seneca Indians, and I reckon Jim's took a big risk."

All evening he followed the trail, which crossed the low hills into the corn-brakes and woodlands of a broader valley. Presently he saw that he had been right, and that Lovelle and the Indian had begun their journey in the night, for the prints showed like those of travellers in darkness. Before sunset Boone grew very anxious. He found traces converging, till a clear path was worn in the grass like a regulation war trail. It was not one of the known trails, so it had been made for a purpose; he found on tree trunks the tiny blazons of the scouts who had been sent ahead to survey it. It was a war party of Mingos, or whoever they might be, and he did not like it. He was puzzled to know what purchase Jim could have with those outland folk.... And yet he had been on friendly terms with the scout he had picked up.... Another fact disturbed him. Lovelle's print had been clear enough till the other Indians joined him. The light was bad, but now that print seemed to have disappeared. It might be due to the general thronging of marks in the trail, but it might be that Jim was a prisoner, trussed and helpless.

He supped off cold jerked bear's meat and slept two hours in the canes, waiting on the moonrise. He had bad dreams, for he seemed to hear drums beating the eerie tattoo which he remembered long ago in Border raids. He woke in a sweat, and took the road again in the moonlight. It was not hard to follow, and it seemed to be making north for the Ohio. Dawn came on him in a grassy bottom, beyond which lay low hills that he knew alone separated him from the great river. Once in the Indian Moon of Blossom he had been thus far, and had gloried in the riches of the place, where a man walked knee deep in honeyed clover. "The dark and bloody land!" He remembered how he had repeated the name to himself, and had concluded that Lovelle had been right and that it was none of the Almighty's giving. Now in the sharp autumn morning he felt its justice. A cloud had come over his cheerful soul. "If only I knowed about Jim," he muttered "I wonder if I'll ever clap eyes onr his old face again." Never before had he known such acute anxiety. Pioneers are wont to trust each other and in their wild risks assume that the odd chance is on their side. But now black forebodings possessed him, born not of reasoning but of instinct. His comrade somewhere just ahead of him was in deadly peril.

And then came the drums.

The sound broke into the still dawn with a harsh challenge. They were war drums, beaten as he remembered them in Montgomery's campaign. He quickened his steady hunter's lope into a run, and left the trail for the thickets of the hill-side. The camp was less than a mile off and he was taking no chances.

As he climbed the hill the drums grew louder, till it seemed that the whole world rocked with their noise. He told himself feverishly that there was nothing to fear; Jim was with friends, who had been south of the river on their own business and would give him the powder he wanted. Presently they would be returning to the camp together, and in the months to come he and Jim would make that broad road through the Gap, at the end of which would spring up smiling farmsteads and townships of their own naming. He told himself these things, but he knew that he lied.

At last, flat on the earth, he peered through the vines on the north edge of the ridge. Below him, half a mile off, rolled the Ohio, a little swollen by the rains There was a broad ford, and the waters had spilled out over the fringe of sand. Just under him, between the bluff and the river, lay the Mingo camp, every detail of it plain in the crisp weather.

In the heart of it a figure stood bound to a stake, and a smoky fire burned at its feet.... There was no mistaking that figure.

Boone bit the grass in a passion of fury. His first impulse was to rush madly into the savages' camp and avenge his friend. He had half risen to his feet when his reason told him it was folly. He had no weapon but axe and knife, and would only add another scalp to their triumph. His Deckard was slung on his back, but he had no powder. Oh, to be able to send a bullet through Jim's head to cut short his torment! In all his life he had never known such mental anguish, waiting there an impotent witness of the agony of his friend. The blood trickled from his bitten lips and film was over his eyes.... Lovelle was dying for him and the others. He saw it all with bitter clearness. Jim had been inveigled to the Mingo camp taking risks as he always did, and there been ordered to reveal the whereabouts of the hunting party. He had refused, and endured the ordeal... Memories of their long comradeship rushed through Boone's mind and set him weeping in a fury of affection. There was never such a man as old Jim, so trusty and wise and kind, and now that great soul was being tortured out of that stalwart body and he could only look on like a baby and cry.

As he gazed, it became plain that the man at the stake was dead. His head had fallen on his chest, and the Indians were cutting the green withies that bound him. Boone looked to see them take his scalp, and so wild was his rage that his knees were already bending for the onslaught which should be the death of him and haply of one or two of the murderers.

But no knife was raised. The Indians seemed to consult together, and one of them gave an order. Deerskins were brought and the body was carefully wrapped in them and laid on a litter of branches. Their handling of it seemed almost reverent. The camp was moving, the horses were saddled, and presently the whole band began to file off towards the forest. The sight held Boone motionless. His fury had gone and only wonder and awe remained. As they passed the dead, each Indian raised his axe in salute, the salute to a great chief. The next minute they were splashing through the ford.

An hour later, when the invaders had disappeared on the northern levels, Boone slipped down from the bluff to the camping place. He stood still a long time by his friend, taking off his deerskin cap, so that his long black hair was blown over his shoulders.

"Jim, boy," he said softly. "I reckon you was the general of us all. The likes of you won't come again. I'd like ye to have Christian burial."

With his knife he hollowed a grave, where he placed the body, still wrapped in its deerskins. He noted on a finger of one hand a gold ring, a queer possession for a backwoodsman. This he took off and dropped into the pouch which hung round his neck. "I reckon it'd better go to Mis' Hanks. Jim's gal 'ud valley it mor'n a wanderin' coyote."

When he had filled in the earth he knelt among the grasses and repeated the Lord's Prayer as well as he could remember it. Then he stood up and rubbed with his hard brown knuckles the dimness from his eyes.

"Ye was allus lookin' for something, Jim," he said. "I guess ye've found it now. Good luck to ye, old comrade."

CHAPTER XIII. THE LAST STAGE

A small boy crept into the darkened hut. The unglazed windows were roughly curtained with skins, but there was sufficient light from the open doorway to show him what he wanted. He tiptoed to a corner where an old travelling trunk lay under a pile of dirty clothes. He opened it very carefully, and after a little searching found the thing he sought. Then he gently closed it, and, with a look towards the bed in the other corner, he slipped out again into the warm October afternoon.

The woman on the bed stirred uneasily and suddenly became fully awake, after the way of those who are fluttering very near death. She was still young, and the little face among the coarse homespun blankets looked almost childish. Heavy masses of black hair lay on the pillow, and the depth of its darkness increased the pallor of her brow. But the cheeks were flushed, and the deep hazel eyes were burning with a slow fire.... For a week the milk-sick fever had raged furiously, and in the few hours free from delirium she had been racked with omnipresent pain and deadly sickness. Now those had gone, and she was drifting out to sea on a tide of utter weakness. Her husband, Tom Linkhorn, thought her mending, and was even now whistling, the first time for weeks, by the woodpile. But the woman knew that she was close to the great change, and so deep was her weariness that the knowledge remained an instinct rather than a thought. She was as passive as a dying animal. The cabin was built of logs, mortised into each other, triangular in shape, with a fireplace in one corner. Beside the fire stood a table made of a hewn log, on which lay some pewter dishes containing the remains of the last family meal. One or two three-legged stools made up the rest of the furniture, except for the trunk in the corner and the bed. This bed was Tom Linkhorn's pride, which he used to boast about to his friends, for he was a tolerable carpenter. It was made of plank stuck between the logs of the wall, and supported at the other end by crotched sticks. By way of a curtain top a hickory post had been sunk in the floor and bent over the bed, the end being fixed in the log wall. Tom meant to have a fine skin curtain fastened to it when winter came. The floor was of beaten earth, but there was a rough ceiling of smaller logs, with a trap in it which could be reached by pegs stuck the centre post. In that garret the children slept. Tom's building zeal had come to an end with the bed. Some day he meant to fit in a door and windows, but these luxuries could wait till he got his clearing in better order.

On a stool by the bed stood a wooden bowl containing gruel. The woman had not eaten for days, and the stuff had a thick scum on it. The place was very stuffy, for it was a hot and sickly autumn day and skins which darkened the window holes kept out the little freshness that was in the air. Beside the gruel was a tin pannikin of cold water which the boy Abe fetched every hour from the spring. She saw the water, but was too weak to reach it.

The shining doorway was blocked by a man's entrance. Tom Linkhorn was a little over middle height, with long muscular arms, and the corded neck sinews which tell of great strength. He had a shock of coarse black hair, grey eyes and a tired sallow face, as of one habitually overworked and underfed. His jaw was heavy, but loosely put together, so that he presented an air of weakness and irresolution. His lips were thick and pursed in a kind of weary good humour. He wore an old skin shirt and a pair of towlinen pants, which flapped about his bare brown ankles. A fine sawdust coated his hair and shoulders, for he had been working in the shed where he eked out his farming by making spinning wheels for his neighbours.

He came softly to the bedside and looked down at his wife. His face was gentle and puzzled.

"Reckon you're better, dearie," he said in a curious harsh toneless voice.

The sick woman moved her head feebly in the direction of the stool and he lifted the pannikin of water to her lips.

"Cold enough?" he asked, and his wife nodded. "Abe fetches it as reg'lar as a clock."

"Where's Abe?" she asked, and her voice for all its feebleness had a youthful music in it.

"I heerd him sayin' he was goin' down to the crick to cotch a fish. He reckoned you'd fancy a fish when you could eat a piece. He's a mighty thoughtful boy, our Abe. Then he was comin' to read to you. You'd like that, dearie?"

The sick woman made no sign. Her eyes were vacantly regarding the doorway.

"I've got to leave you now. I reckon I'll borrow the Dawneys' sorrel horse and ride into Gentryville. I've got the young hogs to sell, and I'll fetch back the corn-meal from Hickson's. Sally Hickson was just like you last fall, and I want to find out from Jim how she got her strength up."

He put a hand on her brow, and felt it cool.

"Glory! You're mendin' fast, Nancy gal. You'll be well in time to can the berries that the childern's picked." He fished from below the bed a pair of skin brogues and slipped them on his feet. "I'll be back before night."

"I want Abe," she moaned.

"I'll send him to you," he said as he went out

Left alone the woman lay still for a little in a stupor of weariness. Waves of that terrible lassitude, which is a positive anguish and not a mere absence of strength, flowed over her. The square of the doorway, which was directly before her eyes, began to take strange forms. It was filled with yellow sunlight, and a red glow beyond told of the sugar-maples at the edge of the clearing. Now it seemed to her unquiet sight to be a furnace. Outside the world was burning; she could feel the heat of it in the close cabin. For a second acute fear startled her weakness. It passed, her eyes cleared, and she saw the homely doorway as it was, and heard the gobble of a turkey in the forest.

The fright had awakened her mind and senses. For the first time she fully realised her condition. Life no longer moved steadily in her body; it flickered and wavered and would soon gutter out.... Her eyes marked every detail of the squalor around her, the unwashed dishes, the foul earthen floor, the rotting apple pile, the heap of rags which had been her only clothes. She was leaving the world, and this was all she had won from it. Sheer misery forced a sigh which seemed to rend her frail body, and her eyes filled with tears. She had been a dreamer, an adept at make-believe, but the poor coverings she had wrought for a dingy reality were now too threadbare to hide it.

And once she had been so rich in hope. She would make her husband a great man, and, when that was manifestly impossible without a rebirth of Tom Linkhorn, she would have a son who would wear a black coat like Lawyer Macneil and Colonel Hardin way back in Kentucky, and make fine speeches beginning "Fellow countrymen and gentlemen of this famous State." She had a passion for words, and sonorous phrases haunted her memory. She herself would have a silk gown and a bonnet with roses in it; once long ago she had been to Elizabethtown and seen just such a gown and bonnet.... Or Tom would be successful in this wild Indiana country and be, like Daniel Boone, the father of a new State, and have places and towns called for him, a Nancyville perhaps or a Linkhorn County. She knew about Daniel Boone, for her grandfather Hanks had been with him.... And there had been other dreams, older dreams, dating far back to the days when she was a little girl with eyes like a brown owl. Someone had told her fairy-tales about princesses and knights, strange beings which she never quite understood, but of which she made marvellous pictures in her head She had learned to read in order to follow up the doings of those queer bright folk, but she had never tracked them down again. But one book she had got called The Pilgrim's Progress, printed by missionaries in a far-away city called Philadelphia, which told of things as marvellous, and had pictures, too, one especially of a young man covered with tin, which she supposed was what they called armour. And there was another called The Arabian Nights, a close-printed thing difficult to read by the winter fire, full of wilder doings than any she could imagine for herself; but beautiful, too, and delicious to muse over, though Tom, when she read a chapter to him, had condemned it as a pack of lies.... Clearly there was a world somewhere, perhaps outside America altogether, far more wonderful than even the magnificence of Colonel Hardin. Once she had hoped to find it herself; then that her children should find it. And the end was this shack in the wilderness, a few acres of rotting crops, bitter starving winters, summers of fever, the deeps of poverty, a penniless futureless family, and for herself a coffin of green lumber and a yard or two of stony soil.

She saw everything now with the clear unrelenting eyes of childhood. The films she had woven for selfprotection were blown aside. She was dying, she had often wondered how she should feel when dying, humble and trustful, she had hoped, for she was religious after a fashion, and had dreamed herself into an affection for a kind fatherly God. But now all that had gone. She was bitter, like one defrauded. She had been promised something, and had struggled on in the assurance of it. And the result was nothing, nothing. Tragic tears filled her eyes. She had been so hungry, and there was to be no satisfying that hunger this side the grave or beyond it. She was going the same way as Betsy Sparrow, a death like a cow's, with nothing to show for life, nothing to leave. Betsy had been a poor crushed creature, and had looked for no more. But she was different. She had been promised something, something fine, she couldn't remember what, or who had promised it, but it had never been out of her mind.

There was the ring, too. No woman in Indiana had the like of that. An ugly thing, but very ancient and of pure gold. Once Tom had wanted to sell it when he was hard-pressed back at Nolin Creek, but she had fought for it like a tigress and scared the life out of Tom. Her grandfather had left it her because she was his favourite and it had been her grandmothers, and long ago had come from Europe. It was lucky, and could cure rheumatism if worn next the heart in a skin bag.... All her thoughts were suddenly set on the ring, her one poor shred of fortune. She wanted to feel it on her finger, and press its cool gold with the queer markings on her eyelids.

But Tom had gone away and she couldn't reach the trunk in the corner. Tears trickled down her cheeks and through the mist of them she saw that the boy Abe stood at the foot of the bed.

"Feelin' comfortabler?" he asked. He had a harsh untunable voice, his father's, but harsher, and he spoke the drawling dialect of the backwoods.

His figure stood in the light, so that the dying mother saw only its outline. He was a boy about nine years old, but growing too fast, so that he had lost the grace of childhood and was already lanky and ungainly. As he turned his face crosswise to the light he revealed a curiously rugged profile, a big nose springing sharply from the brow, a thick underhung lower lip, and the beginning of a promising Adam's apple. His stiff black hair fell round his great ears, which stood out like the handles of a pitcher. He was barefoot, and wore a pair of leather breeches and a ragged homespun shirt. Beyond doubt he was ugly.

He moved round to the right side of the bed where he was wholly in shadow.

"My lines is settin' nicely," he said. "I'll have a fish for your supper. And then I'm goin' to take dad's gun and fetch you a turkey. You could eat a slice of a fat turkey, I reckon."

The woman did not answer, for she was thinking. This uncouth boy was the son she had put her faith in. She loved him best of all things on earth, but for the moment she saw him in the hard light of disillusionment. A loutish backwoods child, like Dennis Hanks or Tom Sparrow or anybody else. He had been a comfort to her, for he had been quick to learn and had a strange womanish tenderness in his ways. But she was leaving him, and he would grow up like his father before him to a life of ceaseless toil with no daylight or honour in it.... She almost hated the sight of him, for he was the memorial of her failure.

The boy did not guess these thoughts. He pulled up a stool and sat very close to the bed, holding his mother's frail wrist in a sunburnt hand so big that it might have been that of a lad half-way through his teens. He had learned in the woods to be neat and precise in his ways, and his movements, for all his gawky look, were as soft as a panther's.

"Like me to tell you a story?" he asked. "What about Uncle Mord's tale of Dan'l Boone at the Blue Licks Battle?"

There was no response, so he tried again.

"Or read a piece? It was the Bible last time, but the words is mighty difficult. Besides you don't need it that much now. You're gettin' better.... Let's hear about the ol' Pilgrim."

He found a squat duodecimo in the trunk, and shifted the skin curtain from one of the window holes to get light to read by. His mother lay very still with her eyes shut, but he knew by her breathing that she was not asleep. He ranged through the book, stopping to study the crude pictures, and then started laboriously to read the adventures of Christian and Hopeful after leaving Vanity Fair, the mine of Demas, the plain called Ease, Castle Doubting, and the Delectable Mountains. He boggled over some of the words, but on the whole he read well, and his harsh voice dropped into a pleasant sing-song.

By and by he noticed that his mother was asleep. He took the tin pannikin and filled it with fresh water from the spring. Then he kissed the hand which lay on the blanket, looked about guiltily to see if anyone had seen him, for kisses were rare in that household and tiptoed out again.

The woman slept, but not wholly. The doorway, which was now filled with the deeper gold of the westering sun, was still in her vision. It had grown to a great square of light, and instead of being blocked in the foreground by the forest it seemed to give on an infinite distance. She had a sense not of looking out of a hut, but of looking from without into a great chamber. Peace descended on her which she had never known before in her feverish dreams, peace and a happy expectation.

She had not listened to Abe's reading, but some words of it had caught her ear. The phrase "delectable mountains" for one. She did not know what "delectable" meant, but it sounded good; and mountains, though she had never seen more of them than a far blue line, had always pleased her fancy. Now she seemed to be looking at them through that magical doorway.... The country was not like anything she remembered in the Kentucky bluegrass, still less like the shaggy woods of Indiana. The turf was short and very green, and the hills fell into gracious folds that promised homesteads in every nook of them. It was a "delectable" country, yes, that was the meaning of the word that had puzzled her.... She had seen the picture before in her head. She remembered one hot Sunday afternoon when she was a child hearing a Baptist preacher discoursing on a Psalm, something about the "little hills rejoicing." She had liked the words and made a picture in her mind. These were the little hills and they were joyful.

There was a white road running straight through them till it disappeared over a crest. That was right, of course. The road which the Pilgrims travelled.... And there, too, was a Pilgrim.

He was a long way off, but she could see him quite clearly. He was a boy, older than Abe, but about the same size, a somewhat forlorn figure, who seemed as if he had a great way to go and was oppressed by the knowledge of it. He had funny things on his legs and feet, which were not proper moccasins. Once he looked back, and she had a glimpse of fair hair. He could not be any of the Hanks or Linkhorn kin, for they were all dark.... But he had something on his left arm which she recognised, a thick ring of gold. It was her own ring, the ring she kept in the trunk and she smiled comfortably. She had wanted it a little while ago, and now there it was before her eyes. She had no anxiety about its safety, for somehow it belonged to that little boy as well as to her.

His figure moved fast and was soon out of sight round a turn of the hill. And with that the landscape framed in the doorway began to waver and dislimn. The road was still there, white and purposeful, but the environs were changing.... She was puzzled, but with a pleasant confusion. Her mind was not on the landscape, but on the people, for she was assured that others would soon appear on the enchanted stage.

He ran across the road, shouting with joy, a dog at his heels and a bow in his hand. Before he disappeared she marked the ring, this time on his finger.... He had scarcely gone ere another appeared on the road, a slim pale child, dressed in some stuff that gleamed like satin, and mounted on a pony.... The spectacle delighted her, for it brought her in mind of the princes she had been told of in fairytales. And there was the ring, worn over a saffron riding glove....

A sudden weakness made her swoon; and out of it she woke to a consciousness of the hut where she lay. She had thought she was dead and in heaven among fair children, and the waking made her long for her own child. Surely that was Abe in the doorway.... No, it was a taller and older lad, oddly dressed, but he had a look of Abe, something in his eyes. He was on the road too, and marching purposefully, and he had the ring. Even in her mortal frailty she had a quickening of the heart. These strange people had something to do with her, something to tell her, and that something was about her son....

There was a new boy in the picture. A dejected child who rubbed the ring on his small breeches and played with it, looking up now and then with a frightened start. The woman's heart ached for him, for she knew her own life-long malady. He was hungry for something which he had small hope of finding.... And then a wind seemed to blow out-of-doors and the world darkened down to evening. But her eyes pierced the gloaming easily, and she saw very plain the figure of a man.

He was sitting hunched up, with his chin in his hands, gazing into vacancy. Without surprise she recognised something in his face that was her own. He wore the kind of hunter's clothes that old folk had worn in her childhood, and a long gun lay across his knees. His air was sombre and wistful, and yet with a kind of noble content in it. He had Abe's puckered-up lips and Abe's steady sad eyes.... Into her memory came a verse of the Scriptures which had always fascinated her. "These all died in faith, not having received the promises, but having seen them afar off, and were persuaded of them, and embraced them, and confessed that they were strangers and pilgrims upon the earth."

She saw it all in a flash of enlightenment. These seekers throughout the ages had been looking for something and had not found it. But Abe, her son, was to find it. That was why she had been shown those pictures.

Once again she looked through the door into bright sunshine. It was a place that she knew beside the Ohio she remembered the tall poplar clump. She did not see the Jacksons' farm which stood south of the trees, but there was the Indian graveyard, which as a little girl she had been afraid to pass. Now it seemed to be fresh made, for painted vermilion wands stood about the mounds. On one of them was a gold trinket, tied by a loop of hide, rattled in the wind. It was her ring. The seeker lay buried there with the talisman above him.

She was awake now, oblivious of the swift sinking of her vital energy. She must have the ring, for it was the pledge of a great glory....

A breathless little girl flung herself into the cabin. It was Sophy Hanks, one of the many nieces who squattered like ducks about the settlement.

"Mammy!" she cried shrilly. "Mammy Linkorn!" She stammered with the excitement of the bearer of ill news. "Abe's lost your ring in the crick. He took it for a sinker to his lines, for Indian Jake telled him a piece of gold would cotch the grit fish. And a grit fish has cotched it. Abe's bin divn' and divn' and can't find it nohow. He reckons it's plumb lost. Ain't he a bad 'un, Mammy Linkhorn?"

It was some time before the dying woman understood. Then she began feebly to cry. For the moment her ring loomed large in her eyes: it was the earnest of the promise, and without it the promise might fail. She had not strength to speak or even to sob, and the tears trickled over her cheeks in dumb impotent misery.

She was roused by the culprit Abe. He stood beside her with his wet hair streaked into a fringe along his brow. The skin of his neck glistened wet in the opening of his shirt. His cheeks too glistened, but not with the water of the creek. He was crying bitterly.

He had no words of explanation or defence. His thick underlip stuck out and gave him the appeal of a penitent dog; the tears had furrowed paler channels down grimy cheeks; he was the very incarnation of uncouth misery.

But his mother saw none of these things.... On the instant he seemed to her transfigured. Something she saw in him of all the generations of pleading boys that had passed before her, something of the stern confidence of the man over whose grave the ring had fluttered. But more, far more. She was assured that the day of the seekers had passed and that the finder had come.... The young features were transformed into the lines of a man's strength. The eyes dreamed but also commanded, the loose mouth had the gold of wisdom and the steel of resolution. The promise had not failed her.... She had won everything from life, for she had given the world a master. Words seemed to speak themselves in her ear... "Bethink you of the blessedness. Every wife is like the Mother of God and has the hope of bearing a saviour of mankind."

She lay very still in her great joy. The boy in a fright sprang to her side, knocking over the stool with the pannikin of water. He knelt on the floor and hid his face in the bed-clothes. Her hand found his shaggy head.

Her voice was very faint now, but he heard it.

"Don't cry, little Abe," she said. "Don't you worry about the ring, dearie. It ain't needed no more."

Half an hour later, when the cabin door was dim with twilight, the hand which the boy held grew cold.

CHAPTER XIV. THE END OF THE ROAD

I

When Edward M. Stanton was associated at Cincinnati in 1857 with Abraham Lincoln in the great McCormick Reaper patent suit, it was commonly assumed that this was the first time the two men had met. Such was Lincoln's view, for his memory was apt to have blind patches in it. But in fact there had been a meeting fifteen years before, the recollection of which in Stanton's mind had been so overlaid by the accumulations of a busy life that it did not awake till after the President's death.

In the early fall of 1842 Stanton had occasion to visit Illinois. He was then twenty-five years of age, and had already attained the position of leading lawyer in his native town of Steubenville in Ohio and acted as reporter of the Supreme Court of that State. He was a solemn reserved young man, with a square fleshy face and a strong ill-tempered jaw. His tight lips curved downwards at the corners and, combined with his bold eyes, gave him an air of peculiar shrewdness and purpose. He did not forget that he came of good professional stock, New England on one side and Virginia on the other, and that he was college-bred, unlike the common backwoods attorney. Also he was resolved on a great career, with the White House at the end of it, and was ready to compel all whom he met to admit the justice of his ambition. The consciousness of uncommon talent and a shining future gave him a self-possession rare in a young man, and a complacence not unlike arrogance. His dress suited his pretensions, the soft rich broadcloth which tailors called doeskin, and linen of a fineness rare outside the eastern cities. He was not popular in Ohio, but he was respected for his sharp tongue, subtle brain, and intractable honesty.

His business finished, he had the task of filling up the evening, for he could not leave for home till the morrow. His host, Mr. George Curtin, was a little shy of his guest and longed profoundly to see the last of him. It was obvious that this alert lawyer regarded the Springfield folk as mossbacks, which might be well enough for St. Louis and Chicago, but was scarcely becoming in a man from Steubenville. Another kind of visitor he might have taken to a chickenfight, but one glance at Stanton barred that solution. So he compromised on Speed's store.

"There's one or two prominent citizens gathered there most nights," he explained. "Like as not we'll find Mr. Lincoln. I reckon you've heard of Abe Lincoln?"

Mr. Stanton had not. He denied the imputation as if he were annoyed.

"Well, we think a mighty lot of him round here. He's Judge Logan's law partner and considered one of the brightest in Illinois. He's been returned to the State Legislature two or three times, and he's a dandy on the stump. A hot Whig and none the worse of that, though I reckon them's not your politics.... We're kind of proud of him in Sangamon county. No, not a native. Rode into the town one day five years back from New Salem with all his belongings in a saddle-bag, and started business next morning in Joe Speed's back room.... He's good company, Abe, for you never heard a better man to tell a story. You'd die of laughing. Though I did hear he was a sad man just now along of being crossed in love, so I can't promise you he'll be up to his usual, if he's at Speed's to-night."

"I suppose the requirements for a western lawyer," said Mr. Stanton acidly, "are a gift of buffoonery and a reputation for gallantry." He was intensely bored, and had small desire to make the acquaintance of provincial celebrities.

Mr. Curtin was offended, but could think of no suitable retort, and as they were close on Speed's store he swallowed his wrath and led the way through alleys of piled merchandise to the big room where the stove was lighted.

It was a chilly fall night and the fire was welcome. Half a dozen men sat smoking round it, with rummers of reeking toddy at their elbows. They were ordinary citizens of the place, and they talked of the last horseraces. As the new-comers entered they were appealing to a figure perched on a high barrel to decide some point in dispute.

This figure climbed down from its perch, as they entered, with a sort of awkward courtesy. It was a very tall man, thin almost to emaciation, with long arms and big hands and feet. He had a lean, powerful-looking head, marred by ugly projecting ears and made shapeless by a mass of untidy black hair. The brow was broad and fine, and the dark eyes set deep under it; the nose, too, was good, but the chin and mouth were too small for the proportions of the face. The mouth, indeed, was so curiously puckered, and the lower lip so thick and prominent, as to give something of a comic effect. The skin was yellow, but stretched so firm and hard on the cheek bones that the sallowness did not look unhealthy. The man wore an old suit of blue jeans and his pantaloons did not meet his coarse unblacked shoes by six inches. His scraggy throat was adorned with a black neckerchief like a boot-lace.

"Abe," said Mr. Curtin, "I would like to make you known to my friend Mr. Stanton of Ohio."

The queer face broke into a pleasant smile, and the long man held out his hand.

"Glad to know you, Mr. Stanton," he said, and then seemed to be stricken with shyness. His wandering eye caught sight of a new patent churn which had just been added to Mr. Speed's stock. He took two steps to it and was presently deep in its mechanism. He turned it all ways, knelt beside it on the floor, took off the handle and examined it, while the rest of the company pressed Mr. Stanton to a seat by the fire.

"I heard Abe was out at Rochester helping entertain Ex-President Van Buren," said Mr. Curtin to the store-keeper.

"I reckon he was," said Speed. "He kept them roaring till morning. Judge Peck told me he allowed Mr. Van Buren would be stiff for a month with laughing at Abe's tales. It's curious that a man who don't use tobacco or whisky should be such mighty good company."

"I wish Abe'd keep it up," said another. "Most of the time now he goes about like a sick dog. What's come to him, Joe?"

Mr. Speed hushed his voice. "He's got his own troubles.... He's a deep-feeling man, and can't forget easily like you and me.... But things is better with him, and I kind of hope to see him wed by Thanksgiving Day.... Look at him with that churn. He's that inquisitive he can't keep his hands off no new thing."

But the long man had finished his inquiry and rejoined the group by the stove.

"I thought you were a lawyer, Mr. Lincoln," said Stanton, "but you seem to have the tastes of a mechanic."

The other grinned. "I've a fancy for any kind of instrument, for I was a surveyor in this county before I took to law."

"George Washington also was a surveyor."

"Also, but not LIKEWISE. I don't consider I was much of a hand with the compass and chains."

"It is the fashion in Illinois, I gather, for the law to be the last in a series of many pursuits, the pool where the driftwood from many streams comes to rest." Mr. Stanton spoke with the superior air of one who took his profession seriously and had been trained for it in the orthodox fashion.

"It was so in my case. I've kept a post-office, and I've had a store, and I've had a tavern, and I kept them so darned bad that I'm still paying off the debts I made in them." The long man made the confession with a comic simplicity.

"There's a deal to be said for the habit," said Speed. "Having followed other trades teaches a lawyer something about human nature. I reckon Abe wouldn't be the man he is if he had studied his books all his days."

"There is another side to that," said Mr. Stanton and his precise accents and well-modulated voice seemed foreign in that homely place. "You are also a politician, Mr. Lincoln?"

The other nodded. "Of a kind. I'm a strong Henry Clay man."

"Well, there I oppose you. I'm no Whig or lover of Whigs. But I'm a lover of the Constitution and the law of the country, and that Constitution and that country are approaching perilous times. There's explosive stuff about which is going to endanger the stability of the noble heritage we have received from our fathers, and if that heritage is to be saved it can only be by those who hold fast to its eternal principles. This land can only be saved by its lawyers, sir. But they must be lawyers profoundly read in the history and philosophy of their profession, and no catchpennny advocates with a glib tongue and an elastic conscience. The true lawyer must approach his task with reverence and high preparation; for as his calling is the noblest of human activities, so it is the most exacting."

The POINT-DEVICE young man spoke with a touch of the schoolmaster, but his audience, who had an inborn passion for fine words, were impressed. Lincoln sat squatted on his heels on a bit of sacking, staring into the open door of the stove.

"There's truth in that," he said slowly. His voice had not the mellow tones of the other's, being inclined to shrillness, but it gave the impression of great power waiting on release somewhere in his massive chest. "But I reckon it's only half the truth, for truth's like a dollar-piece, it's got two sides, and both are wanted to make it good currency. The law and the constitution are like a child's pants. They've got to be made wider and longer as the child grows so as to fit him. If they're kept too tight, he'll burst them; and if you're in a hurry and make them too big all at once, they'll trip him up."

"Agreed," said Stanton, "but the fashion and the fabric should be kept of the same good American pattern."

The long man ran a hand through his thatch of hair.

"There's only one fashion in pants, to make them comfortable. And some day that boy is going to grow so big you won't be able to make the old ones do and he'll have to get a new pair. If he's living on a farm he'll want the same kind of good working pants, but for all that they'll have to be new made."

Stanton laughed with some irritation

"I hate arguing in parables, for in the nature of things they can't be exact. That's a mistake you westerners make. The law must change in detail with changing conditions, but its principles cannot alter, and the respect for these principles is our only safeguard against relapse into savagery. Take slavery. There are fools in the east who would abolish it by act of Congress. For myself I do not love the system, but I love anarchy and injustice less, and if you abolish slavery you abolish every right of legal property, and that means chaos and barbarism. A free people such as ours cannot thus put the knife to their throat. If we were the serfs of a monarchy, accustomed to bow before the bidding of a king, it might be different, but a republic cannot do injustice to one section of its citizens without destroying itself."

Lincoln had not taken his eyes from the stove. He seemed to be seeing things in the fire, for he smiled to himself.

"Well," he drawled, "I reckon that some day we may have to find some sort of a king. The new pants have got to be made."

Mr. Stanton shrugged his shoulders, and the other, quick to detect annoyance, scrambled to his feet and stood looking down from his great height at his dapper antagonist. A kindly quizzical smile lit his homely face. "We'll quit arguing, Mr. Stanton, for I admit I'm afraid of you. You're some years younger than me, but I expect you would have me convinced on your side if we went on. And maybe I'd convince you too, and then we'd be like old Jim Fletcher at New Salem. You'll have heard about Jim. He had a mighty quarrel with his neighbour about a hog, Jim alleging it was one of his lot and the neighbour claiming it for his. Well, they argued and argued, and the upshot was that Jim convinced the neighbour that the hog was Jim's, and the neighbour convinced Jim that the hog was the neighbour's, and neither of them would touch that hog, and they were worse friends than ever."

Mr. Curtin rose and apologised to his companion. He had to see a man about a buggy and must leave Mr. Stanton to find his way back alone.

"Don't worry, George," said the long man. "I'm going round your way and I'll see your friend home." As Mr. Stanton professed himself ready for bed, the little party by the stove broke up. Lincoln fetched from a corner a dilapidated carpet-bag full of papers, and an old green umbrella, handle-less, tied with string about the middle, and having his name sewn inside in straggling letters cut out of white muslin. He and Stanton went out-of-doors into the raw autumn night.

The town lay very quiet in a thin fog made luminous by a full moon. The long man walked with his feet turned a little inwards, accommodating his gait to the shorter stride of his companion. Mr. Stanton, having recovered from his momentary annoyance, was curious about this odd member of his own profession. Was it possible that in the whirligig of time a future could lie before one so uncouth and rustical? A democracy was an unaccountable thing, and these rude westerners might have to be reckoned with.

"You are ambitious of a political career, Mr. Lincoln?" he asked.

The other looked down with his shy crooked smile, and the Ohio lawyer suddenly realised that the man had his own attractiveness.

"Why, no, sir. I shouldn't like to say I was ambitious. I've no call to be, for the Almighty hasn't blessed me with any special gifts. You're different. It would be a shame to you if you didn't look high, for you're a young man with all the world before you. I'm getting middle-aged and I haven't done anything to be proud of yet, and I reckon I won't get the chance, and if I did I couldn't take advantage of it. I'm pretty fond of the old country, and if she wants me, why, she's only got to say so and I'll do what she tells me. But I don't see any clear road I want to travel. ..."

He broke off suddenly, and Stanton, looking up at him, saw that his face had changed utterly. The patient humorous look had gone and it was like a tragic mask, drawn and strained with suffering. They were passing by a little town cemetery and, as if by some instinct, had halted.

The place looked strange and pitiful in the hazy moonlight. It was badly tended, and most of the headstones were only of painted wood, warped and buckled by the weather. But in the dimness the rows of crosses and slabs seemed to extend into the far distance, and the moon gave them a cold, eerie whiteness as if they lay in the light of another world. A great sigh came from Lincoln, and Stanton thought that he had never seen on mortal countenance such infinite sadness.

"Ambition!" he said. "How dare we talk of ambition, when this is the end of it? All these people, decent people, kind people, once full of joy and purpose, and now all forgotten! It is not the buried bodies I mind, it is the buried hearts....I wonder if it means peace...."

He stood there with head bowed and he seemed to be speaking to himself. Stanton caught a phrase or two and found it was verse, banal verses, which were there and then fixed in his fly-paper memory. "Tell me, my secret soul," it ran:

"Oh, tell me, Hope and Faith,
Is there no resting-place
From sorrow, sin, and death?
Is there no happy spot
Where mortals may be blessed,
Where grief may find a balm

And weariness a rest?"

The figure murmuring these lines seemed to be oblivious of his companion. He stood gazing under the moon, like a gaunt statue of melancholy. Stanton spoke to him but got no answer, and presently took his own road home. He had no taste for histrionic scenes. And as he went his way he meditated. Mad, beyond doubt. Not without power in him, but unbalanced, hysterical, alternating between buffoonery and these schoolgirl emotions. He reflected that if the American nation contained much stuff of this kind it might prove a difficult team to drive. He was thankful that he was going home next day to his orderly life.

II

Eighteen years have gone, and the lanky figure of Speed's store is revealed in new surroundings. In a big square room two men sat beside a table littered with the debris of pens, foolscap, and torn fragments of paper which marked the end of a Council. It was an evening at the beginning of April, and a fire burned in the big grate. One of the two sat at the table with his elbows on the mahogany, and his head supported by a hand. He was a man well on in middle life with a fine clean-cut face and the shapely mobile lips of the publicist and orator. It was the face of one habituated to platforms and assemblies, full of a certain self-conscious authority. But to-night its possessor seemed ill at ease. His cheeks were flushed and his eye distracted.

The other had drawn his chair to the fire, so that one side of him was lit by the late spring sun and one by the glow from the hearth. That figure we first saw in the Springfield store had altered little in the eighteen years. There was no grey in the coarse black hair, but the lines in the sallow face were deeper, and there were dark rings under the hollow eyes. The old suit of blue jeans had gone; and he wore now a frock-coat, obviously new, which was a little too full for his gaunt frame. His tie, as of old, was like a boot-lace. A new silk hat, with the nap badly ruffled, stood near on the top of a cabinet.

He smiled rather wearily. "We're pretty near through the appointments now, Mr. Secretary. It's a mean business, but I'm a minority President and I've got to move in zig-zags so long as I don't get off the pike. I reckon that honest statesmanship is just the employment of individual meannesses for the public good. Mr. Sumner wouldn't agree. He calls himself the slave of principles and says he owns no other master. Mr. Sumner's my notion of a bishop."

The other did not seem to be listening. "Are you still set on re-enforcing Fort Sumter?" he asked, his bent brows making a straight line above his eyes.

Lincoln nodded. He was searching in the inside pocket of his frock-coat, from which he extracted a bundle of papers. Seward saw what he was after, and his self-consciousness increased.

"You have read my letter?" he asked.

"I have," said Lincoln, fixing a pair of cheap spectacles on his nose. He had paid thirty-seven cents for them in Bloomington five years before. "A mighty fine letter. Full of horse sense."

"You agree with it?" asked the other eagerly.

"Why, no. I don't agree with it, but I admire it a lot and I admire its writer."

"Mr. President," said Seward solemnly, "on one point I am adamant. We cannot suffer the dispute to be about slavery. If we fight on that issue we shall have the Border States against us."

"I'm thinking all the time about the Border States. We've got to keep them. If there's going to be trouble I'd like to have the Almighty on my side, but I must have Kentucky."

"And yet you will go forward about Sumter, which is regarded by everyone as a slavery issue."

"The issue is as God has made it. You can't go past the bed-rock facts. I am the trustee for the whole property of the nation, of which Sumter is a piece, and if I give up one stick or stone to a rebellious demand I am an unfaithful steward. Surely, Mr. Secretary, if you want to make the issue union or disunion you can't give up Sumter without fatally prejudicing your case."

"It means war."

Lincoln looked again at the document in his hand. "It appears that you are thinking of war in any event. You want to pick a quarrel with France over Mexico and with Spain over St. Domingo, and unite the nation in a war against foreigners. I tell you honestly I don't like the proposal. It seems to me downright wicked.

"If the Lord sends us war, we have got to face it like men, but God forbid we should manufacture war, and use it as an escape from our domestic difficulties. You can't expect a blessing on that."

The Secretary of State flushed. "Have you considered the alternative, Mr. President?" he cried. "It is civil war, war between brothers in blood. So soon as the South fires a shot against Sumter the sword is unsheathed. You cannot go back then."

"I am fully aware of it. I haven't been sleeping much lately, and I've been casting up my accounts. It's a pretty weak balance sheet. I would like to tell you the main items, Mr. Secretary, so that you may see that I'm not walking this road blindfold."

The other pushed back his chair from the table with a gesture of despair. But he listened. Lincoln had risen and stood in front of the fire, his shoulders leaning on the mantelpiece, and his head against the lower part of the picture of George Washington.

"First," he said, "I'm a minority President, elected by a minority vote of the people of the United States. I wouldn't have got in if the Democrats hadn't been split. I haven't a majority in the Senate. Yet I've got to decide for the nation and make the nation follow me. Have I the people's confidence? I reckon I haven't yet. I haven't even got the confidence of the Republican party."

Seward made no answer. He clearly assented.

"Next, I haven't got much in the way of talents. I reckon Jeff Davis a far abler man than me. My friends tell me I haven't the presence and dignity for a President. My shaving-glass tells me I'm a common-looking fellow." He stopped and smiled. "But perhaps the Lord prefers common-looking people, and that's why He made so many of them.

"Next," he went on, "I've a heap of critics and a lot of enemies. Some good men say I've no experience in Government, and that's about true. Up in New England the papers are asking who is this political huckster, this county court advocate? Mr. Stanton says I'm an imbecile, and when he's cross calls me the original gorilla, and wonders why fools wander about in Africa when they could find the beast they are looking for in Washington. The pious everywhere don't like me, because I don't hold that national policy can be run on the lines of a church meeting. And the Radicals are looking for me with a gun, because I'm not prepared right here and now to abolish slavery. One of them calls me 'the slave hound of Illinois.' I'd like to meet that man, for I guess he must be a humorist."

Mr. Seward leaned forward and spoke earnestly. "Mr. President, no man values your great qualities more than I do or reprobates more heartily such vulgar libels. But it is true that you lack executive experience. I have been the Governor of the biggest State in the Union, and possess some knowledge of the task. It is all at your service. Will you not allow me to ease your burden?"

Lincoln smiled down kindly upon the other. "I thank you with all my heart. You have touched on that matter in your letter.... But, Mr. Secretary, in the inscrutable providence of God it is I who have been made President. I cannot shirk the duty. I look to my Cabinet, and notably to you for advice and loyal assistance, and I am confident that I shall get it. But in the end I and I only must decide."

Seward looked up at the grave face and said nothing. Lincoln went on:

"I have to make a decision which may bring war, civil war. I don't know anything about war, though I served a month or two in the Black Hawk campaign and yet, if war comes, I am the Commander-in-Chief of the Union. Who among us knows anything of the business? General Scott is an old man, and he doesn't just see eye to eye with me; for I'm told he talks about 'letting the wayward sisters go in peace.' Our army and navy's nothing much to boast of, and the South is far better prepared. You can't tell how our people will take war, for they're all pulling different ways just now. Blair says the whole North will spring to arms, but I guess they've first got to find the arms to spring to.... I was reviewing some militia the other day, and they looked a deal more like a Fourth of July procession than a battlefield. Yes, Mr. Secretary, if we have to fight, we've first got to make an army.

Remember, too, that it will be civil war, kin against kin, brother against brother."

"I remember. All war is devilish, but ours will be the most devilish that the world has ever known. It isn't only the feeding of fresh young boys to rebel batteries that grieves me, though God knows that's not a thing that bears thinking about. It's the bitterness and hate within the people. Will it ever die down, Mr. Secretary?"

Lincoln was very grave, and his face was set like a man in anguish. Seward, deeply moved, rose and stood beside him, laying a hand on his shoulder.

"And for what, Mr. President?" he cried. "That is the question I ask myself. We are faced by such a problem as no man ever before had to meet. If five and a half million white men deeply in earnest are resolved to secede, is there any power on earth that can prevent them? You may beat them in battle, but can you ever force them again inside the confines of the nation? Remember Chatham's saying: 'Conquer a free population of three million souls, the thing is impossible.' They stand on the rights of democracy, the right of self-government, the right to decide their own future."

Lincoln passed a hand over his brow. His face had suddenly became very worn and weary.

"I've been pondering a deal over the position of the South," he said. "I reckon I see their point of view, and I'll not deny there's sense in it. There's a truth in their doctrine of State rights, but they've got it out of focus. If I had been raised in South Carolina, loving the slave-system because I had grown up with it and thinking more of my State than of the American nation, maybe I'd have followed Jeff Davis. I'm not saying there's no honesty in the South, I'm not saying there's not truth on their side, but I do say that ours is the bigger truth and the better truth. I hold that a nation is too sacred a thing to tamper with, even for good reasons. Why, man, if you once grant the right of a minority to secede you make popular government foolish. I'm willing to fight to prevent democracy becoming a laughing-stock."

"It's a fine point to make war about," said the other.

"Most true points are fine points. There never was a dispute between mortals where both sides hadn't a bit of right. I admit that the margin is narrow, but if it's made of good rock it's sufficient to give us a foothold. We've got to settle once for all the question whether in a free Government the minority have a right to break up the Government whenever they choose. If we fail, then we must conclude that we've been all wrong from the start, and that the people need a tyrant, being incapable of governing themselves."

Seward wrung his hands. "If you put it that way I cannot confute you. But, oh, Mr. President, is there not some means of building a bridge? I cannot think that honest Southerners would force war on such a narrow issue.

"They wouldn't but for this slavery. It is that accursed system that obscures their reason. If they fight, the best of them will fight out of a mistaken loyalty to their State, but most will fight for the right to keep their slaves.... If you are to have bridges, you must have solid ground at both ends. I've heard a tale of some church members that wanted to build a bridge over a dangerous river. Brother Jones suggested one Myers, and Myers answered that, if necessary, he could build one to hell. This alarmed the church members, and Jones, to quiet them, said he believed his friend Myers was so good an architect that he could do it if he said he could, though he felt bound himself to express some doubt about the abutment on the infernal side."

A queer quizzical smile had relieved the gravity of the President's face. But Seward was in no mood for tales.

"Is there no other way?" he moaned, and his suave voice sounded cracked and harsh.

"There is no other way but to go forward. I've never been a man for cutting across lots when I could go round by the road, but if the roads are all shut we must take to open country. For it is altogether necessary to go forward."

Seward seemed to pull himself together. He took a turn down the room and then faced Lincoln.

"Mr. President," he said, "you do not know whether you have a majority behind you even in the North. You have no experience of government and none of war. The ablest men in your party are luke-warm or hostile towards you. You have no army to speak of, and will have to make everything from the beginning. You feel as I do about the horror of war, and above all the horrors of civil war. You do not know whether the people will support you. You grant that there is some justice in the contention of the South, and you claim for your own case only a balance of truth. You admit that to coerce the millions of the South back into the Union is a kind of task which has never been performed in the world before and one which the wise of all ages have pronounced impossible. And yet, for the sake of a narrow point, you are ready, if the need arises, to embark on a war which must be bloody and long, which must stir the deeps of bitterness, and which in all likelihood will achieve nothing. Are you entirely resolved?"

Lincoln's sad eyes rested on the other. "I am entirely resolved. I have been set here to decide for the people according to the best of my talents, and the Almighty has shown me no other road."

Seward held out his hand.

"Then, by God, you must be right. You are the bravest man in this land, sir, and I will follow you to the other side of perdition."

III

The time is two years later, a warm evening in early May. There had been no rain for a week in Washington, and the President, who had ridden in from his summer quarters in the Soldiers' Home, had his trousers grey with dust from the knees down. He had come round to the War Department, from which in these days he was never long absent, and found the

Secretary for War busy as usual at his high desk. There had been the shortest of greetings, and, while Lincoln turned over the last telegrams, Stanton wrote steadily.

Stanton had changed much since the night in the Springfield store. A square beard, streaked with grey, covered his chin, and his face had grown heavier. There were big pouches below the short-sighted eyes, and deep lines on each side of his short shaven upper lip. His skin had an unhealthy pallor, like that of one who works late and has little fresh air. The mouth, always obstinate, was now moulded into a settled grimness. The ploughs of war had made deep furrows on his soul.

Lincoln, too, had altered. He had got a stoop in his shoulders as if his back carried a burden. A beard had been suffered to grow in a ragged fringe about his jaw and cheeks, and there were silver threads in it. His whole face seemed to have been pinched and hammered together, so that it looked like a mask of pale bronze, a death mask, for it was hard to believe that blood ran below that dry tegument. But the chief change was in his eyes. They had lost the alertness they once possessed, and had become pits of brooding shade, infinitely kind, infinitely patient, infinitely melancholy.

Yet there was a sort of weary peace in the face, and there was still humour in the puckered mouth and even in the sad eyes. He looked less harassed than the Secretary for War. He drew a small book from his pocket, at which the other glanced malevolently.

"I give you fair warning, Mr. President," said Stanton. "If you've come here to read me the work of one of your tom-fool funny men, I'll fling it out of the window."

"This work is the Bible," said Lincoln, with the artlessness of a mischievous child. "I looked in to ask how the draft was progressing."

"It starts in Rhode Island on July 7, and till it starts I can say nothing. We've had warning that there will be fierce opposition in New York. It may mean that we have a second civil war on our hands. And of one thing I am certain, it will cost you your re-election."

The President did not seem perturbed. "In this war we've got to take one step at a time," he said. "Our job is to save the country, and to do that we've got to win battles. But you can't win battles without armies, and if men won't enlist of their own will they've got to be compelled. What use is a second term to me if I have no country.... You're not weakening on the policy of the draft, Mr. Stanton?"

The War Minister shrugged his shoulders. "No. In March it seemed inevitable. I still think it is essential, but I am forced to admit the possibility that it may be a rank failure. It is the boldest step you have taken, Mr. President. Have you ever regretted it?"

Lincoln shook his head. "It don't do to start regretting. This war is managed by the Almighty, and if it's his purpose that we should win He will show us how. I regard our fallible reasoning and desperate conclusions as part of His way of achieving His purpose. But about that draft.

I'll answer you in the words of a young Quaker woman who against the rules had married a military man. The elders asked her if she was sorry, and she replied that she couldn't truly say that she was sorry, but that she could say she wouldn't do it again. I was for the draft, and I was for the war, to prevent democracy making itself foolish."

"You'll never succeed in that," said Stanton gravely.

"If Congress is democracy, there can't be a more foolish gathering outside a monkey-house."

The President grinned broadly. He was humming the air of a nigger song, "The Blue-tailed Fly," which Lamon had taught him.

"That reminds me of Artemus Ward. He observes that at the last election he voted for Henry Clay. It's true, he says, that Henry was dead, but since all the politicians that he knew were fifteenth-rate he preferred to vote for a first-class corpse."

Stanton moved impatiently. He hated the President's pocket humorists and had small patience with his tales. "Was ever a great war fought," he cried, "with such a camp-following as our Congressmen?"

Lincoln looked comically surprised.

"You're too harsh, Mr. Stanton. I admit there are one or two rascals who'd be better hanged. But the trouble is that most of them are too high-principled. They are that set on liberty that they won't take the trouble to safeguard it. They would rather lose the war than give up their little notions. I've a great regard for principles, but I have no use for them when they get so high that they become foolishness."

"Every idle pedant thinks he knows better how to fight a war than the men who are labouring sixteen hours a day at it," said Stanton bitterly.

"They want to hurry things quicker than the Almighty means them to go. I don't altogether blame them either, for I'm mortally impatient myself. But it's no good thinking that saying a thing should be so will make it so. We're not the Creator of this universe. You've got to judge results according to your instruments. Horace Greeley is always telling me what I should do, but Horace omits to explain how I am to find the means. You can't properly manure a fifty-acre patch with only a bad smell."

Lincoln ran his finger over the leaves of the small Bible he had taken from his pocket. "Seems to me Moses had the same difficulties to contend with. Read the sixteenth chapter of the book of Numbers at your leisure, Mr. Secretary. It's mighty pertinent to our situation. The people have been a deal kinder to me than I deserve and I've got more cause for thankfulness than complaint. But sometimes I get just a little out of patience with our critics. I want to say to them as Moses said to Korah, Dathan, and Abiram, 'Ye take too much upon you, ye sons of Levi!'"

Lincoln's speech had broadened into something like the dialect of his boyhood. Stanton finished the paper on which he had been engaged and stepped aside from his desk. His face was heavily preoccupied and he kept an eye always on the door leading to his private secretary's room.

"At this moment," he said, "Hooker is engaged with Lee." He put a finger on a map which was stretched on a frame behind him. "There! On the Rappahannock, where it is joined by the Rapidan.... Near the hamlet of Chancellorsville.... Battle was joined two days ago, and so far it has been indecisive. Tonight we should know the result. That was the news you came here to-night about, Mr. President?"

Lincoln nodded. "I am desperately anxious. I needn't conceal that from you, Mr. Stanton."

"So am I. I wish to God I had more confidence in General Hooker. I never liked that appointment, Mr. President. I should have preferred Meade or Reynolds. Hooker is a blustering thick-headed fellow, good enough, maybe, for a division or even a corps, but not for an army."

"I visited him three weeks back," said Lincoln, "and I'm bound to say he has marvellously pulled round the Army of the Potomac. There's a new spirit in their ranks. You're unjust to Joe Hooker, Mr. Stanton. He's a fine organiser, and he'll fight, he's eager to fight, which McClellan and Burnside never were."

"But what on earth is the good of being willing to fight if you're going to lose? He hasn't the brains to command. And he's opposed by Lee and Jackson. Do you realise the surpassing ability of those two men? We have no generals fit to hold a candle to them."

"We've a bigger and a better army. I'm not going to be depressed, Mr. Stanton. Joe has two men to every one of Lee's, he's safe over the Rappahannock, and I reckon he will make a road to Richmond. I've seen his troops, and they are fairly bursting to get at the enemy. I insist on being hopeful. What's the last news from the Mississippi?"

"Nothing new. Grant has got to Port Gibson and has his base at Grand Gulf. He now proposes to cut loose and make for Vicksburg. So far he has done well, but the risk is terrific. Still, I am inclined to think you were right about that man. He has capacity."

"Grant stops still and saws wood," said Lincoln "He don't talk a great deal, but he fights. I can't help feeling hopeful to-night, for it seems to me we have the enemy in a fix. You've heard me talk of the shrinking quadrilateral, which is the rebel States, as I see the proposition."

"Often," said the other drily.

"I never could get McClellan rightly to understand it. I look on the Confederacy as a quadrilateral of which at present we hold two sides, the east and the south, the salt-water sides. The north side is Virginia, the west side the line of the Mississippi. If Grant and Farragut between them can win the control of the Father of Waters, we've got the west side. Then it's the business of the Armies on the Mississippi to press east and the Army of the Potomac to press south. It may take a time, but if we keep a stiff upper lip we're bound to have the rebels whipped. I reckon they're whipped already in spite of Lee. I've heard of a turtle that an old nigger man decapitated. Next day he was amusing himself poking sticks at it and the turtle was snapping back. His master comes along and says to him, 'Why, Pomp, I thought that turtle was dead.' 'Well, he am dead, massa,' says Pompey, 'but the critter don't know enough ter be sensible ob it.' I reckon the Confederacy's dead, but Jeff Davis don't know enough to be sensible of it."

A young man in uniform came hurriedly through the private secretary's door and handed the Secretary for War a telegram. He stood at attention, and the President observed that his face was pale. Stanton read the message, but gave no sign of its contents. He turned to the map behind him and traced a line on it with his forefinger.

"Any more news?" he asked the messenger.

"Nothing official, sir," was the answer. "But there is a report that General Jackson has been killed in the moment of victory."

The officer withdrew and Stanton turned to the President. Lincoln's face was terrible in its strain, for the words "in the moment of victory" had rung the knell of his hopes.

When Stanton spoke his voice was controlled and level. "Unlike your turtle," he said, "the Confederacy is suddenly and terribly alive. Lee has whipped Hooker to blazes. We have lost more than fifteen thousand men. To-day we are back on the north side of the Rappahannock."

Lincoln was on his feet and for a moment the bronze mask of his face was distorted by suffering.

"My God!" he cried. "What will the country say? What will the country say?"

"It matters little what the country says. The point is what will the country suffer. In a fortnight Lee will be in Maryland and Pennsylvania. Your quadrilateral will not shrink, it will extend. In a month we shall be fighting to hold Washington and Baltimore, aye, and Philadelphia."

The bitterness of the words seemed to calm Lincoln. He was walking up and down the floor, with his hands clasped behind his back, and his expression was once again one of patient humility.

"I take all the blame," he said. "You have done nobly, Mr. Stanton, and all the mistakes are mine. I reckon I am about the poorest effigy of a War President that ever cursed an unhappy country."

The other did not reply. He was an honest man who did not deal in smooth phrases.

"I'd resign to-morrow," Lincoln went on. "No railsplitter ever laid down his axe at the end of a hard day so gladly as I would lay down my office. But I've got to be sure first that my successor will keep faith with this nation. I've got to find a man who will keep the right course."

"Which is?" Stanton asked.

"To fight it out to the very end. To the last drop of blood and the last cent. There can be no going back. If I surrendered my post to any successor, though he were an archangel from heaven, who would weaken on that great purpose, I should deserve to be execrated as the betrayer of my country."

Into Stanton's sour face there came a sudden gleam which made it almost beautiful.

"Mr. President," he said, "I have often differed from you. I have used great freedom in criticism of your acts, and I take leave to think that I have been generally in the right. You know that I am no flatterer. But I tell you, sir, from my inmost heart that you are the only man to lead the people, because you are the only man whose courage never fails. God knows how you manage it. I am of the bull-dog type and hold on because I do not know how to let go. Most of my work I do in utter hopelessness. But you, sir, you never come within a mile of despair. The blacker the clouds get the more confident you are that there is sunlight behind them. I carp and cavil at you, but I also take off my hat to you, for you are by far the greatest of us."

Lincoln's face broke into a slow smile, which made the eyes seem curiously child-like.

"I thank you, my old friend," he said. "I don't admit I have your courage, for I haven't half of it. But if a man feels that he is only a pipe for Omnipotence to sound through, he is not so apt to worry. Besides, these last weeks God has been very good to me and I've been given a kind of assurance. I know the country will grumble a bit about my ways of doing things, but will follow me in the end. I know that we shall win a clean victory. Jordan has been a hard road to travel, but I feel that in spite of all our frailties we'll be dumped on the right side of that stream. After that..."

"After that," said Stanton, with something like enthusiasm in his voice, "you'll be the first President of a truly united America, with a power and prestige the greatest since Washington."

Lincoln's gaze had left the other's face and was fixed on the blue dusk now gathering in the window.

"I don't know about that," he said. "When the war's over, I think I'll go home."

IV

Two years passed and once again it was spring in Washington, about half-past ten of the evening of the 14th of April, Good Friday, the first Eastertide of peace. The streets had been illuminated for victory, and the gas jets were still blazing, while a young moon, climbing the sky, was dimming their murky yellow with its cold pure light. Tenth Street was packed from end to end by a silent mob. As a sponge cleans a slate, so exhilaration had been wiped off their souls. On the porch of Ford's Theatre some gaudy posters advertised Tom Taylor's comedy, Our American Cousin, and the steps were littered with paper and orange peel and torn fragments of women's clothes, for the exit of the audience had been hasty. Lights still blazed in the building, for there was nobody to put them out. In front on the side-walk was a cordon of soldiers.

Stanton elbowed his way through the throng to the little house, Mr. Peterson's, across the street. The messenger from the War Department had poured wild news into his ear, wholesale murder, everybody, the President, Seward, Grant. Incredulous he had hurried forth and the sight of that huge still crowd woke fear in him. The guards at Mr. Peterson's door recognised him and he was admitted. As he crossed the threshold he saw ominous dark stains.

A kitchen candle burned below the hat-rack in the narrow hall, and showed further stains on the oilcloth. From a room on the left hand came the sound of women weeping.

The door at the end of the passage was ajar. It opened on a bare little place, once perhaps the surgery of some doctor in small practice, but now a bedroom. A door gave at the farther side on a tiny verandah, and this and the one window were wide open. An oil lamp stood on a table by the bed and revealed a crowd of people. A man lay on the camp-bed, lying aslant for he was too long for it. A sheet covered his lower limbs, but his breast and shoulders had been bared. The head was nearest to the entrance, propped on an outjutting bolster.

A man was leaving whom Stanton recognised as Dr. Stone, the Lincoln family physician. The doctor answered his unspoken question. "Dying," he said. "Through the brain. The bullet is now below the left eye. He may live for a few hours, scarcely the night."

Stanton moved to the foot of the bed like one in a dream. He saw that Barnes, the Surgeon-General, sat on a deal chair on the left side, holding the dying man's hand. Dr. Gurley, the minister, sat beside the bed. He noted Sumner and Welles and General Halleck and Governor Dennison, and back in the gloom the young Robert Lincoln. But he observed them only as he would have observed figures in a picture. They were but shadows; the living man was he who was struggling on the bed with death.

Lincoln's great arms and chest were naked, and Stanton, who had thought of him as meagre and shrunken, was amazed at their sinewy strength. He remembered that he had once heard of him as a village Hercules. The President was unconscious, but some tortured nerve made him moan like an animal in pain. It was a strange sound to hear from one who had been wont to suffer with tight lips. To Stanton it heightened the spectral unreality of the scene. He seemed to be looking at a death in a stage tragedy.

The trivial voice of Welles broke the silence. He had to give voice to the emotion which choked him.

"His dream has come true," he said, "the dream he told us about at the Cabinet this morning. His ship is nearing the dark shore. He thought it signified good news from Sherman."

Stanton did not reply. To save his life he could not have uttered a word.

Then Gurley, the minister, spoke, very gently, for he was a simple man sorely moved.

"He has looked so tired for so long. He will have rest now, the deep rest of the people of God.... He has died for us all.... To-day nineteen hundred years ago the Son of Man gave His life for the world.... The President has followed in his Master's steps."

Sumner was repeating softly to himself, like a litany, that sentence from the second Inaugural, "With malice toward none, with charity for all."

But Stanton was in no mood for words. He was looking at the figure on the bed, the great chest heaving with the laboured but regular breath, and living again the years of colleagueship and conflict. He had been Loyal to him: yes, thank God! he had been loyal. He had quarrelled, thwarted, criticised, but he had never failed him in a crisis. He had held up his hands as Aaron and Hur held up the hands of Moses....

The Secretary for War was not in the habit of underrating his own talents and achievements. But in that moment they seemed less than nothing. Humility shook him like a passion. Till his dying day his one boast must be that he had served that figure on the camp-bed. It had been his high fortune to have his lot cast in the vicinity of supreme genius. With awe he realised that he was looking upon the passing of the very great.... There had never been such a man. There could never be such an one again. So patient and enduring, so wise in all great matters, so potent to inspire a multitude, so secure in his own soul.... Fools would chatter about his being a son of the people and his career a triumph of the average man. Average! Great God, he was a ruler of princes, a master, a compeller of men.... He could imagine what noble nonsense Sumner would talk.... He looked with disfavor at the classic face of the Bostonian.

But Sumner for once seemed to share his feelings. He, too, was looking with reverent eyes towards the bed, and as he caught Stanton's gaze he whispered words which the Secretary for War did not condemn: "The beauty of Israel is slain upon thy high places."

The night hours crawled on with an intolerable slowness. Some of the watchers sat, but Stanton remained rigid at the bed-foot. He had not been well of late and had been ordered a long rest by his doctor, but he was not conscious of fatigue. He would not have left his post for a king's ransom, for he felt himself communing with the dying, sharing the last stage in his journey as he had shared all the rough marches. His proud spirit found a certain solace in the abasement of its humbleness.

A little before six the morning light began to pale the lamps. The window showed a square of grey cloudy sky, and outside on the porch there was a drip of rain. The faces revealed by the cold dawn were as haggard and yellow as that of the dying man. Wafts of the outer air began to freshen the stuffiness of the little room.

The city was waking up. There came the sound of far-away carts and horses, and a boy in the lane behind the house began to whistle, and then to sing. "When I was young," he sang -

"When I was young I used to wait
At Magea'n table 'n' hand de plate
An' pais de bottie when he was dry,
An' brush away de blue-tailed fly."

"It's his song," Stanton said to himself, and with the air came a rush of strange feelings. He remembered a thousand things, which before had been only a background of which he had been scarcely conscious. The constant kindliness, the gentle healing sympathy, the homely humour which he once thought had irritated but which he now knew had soothed him.... This man had been twined round the roots of every heart. All night he had been in an ecstasy of admiration, but now that was forgotten in a yearning love. The President had been part of his being, closer to him than wife or child. The boy sang -

"But I can't forget, until I die
Ole Massa an' de blue-tailed fly."

Stanton's eyes filled with hot tears. He had not wept since his daughter died.

The breathing from the bed was growing faint. Suddenly the Surgeon-General held up his hand. He felt the heart and shook his head. "Fetch your mother," he said to Robert Lincoln. The minister had dropped on his knees by the bedside and was praying.

"The President is dead," said the Surgeon-General, and at the words it seemed that every head in the room was bowed on the breast.

Stanton took a step forward with a strange appealing motion of the arms. It was noted by more than one that his pale face was transfigured.

"Yesterday he was America's," he cried. "Our very own. Now he is all the world's.... Now he belongs to the ages."

EPILOGUE

Mr. Francis Hamilton, an honorary attache of the British Embassy, stood on the steps of the Capitol watching the procession which bore the President's body from the White House to lie in state in the great Rotunda. He was a young man of some thirty summers, who after a distinguished Oxford career was preparing himself with a certain solemnity for the House of Commons. He sought to be an authority on Foreign affairs, and with this aim was making a tour among the legations. Two years before he had come to Washington, intending to remain for six months, and somewhat to his own surprise had stayed on, declining to follow his kinsman Lord Lyons to Constantinople. Himself a staunch follower of Mr. Disraeli, and an abhorrer of Whiggery in all its forms, he yet found in America's struggle that which appealed both to his brain and his heart. He was a believer, he told himself, in the Great State and an opponent of parochialism; so, unlike most of his friends at home, his sympathies were engaged for the Union. Moreover he seemed to detect in the protagonists a Roman simplicity pleasing to a good classic.

Mr. Hamilton was sombrely but fashionably dressed and wore a gold eyeglass on a black ribbon, because he fancied that a monocle adroitly used was a formidable weapon in debate. He had neat small sidewhiskers, and a pleasant observant eye. With him were young Major Endicott from Boston and the eminent Mr. Russell Lowell, who, as Longfellow's successor in the Smith Professorship and one of the editors of The North American Review, was a great figure in cultivated circles. Both were acquaintances made by Mr. Hamilton on a recent visit to Harvard. He found it agreeable to have a few friends with whom he could have scholarly talk.

The three watched the procession winding through the mourning streets. Every house was draped in funeral black, the passing bell tolled from every church, and the minute-guns boomed at the City Hall and on Capitol Hill. Mr. Hamilton regarded the cortege at first with a critical eye. The events of the past week had wrought in him a great expectation, which he feared would be disappointed. It needed a long tradition to do fitting honour to the man who had gone. Had America such a tradition? he asked himself.... The coloured troops marching at the head of the line pleased him. That was a happy thought. He liked, too, the business-like cavalry and infantry, and the battered field-pieces.... He saw his Chief among the foreign Ministers, bearing a face of portentous solemnity.... But he liked best the Illinois and Kentucky delegates; he thought the dead President would have liked them too.

Major Endicott was pointing out the chief figures. "There's Grant... and Stanton, looking more cantankerous than ever. They say he's brokenhearted." But Mr. Hamilton had no eye for celebrities. He was thinking rather of those plain mourners from the west, and of the poorest house in Washington decked with black. This is a true national sorrow, he thought. He had been brought up as a boy from Eton to see Wellington's funeral, and the sight had not impressed him like this. For the recent months had awakened odd emotions in his orderly and somewhat cynical soul. He had discovered a hero.

The three bared their heads as the long line filed by. Mr. Lowell said nothing. Now and then he pulled at his moustaches as if to hide some emotion which clamoured for expression. The mourners passed into the Capitol, while the bells still tolled and the guns boomed. The cavalry escort formed up on guard; from below came the sound of sharp commands.

Mr. Hamilton was shaken out of the admirable detachment which he had cultivated. He wanted to sit down and sob like a child. Some brightness had died in the air, some great thing had gone forever from the world and left it empty. He found himself regarding the brilliant career which he had planned for himself with a sudden disfavour. It was only second-rate after all, that glittering old world of courts and legislatures and embassies. For a moment he had had a glimpse of the firstrate, and it had shivered his pretty palaces. He wanted now something which he did not think he would find again.

The three turned to leave, and at last Mr. Lowell spoke.

"There goes," he said, "the first American!"

Mr. Hamilton heard the words as he was brushing delicately with his sleeve a slight berufflement of his silk hat.

"I dare say you are right, Professor," he said. "But I think it is also the last of the Kings."

John Buchan – A Short Biography

The Scottish novelist John Buchan's full list of titles bespeaks a remarkable career as a Unionist politician, a historian and a Governor General. He was born John Buchan on the 26th August 1875 and would go on to add 1st Baron Tweedsmuir PC GCMG GCVO CH to his name. His father, also John, was a minister in the Free Church of Scotland who lived in Perth with his wife Helen Jane.

Though Buchan was born in Perth he was raised in Kirkcaldy, Fife, spending summers in Broughton in the Scottish Borders with his grandparents. He was enchanted by the geographical and natural beauty of the area and quickly became a keen walker, finding it the most effective way of exploring and immersing himself in the scenery. The value of this youthful education in nature becomes apparent in his writing; some novels are set there, all are written with a keen eye for natural detail and even some significant characters' names derive from local place names, notably Sir Edward Leithen whose surname is taken from Leithen Water, a River Tweed tributary.

Buchan studied at Hutchesons' Grammar School in Glasgow until he was seventeen, when he won a scholarship to the University of Glasgow to study classics. While there he began to write poetry and enjoyed success as a published author. In 1895 he took a junior Hulme scholarship and transferred to Brasenose College in Oxford to study *Literae Humaniores*, or 'the Classics'. His first work was published in 1896; the novel *Sir Quixote of the Moors* and the non-fiction *Scholar-Gipsies*. From now on he published work at a relatively steady rate, consistently producing both novels and non-fiction work including biographies, historical papers and political analysis and propaganda. At Brasenose he became friends with the Anglo-French writer and historian Hilaire Belloc, the barrister Raymond Asquith, and the diplomat and traveller Aubrey Herbert. In 1897 Buchan won the Stanhope Essay Prize, an undergraduate history prize, and in 1898 the Newdigate Prize for poetry. Also in 1898 he was elected president of the Oxford Union and *John Burnet of Barns*, his second novel, was published. In 1900, at the time of his graduation from Oxford, he sat for his first portrait by the young Sholto Johnstone Douglas.

After his graduation from Oxford Buchan moved towards diplomacy, becoming Alfred Milner's private secretary. At that time Milner was the High Commissioner for Southern Africa, Governor of Cape Colony, and the colonial administrator of Transvaal and the Orange Free State. Buchan became one of several Britons working in the South African Civil Service under Lord Milner who would attain their own public prominence built on their experience working under Milner, and this group and the South African Civil Service itself became known as 'Milner's Kindergarten' thanks to its incubatory nature. He found equal inspiration in the South African landscape as he had in the Scottish Borders, and the area would become another setting for much of his future work. He resumed this writing on his return to London, establishing a partnership with Thomas Nelson and Son publishing house and taking on an editorial role with *The Spectator*. During this time he had read law and was called to the bar in 1901, though he never actually practiced. For the next few years he published fewer books, much of his time being taken up by his responsibilities at *The Spectator* and as a partner.

On the 15th of July 1907 Buchan married Susan Charlotte Grosvenor. Her father was Norman Grosvenor and she was the cousin of the Duke of Westminster. In 1910 Buchan wrote *Prester John* which was the first of a series of adventure novels which he set in South Africa having taken inspiration from his time in the Civil Service there. The novel deals with the social and political ramifications of a fictional Zulu uprising through an account of the adventures of its protagonist David Crawfurd. Buchan's Imperial and Commonwealth support is clear throughout the novel, as is his intimate knowledge of South African landscape and customs. The novel remains in print thanks to its delicate treatment of the issue of cultural clash and ideas of imperialism. The couple's first child Alice was born the same year.

In 1911 Buchan entered the political arena running as a Unionist candidate in a constituency in the Scottish Borders. Principle among his concerns were the support of free trade, women's suffrage, national insurance, and a reduction in the power of the House of Lords. He opposed the "class hatred" of Liberals such as future Prime Minister David Lloyd George, and disagreed with the Liberal party's welfare reforms. The couple's second child and first son, John Norman Stuart Buchan, was born on the 25th November 1911. He would succeed Buchan as Lord Tweedsmuir, and was once described as a "brilliant fisherman and naturalist, a gallant soldier and fine writer of English, an explorer, colonial administrator and man of business." The outbreak of the First World War saw Buchan writing for the War Propaganda Bureau and as a *Times* correspondent in France. He was able to continue his writing and, in 1915, published *The Thirty-Nine Steps*, his most famous book. It is the first appearance of Richard Hannay, a character he based on his friend Edmund Ironside whom he had known in South Africa. It was first serialised in *Blackwood's Magazine* and published the following year by William Blackwood and Sons in Edinburgh. The second novel, *Greemantle*, was published in 1916. William Buchan was born on the 10th January 1916. He succeeded his brother as Lord Tweedsmuir following John Buchan 2nd Baron's death. He was himself an accomplished writer.

In 1916 Buchan enlisted in the British Army, taking a commission in the Intelligence Corps as second lieutenant. His responsibilities included writing speeches for Sir Douglas Haig. His talent was quickly recognised and in 1917 he was appointed Director of Information under Lord Beaverbrook. Buchan once called it "the toughest job [he] ever took on". Despite the difficulty of this role, alongside it he assisted in the publication of a magazine detailing the history of the war. It was overseen by Charles Masterman and later published in a 24 volume edition, entitled *Nelson's History of the War*. One of the main challenges was the need to be unbiased and critical where appropriate of the conduct of the British Army and its leaders, owing to his close relationships with several of its key figures. His fourth child, Alistair Francis, was born on the 9th September 1918, and would go on to become a respected writer of defence studies.

After the war was over Buchan continued his novel writing and began to focus attention on his historical studies. He lived in Elsfield and by 1925 had become a trustee of the National Library of Scotland and President of the Scottish Historical Society. In 1927 Buchan became the Unionist Party Member of Parliament for the Combined Scottish Universities. In a speech to Parliament he said "I believe every Scotsman should be a Scottish nationalist. If it could be proved that a Scottish parliament were desirable... Scotsmen should support it." His speeches and writing on the issue of Scottish independence and their place within the Empire has found a new relevance in the twenty-first century thanks to its pertinence to the issue of Scottish Independence and the question of its European interests. Moreover, in that same speech (and in reference to the high emigration from Scotland after the Scottish Great Depression), Buchan remarked that "we do not want to be like the Greeks, powerful and prosperous wherever we settle, but with a dead Greece behind us". Again, his political considerations are reflected in the contemporary political climate of the twenty-first century, with a Greece crippled by financial crisis.

Over the course of the next few years Buchan continued to accomplish himself politically and as a cultural commentator and figurehead. He was an elder of St. Columba's Church in London, of the Oxford Presbyterian Parish, he became King George V's Lord High Commissioner to the General Assembly of the Church of Scotland, an ally of the Zionist

Palestine All Party Parliamentary Group and on the 1st January 1932 was inducted into the Order of the Companions of Honour. Throughout this time he continued to write, both fiction and non-, continuing his successful Hannay novels. In 1935 Alfred Hitchcock released his adaptation of *The Thirty-Nine Steps*, though the story was heavily altered. Buchan had little involvement in the making of the film, though his reaction to it was positive. He was appointed to the Order of St. Michael and St. George on the 23rd of May that year, and on the 1st of June became 1st Baron Tweedsmuir of Elsfield in the County of Oxford. This peerage came from Buchan's destination as Governor General in Canada; the Canadian Prime Minister, Richard Bennett, consulted William Lyon Mackenzie King, the Leader of His Majesty's Loyal Opposition, who recommended Buchan to serve as viceroy; though George V agreed with Buchan as a candidate, he insisted that he be represented by a peer. Mackenzie King had entertained Buchan and his wife at his estate, Kingsmere, ten years previously, and at that time Mackenzie King had put Buchan forward to George V for consideration for the governor generalcy, stating at the time that "I know now man I would rather have as a friend, a beautiful, noble soul, kindly and generous in though and word and act, informed as few men in this world have ever been, modest, humble, true, man after God's own heart". Buchan had been reluctant to take the post following correspondence with the Lord Byng of Vimy in which Byng wrote disparagingly of Mackenzie King.

On the 10th of August 1935 the Canadian Prime Minister's office announced the King's approval of Buchan as the vice regal representative by commission under the royal sign-manual and signet. Buchan left for Canada shortly thereafter and was sworn in on the 2nd of November 1935 in the Quebec parliament buildings. In an unprecedented move he resolved to travel all over Canada, including the Arctic regions, in order that he might gain a better picture of the country. He said "a Governor General is in a unique position for it is his duty to know the whole of Canada ad all the various types of her people". Having already enjoyed his explorations of the Scottish Borders as a boy, and South Africa as a young man, he was well suited to this new exploratory undertaking. Having crossed the length and breadth of the country, he saw the cultural shift between areas and their common ground, and was able to bring about a clear national Canadian identity which helped rally the people during the Great Depression. In response to challenges for imperialists angry at his statement that "a Canadian's first loyalty is not to the British Commonwealth of Nations, but to Canada and Canada's King", he said "the strongest nations are those that are made up of different racial elements" and that individual ethnic groups within a population should "retain their individuality and each make its contribution to the national character". The death of George V the following year led to a period of monarchical turmoil, as the succession of Prince Edward and his unfolding relationship with American divorcée Wallis Simpson threatened Imperial support of the royal family and jeopardised their authority and governance in Canada. Finally Edward abdicated and was succeeded by his younger brother Albert, the Duke of York, who became George VI.

A royal tour by George VI and Queen Elizabeth in May and June 1939 was conceived and executed by Buchan, though for its duration he returned on personal holiday to his home near Oxford since he believed that, while the King he represented was himself visiting the country in which he represented that King, his own viceregal position was suspended. He said "I cease to exist as Viceroy, and retain only a shadowy legal existence as Governor-General in Council". The royal couple took part in various official public engagements such as the opening of the Lions Gate Bridge. The tour was conceived both to maintain support of the royal family following the scandalous conditions of George VI's ascension to the throne, and in the face of the Second World War as a popularity campaign to garner American political and military support ahead of mounting hostility with Nazi Germany. He, Mackenzie King and Franklin D. Roosevelt were all three in favour of avoiding another war. Though his own military experience and Liberal attitude meant he was entirely against conflict, it was he who officially authorised Canada's declaration of war against Germany which came shortly after the British declaration. He then became Commander-in-Chief of the Canadian Armed Forces.

On the 6th of February 1940 he had a stroke and collapsed, sustaining a very serious head injury as he fell. He was at his Canadian Home, Rideau Hall, and so was treated by Doctor Wilder Penfield of the Montreal Neurological Institute who conducted two rounds of surgery in an attempt to stabilise Buchan's condition. These surgeries were unsuccessful and Buchan died on the 11th February as a result of complications after his head injury. He was eulogised on the radio by Mackenzie King, who said "In the passing of His Excellency, the people of Canada have lost one of the greatest and most revered of their Governors General, and a friend who, from the day of his aerial in this country, dedicated his life to their service". Buchan had forged a strong relationship with Mackenzie King, who spoke of his "sterling rectitude" and "disinterested purpose" though he noted as a vice Buchan's pursuit of titles. Buchan's state funeral was held at St. Andrew's Presbyterian Church in Ottawa, and his ashes were returned to his estate in Oxfordshire.

John Buchan – A Concise Bibliography

Fiction
Sir Quixote of the Moors (1896)
John Burnet of Barns (1898)
No-Man's Land (1899)
Grey Weather (1899)
A Lost Lady of Old Years (1899)
The Half-Hearted (1900)
The Watcher by the Threshold (1902)
A Lodge in the Wilderness (1906)
Prester John (1910)
The Moon Endureth (1912)
Salute to Adventurers (1915)
The Thirty-Nine Steps (1915)
The Power House (1916)
Greenmantle (1916)
Mr Standfast (1919)
The Path of the King (1921)
Huntingtower (1922)
Midwinter (1923)
The Three Hostages (1924)

John Macnab (1925)
The Dancing Floor (1926)
Witch Wood (1927)
The Runagates Club (1928)
The Courts of the Morning (1929)
Castle Gay (1930)
The Blanket of the Dark (1931)
The Gap in the Curtain (1932)
The Magic Walking Stick (1932)
A Prince of the Captivity (1933)
The Free Fishers (1934)
The House of the Four Winds (1935)
The Island of Sheep (1936)
Sick Heart River (US title: Mountain Meadow) (1941)
The Long Traverse (US title: Lake of Gold) (1941)
The Far Islands and Other Tales of Fantasy (1984)

Non-fiction
Scholar-Gipsies (1896)
The African Colony (1903)
The Law Relating to the Taxation of Foreign Income (1905)
Some Eighteenth Century Byways (1908)
Sir Walter Raleigh (1911)
What the Home Rule Bill Means (1912)
The Marquis of Montrose (1913)
Andrew Jameson, Lord Ardwall (1913)
Nelson's History Of The War. 24 volumes (1914–1919)
Britain's War by Land (1915)
The Achievement of France (1915)
Ordeal by Marriage (1915)
The Future of the War (1916)
The Battle of the Somme, First Phase (1916)
The Purpose of War (1916)
The Battle of Jutland (1916)
Poems, Scots and English (1917)
The Battle of the Somme, Second Phase (1917)
These for Remembrance (1919)
The Battle Honours of Scotland 1914–1918 (1919)
The History of the South African Forces in France (1920)
Francis and Riversdale Grenfell (1920)
The Long Road to Victory (1920)
A History of the Great War (1922)
A Book of Escapes and Hurried Journeys (1922)
The Last Secrets (1923)
A History of English Literature (1923)
Days to Remember (1923)
Some Notes on Sir Walter Scott (1924)

Lord Minto, a Memoir (1924)
The History of the Royal Scots Fusiliers 1678–1918 (1925)
The Man and the Book: Sir Walter Scott (1925)
Two Ordeals of Democracy (1925)
Homilies and Recreations (1926)
The Kirk in Scotland (with George Adam Smith) (1930)
Montrose and Leadership (1930)
Lord Rosebery, 1847–1929 (1930)
The Novel and the Fairy Tale (1931)
Julius Caesar (1932)
Andrew Lang and the Borders (1932)
The Massacre of Glencoe (1933)
The Margins of Life (1933)
Gordon at Khartoum (1934)
Oliver Cromwell (1934)
The King's Grace (1935)
Augustus (1937)
Naval Episodes Of The Great War (1938)
The Interpreter's House (1938)
Presbyterianism Yesterday, Today and Tomorrow (1938)
Memory Hold-the-Door (US title: Pilgrim's Way) (1940)
Comments and Characters (1940)
Canadian Occasions (1940)